I like Todd. I like the way he's
quiet. I like his company, like
music to me and doesn't think I'm silly to waste my time reading books.

Part of me that knows Josh should come before any other guy in my life – but I know that doesn't mean I can't have guy friends, like Todd. I've already lost a best friend because of my relationship with Josh. Maybe it's time I found a new one.

Allie and I used to do everything together, back when she was my best friend. We learned to ride a bike at the same time. We used to have sleepovers and paint each other's nails and gossip about the boys we had crushes on all the time. And when we got older, we used to go to Denny's for milkshakes after school on a Friday. She was my other half.

People use that phrase a lot: 'other half'. Like they're incomplete without someone to kiss them and hold their hand, or something. Usually, they're talking about a boyfriend or girlfriend.

But losing my best friend was like losing half of myself.

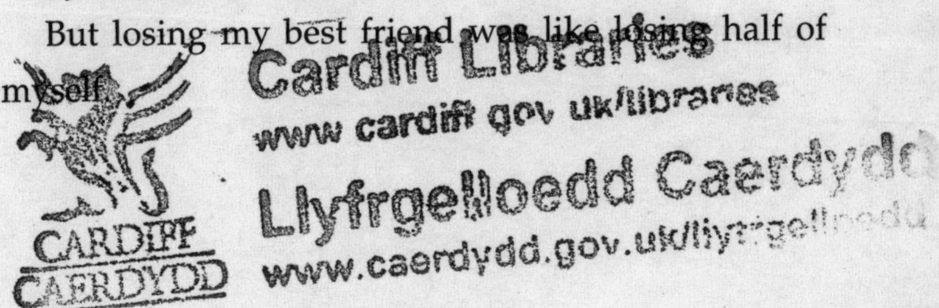

Beth is from South Wales and is currently studying Physics at the University of Exeter. She is an undeniable bookworm and avid drinker of tea.

Beth's novel *The Kissing Booth* became the most-viewed, most-commented-on teen fiction title on Wattpad in 2012 – 19 million reads and 40,000 comments. *The Kissing Booth* was winner of the Most Popular Teen Fiction Watty Award, and the digital edition topped the YA iBooks chart on release.

In 2013, Beth was named as one of *Time* magazine's Top Influential Teens.

# OUT OF TUNE

BETH REEKLES

CORGI

OUT OF TUNE
A CORGI BOOK 978 0 552 56883 8

Published in Great Britain by Corgi Books,
an imprint of Random House Children's Publishers UK
A Random House Group Company

This edition published 2014

1 3 5 7 9 10 8 6 4 2



The Random House Group Limited supports The Forest Stewardship Council® (FSC®), the leading international forest-certification organisation. Our books carrying the FSC label are printed on FSC®-certified paper. FSC is the only forest-certification scheme supported by the leading environmental organisations, including Greenpeace. Our paper procurement policy can be found at www.randomhouse.co.uk/environment

Set in 11/17 pt Palatino by Falcon Oast Graphic Art Ltd.

Corgi Books are published by Random House Children's Publishers UK,
61–63 Uxbridge Road, London W5 5SA

www.**randomhousechildrens**.co.uk
www.**totallyrandombooks**.co.uk
www.**randomhouse**.co.uk

Addresses for companies within The Random House Group Limited can be found at: www.randomhouse.co.uk/offices.htm

THE RANDOM HOUSE GROUP Limited Reg. No. 954009
A CIP catalogue record for this book is available from the British Library.

Printed and bound in Great Britain by
CPI Group (UK) Ltd, Croydon, CR0 4YY

*To Gransha, my biggest fan*

# Chapter 1

Number thirty-one Maple Drive has been vacant for as long as I've lived here.

At least, it was empty, until 6:27a.m. on the Friday morning before school starts. That's the exact time I'm woken up by the incessant *beep-beep-beep* of a truck reversing outside. Curiosity gets the better of me, and I drag myself out of bed, pulling the comforter with me, to peek through the drapes. I refrain from yelling out of my window that some of us are trying to sleep, as I try to get a good look at our new neighbors.

The 'For Sale' sign in their yard disappeared a week ago, and I'm still eager to know who exactly is moving in next door. I can't see much of them from here, though: a new-looking blue Ford, and the back of a man's head as he talks to a guy in a red uniform polo shirt climbing out from the driver's seat of the moving truck.

I'm tempted to stay longer at the window and see

more of them, but when I yawn and realize my eyes are drooping, I crawl back into bed. Mom will make us go over and introduce ourselves soon enough anyway.

It's Sunday afternoon when we meet the new neighbors.

'Ashley!' Mom yells up the stairs.

'What?' I shout back, sounding exactly the way I feel – ever the uncooperative, angsty teenager. Much as I want to know who's moved in next door, I really don't want to have to go over there with a big, bright, fake smile and welcome them to the neighborhood. To be honest, I'm kind of nervous. What if they've got some horrible teenage daughter who looks down her nose at me, even if she's a year or two younger than me? Or some spoilt, bratty kid I'll be obligated to babysit? The thought makes me shudder.

*You're being too pessimistic,* I tell myself. My mood lifts when I wonder what it would be like if it was someone my age there next door – a girl, maybe, who's not horrible and someone I can actually talk to, have something in common with.

I don't get my hopes up too much, though. Not yet.

I'd much rather just meet them from a distance. Like, from the safety of my bedroom window.

'We're going to welcome the neighbors. Come on.'

'Tell them I'm . . . I'm doing homework!'

'Ashley Bennett, they will not buy the homework excuse when school hasn't even started yet!'

'Then tell them I'm an honors student!'

She laughs at that, before the stern tone returns and she yells, 'Get your butt down here right now, or—'

'All right, all right! I'm coming!'

I huff and dog-ear the page I am reading before tossing my book onto my bed. My mom hates when I do that, but I'm always losing the bookmarks she buys me.

Throwing my legs off my bed, I shove my feet into the nearest pair of footwear I can see, which happen to be a pair of blue canvas shoes that clash horrendously with my green shorts. I duck down quickly to check my appearance in the mirror over my dresser, and shrug; my hair is fine, but I slap some make-up over my freckles before I head downstairs.

Mom waits impatiently at the foot of the stairs, next to the front door, tapping her foot pointedly – loudly. I roll my eyes at her.

'Here.' She places a basket in my hands.

I swear to God, it's an actual wicker basket, with cookies inside that are still warm. I don't know from where my mom gets this stuff.

'Hold up, let me just go grab my red cloak – you

know, the one with the hood – and I'll be right with you.'

She laughs, even though she tries to maintain the 'I'm-not-in-the-mood-for-your-sarcasm' expression. But there's more important business at hand than scolding me. Mom has been itching to go over and properly introduce herself to the new neighbors, but she's left it this long since she didn't feel it prudent to interrupt them – after all, they were most likely extremely busy settling in.

Now I know why Dad took an impromptu trip to the hardware store declaring he was finally going to fix that broken stair after procrastinating over it for like, the last eight months. Lucky escape for someone at least . . .

Mom picks up the bottle of expensive-looking wine on the table by the door and we leave.

Waiting on the porch of thirty-one Maple Drive, I realize it doesn't have that desolate feel about it any more. I look around. There's a small yet distinctive hole where the realtor's sign was in the lawn. The new neighbors have already hung up drapes at the windows of the room at the front of the house alongside the porch. Behind the peach curtains, there's a TV on a stand with an Xbox and DVD player hooked up, and I can see a bookshelf that's only about a third full.

The door opens before I can look at any more of the house.

It's a guy, around my age I'd guess, with messy brown hair and a loose-fitting Blink-182 T-shirt. He looks at my mom and me for a brief second, as though we're from another planet, before breaking the silence with a stiff, 'Hi.'

'Hello!' Mom trills. 'We're just dropping by to welcome you to the area. We're your new next-door neighbors.'

'Todd!' someone yells from inside – a male voice. 'Who is it?'

'Next-door!' he bellows back over his shoulder.

Then, with all the grace of a bear running downhill, a man around his mid-forties comes barreling down the staircase into sight. He runs a hand through his graying hair to smooth it down, make it more presentable.

'Hello, there. I'm Callum.' He offers a hand, and Mom shakes it. 'And this is my son, Todd.'

'Great to meet you. I'm Isabelle,' Mom introduces herself. 'Isabelle Bennett. My husband, Jeff, is at the hardware store at the moment – but I'm sure he'll drop by as soon as he gets back.' What she means is, she'll make him come over and introduce himself. 'And this is our daughter, Ashley.'

'Hey,' I say, because I feel like I have to say something.

'Anyway,' says Mom. 'We were just dropping by to introduce ourselves and give you a little housewarming gift.' She gestures to my wicker basket with her bottle of wine.

'Oh, thank you so much. Please, come in. Would you like some coffee? Tea? A soda?'

'I'm good, thanks,' I say, when he looks at me.

'We wouldn't want to impose . . .'

'It's fine, honestly, don't worry!'

'In that case, a coffee would be wonderful, thank you,' Mom says graciously, and steps inside, leaving me to follow.

I make to wipe my feet on the welcome mat outside the door, but there isn't one, so my foot kind of just hovers in the air for a second before I step inside. The guy who opened the door – Todd, I suppose – watches me with the tiniest hint of amusement on his face. That is, until I look him in the eye, and he turns away and walks ahead of me to the kitchen.

I know it's the kitchen because the layout of this house – and every other house on Maple Drive, for that matter – has more or less the same layout as my house.

The kitchen's a mess, for which Callum apologizes. I like that it's messy, though. It makes the place feel like somebody's *home*, not just a bland show home with nobody living there.

'So, what brings you to Greendale?' Mom asks with a polite smile.

There's a brief, somewhat awkward pause. I want to slap my forehead.

Todd opens his mouth, but Callum says hastily, 'We just needed a change.'

I look at Todd, who's staring at his bare feet and wiggling his toes. A smirk tweaks at his lips for a split second. I get the impression that whatever his response would have been, it wouldn't have been as vague and polite as his dad's.

I can tell Mom is wondering if there's a politely inquisitive way to find out what that story is, but since she doesn't ask, I know she can't find one.

'Todd's going to be attending the local high school,' Callum says, flipping the switch on their electric kettle. 'Is that where you go?'

Oh, right, me.

'Yeah. I'll be a junior.'

'Hey, isn't that great! So will Todd.' He smiles to me. 'How do you find the school?'

I shrug my shoulders one after the other. What does he want me to say? 'Oh, yeah, it's great. All the teachers are wonderful and don't give so much homework it drives you to insanity. There are never any fights and everyone gets on and everything's always fine and dandy.'

But it's high school – who'd believe that answer?

'It's all right,' I say. 'It's just high school. Most of the teachers are okay, and the people aren't too bad, I guess. Like I said, it's just high school.'

Mom cuts me a look. 'The SAT scores are some of the best in the state every year.'

Callum nods. 'Can't ask for much more than that, can you?' The kettle switch flips off and there's a quiet *ding!* to signal that it's done boiling water. He pours it into two mugs for coffee.

'Do you take sugar? Milk?'

'No, thank you.'

'Okay.'

There's a two-second burst of music from my back pocket, and I reach for my cellphone to answer the text. It's probably Josh, finally replying to the text I sent him earlier. But as my hand creeps to my back pocket, Mom clears her throat and I get the message loud and clear, and drop my hand. The better I cooperate now, the sooner we can get out of here. I hope.

We stand around the kitchen making small talk for a couple of minutes before Callum says, 'I'm sorry, would you like to sit down? I apologize in advance for the state of the living room, we haven't finished unpacking yet . . .'

Mom laughs. 'It's not that bad. Besides, every house is a bit hectic right after you move in.'

Todd speaks for the first time since he answered the door. 'I'm just going to head back upstairs, and—'

'You can show Ashley around the house,' his dad suggests. But we all catch the undertone that makes it more of a command than an option.

'I'm sure Ashley doesn't need a tour of the house,' he replies curtly. Callum gives him a look and Todd sighs. 'Sure. Whatever. Come on.'

He doesn't even look at me, just walks out and expects me to follow. But I'd feel rude if I stayed, so I have no choice but to follow him out of the kitchen and down the hallway.

All right, so the new neighbors don't have some bratty kid, or some cheerleader-type daughter, either, so things could be worse. But Todd has barely said a word, and I don't know what to make of him. I don't know that obnoxious is quite the right word to describe him. Or even arrogant . . . Aloof, maybe. That seems the best fit. It's something more than plain indifference.

He turns to me at the bottom of the stairs, one foot on the lowest step and the other on the floor; his eyes are focused on his feet. 'Look, I don't want to be in this situation any more than you do, so you'll forgive me for not showing you round the place.'

'It's okay,' I say. 'My house is laid out exactly the same.'

'Right.'

He starts up the stairs and I hesitate. Am I supposed to follow him?

I do, just because I have no idea what else to do.

'Where are you going?' I ask, though the options are limited.

'Narnia. Where'd you think?'

I bite back a laugh.

He seems to realize that I'm not going anywhere, and I guess our friendship isn't yet at the level where he'll invite me to his bedroom to sit down. And neither of us really want to sit with our parents, with the risk of being asked about our academic achievements and extracurricular activities, or anything like that. So he turns and sits on a step most of the way up the stairs instead of carrying on going up. I sit on the stair below him, my back to the wall and my feet propped against the banister.

I look at Todd out of the corner of my eye, trying not to be obvious about it. He's a few inches taller than me. His lean build reminds me of a soccer player, but he doesn't look much like the sporty type. The movement of his hands distracts me; he's twirling a dark gray guitar pick over and over between his fingers. His eyes are downcast, concentrating on the motion of the guitar pick – but then he looks up at me, saying, 'What?' and I frown a little, because I can't quite determine if his eyes are blue or gray.

'Nothing.'

He shrugs his left shoulder and holds my gaze for a brief second before looking down again. I cock my head a little to the side as I scrutinize him. God, those cheek-bones are to die for! If he wasn't acting so aloof and brooding, I'd think him handsome – but I refuse to, just on principle.

'So you play guitar?'

'Evidently,' he says, making a gesture with the pick. He opens his mouth to say something then closes it again, forehead puckered in a scowl.

'That's cool. What kind of stuff do you play?'

He takes a moment before answering, which he does quite grudgingly – I can see it in the curl of his lips. 'Mostly things I come up with myself. I, uh, I took to writing music a couple of years ago.'

I nod, not knowing what to reply. He clearly doesn't want to talk to me much. Well, maybe I don't want to talk to him. Stubbornly, I sit in silence for a few minutes. We both sit there on the stairs and listen to my mom and his dad talking and laughing in the lounge. Their voices float up through the open door, but not quite loud enough for us to make out what they're saying.

I know that I should try and be friendly toward Todd; he's probably nervous about making new friends here, about fitting in, because friendships have already been forged long ago, cliques have been set in place, and he's the new guy. I know I'd be terrified. Being friendly would be the right thing to do, and I know my mom would want me to be nice to him. But he's a big boy, I'm sure he can make his own friends.

My cellphone sounds again in my pocket. I'd forgotten I had a text earlier. I catch Todd looking at me, but I ignore him and take out my cell.

Both texts are from Josh.

*Good thanks, want to come over later for dinner? XXXXX* is the reply to my earlier 'Hey, how are you?' text.

*Babe? Hello? XXXXX*

I type a reply to say that sure, dinner sounds great, and sorry for the late response – we're visiting the new neighbors.

'Boyfriend?' Todd says, startling me.

'Yeah.'

He nods. 'How long have you guys been together?'

'Year and a half.'

'That's nice.'

'What about you?' I blurt before I can stop myself. 'Any broken hearts left back in . . . Where'd you live before, anyway?'

'Idaho. And no, no broken hearts left behind.' There's a note of laughter in his voice, and the corner of his mouth tweaks up like he finds the idea amusing. I wonder if maybe he's a player, not into serious commitment in a relationship. Because a guy who looks as attractive as he does must have had girlfriends. Or maybe it's that someone broke up with him instead.

After that, conversation dies out pretty quickly. So he sits there fiddling with the guitar pick, and I sit there texting Josh, until we hear my mom and Callum saying goodbye to each other, at which point there seems to be an unspoken mutual decision between Todd and I to move to the front door.

There's the usual kind of thing: *thanks for the cookies and the wine, if you need anything don't hesitate to ask, we should have dinner sometime* – and, finally, *goodbye*.

We walk through our own front door and my mom starts asking me what Todd and I had spoken about, and how we'd gotten along.

'I don't know. He doesn't talk much.'

'Callum said he's quite shy.'

I snort dubiously. 'I don't know about shy. Stand-offish, maybe. It was like he thought he was too good to talk to me, you know?'

'Ashley . . .'

'I'm going over Josh's for dinner tonight, I need to jump in the shower.'

And that's all we say about the new neighbors at thirty-one Maple Drive.

# Chapter Two

'*No.*'

No way. No. No! I refuse. I am not doing this. No. She can't make me.

I cross my arms and narrow my eyes at my mom to make my point. Not in a million years will I agree to this.

'Oh, come on, Ashley. Do the poor kid a favor; it'll be his first day at a new school, the least you can do is—'

'No way! I'm sure he can handle himself. He's not *twelve*.'

'Did I ask you to be his new best friend? Look, I'm not saying you should walk him to all his classes and be—'

'Mom. What part of "no" didn't you understand? Was it the *N* or the *O*?'

Her retort to that is a cutting look, and she plants her hands on her hips. 'Just give him a ride to school. That's all I'm asking. Besides, he lives next door, it makes sense that you two carpool.'

'I'm not driving to school tomorrow though, Josh is. I'm doing the kid a favor by not giving him a ride – he'll only feel like a total third wheel.'

'I'm sure Josh will understand.'

I snort cynically.

Mom's voice then takes on a pleading tone – 'I'll give you gas money to fill up the tank if you take him to school. Just for this first week. Five days. Then he can make his own way there if you're going to be so stupid as to insist on not carpooling.'

My ears have pricked up at hearing the first sentence. Gas money to fill the whole tank . . . And my fuel gauge is looking pretty low at the moment . . .

I am sorely tempted.

'Maybe he doesn't want a ride with me, did you think about that?'

'Ask him, then, no harm in trying. If he says no, then you don't have to drive him.'

'Fine, fine,' I sigh heavily, glaring still, but caving in at last. 'But only – *only* – for the gas money.'

'Sure,' Mom agrees, trying hard not to laugh. 'Not because under all that cynicism is a lovely girl, or anything.'

'Exactly.'

She lets out a laugh then and shakes her head at me. I huff and stomp back up to my room, although by the time I slam my door shut, I only do it for the sake of it. The initial irritation has ebbed away and now I'm just dreading having to walk over later and speak to Todd.

The thing about houses on Maple Drive is that they are all pretty much identical in design, but someone thought it would be a nice idea to build them in sort of symmetrical pairs. My bedroom has a large window on the side of the house with a window seat (which is a feature I absolutely adore). And the house next door, which my bedroom faces has an identically constructed bedroom facing mine.

Which has never been a problem before.

This morning, I got out of the shower and walked back to my room with my towel wrapped around me. I ran a brush through my damp hair, singing to myself, and picked out some underwear from a drawer. I was about to drop the towel and get dressed when I heard a loud, 'Hey!'

Frowning, I looked around, before realizing it had come from outside my open window. Clutching my towel tightly around me, I moved to the window seat to see Todd leaning out of his window.

'You might want to shut the drapes or something,' he yelled over, with a pointed look at my towel.

'Pervert!' I shouted back.

'Protecting your modesty!' he retorted, then sat back in the window seat, closing the window behind him and pointedly turning his head away. With a huff of anger, I yanked the rope on the shutters and they clattered down to cover the open window.

Now, I find myself walking over to next door and really hoping that Todd won't want a ride to school tomorrow. I just feel completely humiliated after this morning.

I ring the doorbell and bounce on the balls of my feet, my stomach twisting into knots. Maybe Callum will answer, and he'll say, 'No, don't worry about it, I'll drive Todd to school tomorrow,' and I won't have to be subjected to this ordeal.

Todd opens the door. His eyebrows go up, surprised to see me.

'Oh, hi.'

'Look, my mom told me I should offer you a ride to school tomorrow, so if you want a ride that's fine, I guess, but don't expect me to be all buddy-buddy with you, got that?'

I don't mean to sound so horrible, but I want to get out of here as quickly and painlessly as possible. He saw me in nothing but a towel this morning and I'm worried that image might still be in his head. Not in a vain way, but seeing your neighbor almost naked probably isn't the kind of thing you easily forget. And I'm still cringing over it, hours later.

'Uh . . . sure, yeah, a ride would be great. I don't know my way to the school yet.'

'Fine. I'll be outside at eight, school starts at eight thirty.'

'Thanks.'

I nod briskly. I turn on my heel and start walking down the path because I really don't want to hang around there any longer – but then he calls out to me. I stop and turn back.

'For the record, I don't expect you to help me try to fit in. I'm a big boy, I can handle myself.'

I give him a small smile. 'Good. Glad to hear we're in agreement on that.'

He returns my smile with one of his own, and then steps back and pushes the door shut; I take that as my cue to leave.

*Beeeeeeeeep, beeeeeeeeep!*

I slam my hand on the snooze button and bury my face in my pillow. When the alarm goes again five minutes later, I'm tempted to shut it off and go back to sleep – then I remember why my alarm is going off: it's the first day of school.

Dragging myself out of bed and into the shower, I try to plan out what to wear today. Everyone makes an effort on the first day, even if they end up wearing sweatpants the next week.

I tease my curly hair back into a ponytail and stand in front of my wardrobe, eyeing everything as critically as other people will today. I settle on denim cut-offs that give my butt some lift, and a sleeveless, pale blue blouse with a black Peter Pan collar, and I grab a sweater to toss in the car, in case it gets colder later.

Cute, but not too over the top, I think with a smile as I look myself over in the mirror.

I put some eyeliner on, and cover up my freckles with concealer and powder. I hate my freckles. I don't have a couple of cute ones over the bridge of my nose like some people; my face and even my shoulders are covered in freckles. I hate it.

It's three minutes to eight, so I grab my satchel and head downstairs, tossing my book in my bag at the last minute in case I'm lucky enough to have a free period today. I swallow a piece of toast Dad has made for me as quickly as is humanly possible and call goodbye to my mom, who's in her office upstairs. Dad's sitting at the breakfast bar reading the biography of some footballer I've never heard of, and I give him a kiss on the cheek.

'Have a good first day back,' he says.

'Thanks.'

My car, the old red Buick with the bad paint job, grumbles to life as I turn the key in the ignition, my keychains jangling together noisily. The exhaust sputters when I stop outside Todd's house. I honk the horn in two short bursts to get his attention, and a moment later he wanders down the path and climbs in the passenger seat, his legs splayed awkwardly in the tight space. He reaches behind him to try and find the lever to move the seat back, and it jerks back a whole foot and a half in one go.

'Nice car.'

'Is that sarcasm?' I ask sharply, scowling a little as I drive down the street. I know it's not the best car – but I bought it with my own money, from Old Man Davies down the street, and I've got to save up for college, so unless this old thing catches fire, I'm not paying out to have it fixed up while it still gets me from A to B.

'No,' he says. 'It's a nice car.'

'Oh. Well. Okay, then.' I feel a blush creeping over my face for snapping at him.

He smiles a little – I see it out of the corner of my eye, and realize that's the first time I've seen him smile.

It makes him look so much warmer, and less sulky.

I turn on the stereo and the Imagine Dragons disc whirs to life and starts to play from where it left off mid-song. I don't care what he thinks about the music, I just can't bear a whole car ride in awkward silence.

'You have good taste in music,' Todd comments.

'Duh.'

He chuckles, but it's very quiet, and he stops himself, fighting away the smile on his face.

It's pretty busy when we get to school. People are buzzing with excitement at seeing their friends after the summer, gossiping and chattering like they've been somewhere with no Wi-Fi, no social networks or cellphones. I roll my eyes as some girl squeals to someone she probably saw just last week that it's been '*way* too long', and I carry on walking past. I know where my friends will be hanging out.

I don't know what to do about Todd though. Should I introduce him to my friends, or stay here with him for the next seven minutes until the bell rings?

'Um . . .' I hesitate, gnawing on my lip.

'Could you at least tell me where to find my homeroom? They mailed me a bunch of papers – like the school rules, dress code, map – and told me which homeroom I'm in. It's okay, you don't have to babysit me, but . . .'

'If you have a map, why do you need me to tell you where it is?' I smile though, so he knows I'm not being mean.

'Because the map looks like something a five-year-old drew. It's impossible to decipher.'

I laugh, deciding not to argue, so he tells me where his homeroom is and I lead him there down a few corridors, through the throngs of people.

'Thanks.'

'That's okay.'

He's fiddling with that guitar pick again. He puts it back in the pocket of his jeans but then takes it out again after a second or two.

'Look,' I sigh, and grab his hand. I dig into the side pocket of my satchel and pull out a pen. I bite the lid between my teeth and scribble my number on his hand. 'If you need someone to eat lunch with, I guess, send me a text. Only to be used in case of emergency, though, got that?'

I can't help it! I feel bad for the guy. I've never really been the new kid, never been ostracized or anything like he might be. I can't imagine what he feels like. He'll make friends, I'm sure, and I don't doubt that there will be girls queued up trying to talk to him by the end of the week, especially with those cheekbones and those eyes. But I feel for him.

There's that reluctant smile again, and for once he looks me right in the eyes. 'Thanks, Ashley.'

I smile back and shrug. Then I remember to let go of his hand, which falls back to his side.

'Hey! Ashley!'

I turn at the familiar voice and see the hulking form of my boyfriend making his way down the corridor toward us. I smile and as he reaches us I go on my tiptoes to give him a quick kiss. 'Hey.'

'You didn't come to meet us. One of the football guys said he saw you come this way.'

'Yeah, I was showing Todd to his homeroom. This is Todd, by the way,' I say, pointing between them. Todd scuffs the toe of his shoe against the floor, head down. 'My new neighbor, you know I told you about him? Todd, this is my boyfriend, Josh.'

They both nod their heads in acknowledgement of each other with a blunt, 'Hey, what's up,' and the bell rings. Relief washes over me that we can get out of here before things have chance to get awkward. I slip my hand into Josh's and say, 'See you,' to Todd, and we head off down the corridor to our own homeroom.

'Were you giving him your number?' Josh mumbles, bending to speak in my ear.

'Yeah, just in case he needs some help. It's his first day. I was just trying to be nice.'

He grunts. I stop walking and step to the side of the corridor, tugging at Josh so that he steps beside me. I rub my hand up and down his forearm, over the muscles there.

'You're not jealous?'

He lets out a sigh and smiles. 'I love you.'

'I love you too,' I say back. Smiling, Josh tilts my face up so he can kiss me.

A throat clears loudly, followed by, 'Miss Bennett, Mr Parker. I think you ought to be on your way to homeroom now.'

'Yes, sir,' Josh drawls at the geography teacher, who carries on down the corridor. I'm blushing furiously. Then Josh gives me another kiss, and we walk on to our first class.

# Chapter Three

Todd O'Connor isn't the only new kid, of course, but he's by far the most talked about. I don't see him for the rest of the morning, but I hear snatches of gossip about him. Although nobody seems to know that much about him at all, not really.

'Where did he even come from?'

'Someone told me he used to go to boarding school in New York. Apparently, they caught him smoking pot in the library. Can you believe it?'

'Well *I* heard he used to live in California. Got kicked out for selling drugs on the football pitch, you know?'

'No, he moved from a juvie centre in North Dakota, I heard someone telling Olivia Riley.'

Not that I know much about him – but come on, people really believe all the rumors that are spilling around the school? I don't pay them any attention. The bell finally rings for lunch, and I make my way to the cafeteria and over to my usual table.

Josh and Austin are already there with Naomi. Then the twins, Sam and Neil, turn up just as I get there. I glance around the rest of the room, looking at the cliques and the groups of friends joking about, or having playful, yet still heated, debates about something.

I look back at my usual table as I draw closer, and there's the usual feeling of disappointment in the pit of my stomach. It's not that they're bad people, or anything, it's just . . . we don't exactly have much in common. I never have much to say to them.

Josh pulls me into the empty space beside him and gives me a kiss full on the mouth as I sit down.

After a few minutes, the last of our little group arrive – Eliza and Danielle. I sit and pull apart the tuna salad sandwich I bought from the counter. It's all the usual first-day-back talk: they moan about their classes, or say how relieved they are about the teacher they got for English this year. At least this is one conversation I can actually join in with.

'Have you guys picked an elective yet?' Neil asks.

'I'll probably end up choosing Film Studies,' Austin says. 'Watching movies for homework sounds like a piece of cake if you ask me.'

'I don't know. Choir again?' Eliza is the kind of person who phrases most of her sentences like a question. 'Totally boring, but the easiest class I've ever taken, you know?'

That goes on for a while. I don't have any input: I don't want to tell them which elective I'm planning on taking. They'd only laugh.

I never really have a lot to say in our conversations. They were all Josh's friends before they were mine; I started to hang out with them once I began dating Josh, and truthfully, I don't have that much in common with them.

In freshman year English class, we'd had a new teacher partway through the spring semester. She introduced a seating chart, and I'd ended up sat right next to Josh Parker. I'd had a crush on him for a while – he had that whole 'golden boy' image going for him, what with the blond hair, the dazzling smile, the green eyes that were set just a little too far apart that gave him an endearing flaw.

Allie used to roll her eyes when I'd say maybe I had a shot with him. Back when she was my best friend.

I used to blush a lot whenever he joked around with me, but I was never very bold when it came to boys. I tried all the magazine techniques – smiling like I had a secret, talking about other boys to try and pique his interest . . . It seems so stupid now, thinking I used to act like that around him.

But Josh was one of the cool kids; he just had the right aura and the right look that made him one of them from the off. Allie and me on the other hand . . . we were still trying to find where we fitted in at high school. She'd joined the school paper, and I'd joined the swim team, but neither did us much good when it came to popularity. We were both totally invisible. Irrelevant.

When Josh finally asked me out, it was like my wildest dreams had come true. He was cute and funny, and he was *popular*, too.

Allie didn't exactly see it that way.

I shake myself. I'm being way too nostalgic. It's the first day back at school, shouldn't it be like a fresh start? Shouldn't I have put everything that had gone on between me and my ex-best friend behind me by now?

I try and pitch in with the conversation at the lunch table, but I seem to have even less to say than usual.

As we're heading to our afternoon classes, Josh pulls me aside. I don't know what it's about, but he looked preoccupied through most of lunch. Maybe it's about one of his classes – maybe he has to re-take Algebra I, which he took last year. It wouldn't surprise me.

'How much do you know about that O'Connor kid?'

So definitely not about Algebra I . . .

My first instinct is to point out that he's not a kid;

he's the same age as us. But Josh wouldn't exactly appreciate that, I think.

Instead, I say, 'Not a lot. He's not particularly talkative. I don't know, I only spoke to him a little the other day. Why? What's wrong?'

He shrugs, looking around. 'People are saying all kinds of things about him, that's all. I don't know that I like the kid. I know it's a lot of rumors, but some of it could be true. You don't know what kind of person he is.'

'What does it matter?'

Josh gives me a flat look. 'If you're going to be driving him back and forth to school all week—'

'Oh, come *on*.' I clench my teeth for a second, trying not to let it show how exasperated I am with him. 'I don't know much about Todd, but he's not a bad guy. You're honestly not paying attention to all those stupid rumors, are you?'

'Those "stupid rumors" have got to start somewhere, haven't they?' he argues.

I shake my head. 'Whatever. I have to get to class.'

'I love you.'

'I love you, too.' He leans down to kiss me, but I make sure it's only a short one; I do have to get to class. As I turn to walk off, he smacks my butt lightly. I glance back just enough to roll my eyes at him. Then I see someone looking at me with a pair of big, gray-blue eyes, from underneath a mess of dark brown hair. There's a set of headphones around his neck, which he pulls up over his ears. Then he ducks his head back down and carries on walking.

Josh walks off behind me.

I'm tempted to catch up with Todd. Ask him what he was staring at. Ask him how his first day is going. But all I can do for the moment is stand there and wonder why he was looking at me like that. And . . . was that hurt in his eyes, or something else? What if he overheard Josh talking about him?

The bell goes, jerking me out of my thoughts as people move around me to their classes, and I head off to chemistry.

Todd meets me back at my car after school. I'm already there, sat in the driver's seat. He climbs in the passenger seat, shoves his backpack between his knees and says, 'Hey.'

I start up the engine. 'How'd your first day go?'

He shrugs. 'Well, apparently I'm some kid who went to boarding school in North Dakota – *and* New York, or maybe it was Vermont? – and got kicked out of my old school, wherever it was, for blowing up a science lab, taking and/or selling drugs, depending on who you talk to . . .' He shakes his head and lets out a breath of laughter. 'Gotta love high school.'

My mouth twists up in a smile. 'Really? I heard that you'd been in juvie in Florida. Or maybe *that* was North Dakota, now I think about it . . .'

'Is that so?' He gives that same skeptical laugh again. 'Well, you learn something new about yourself every day, huh?'

There's a couple of minutes silence.

'So you found somebody to sit with at lunch?'

He nods. 'Yeah. Some guys from my French class. They seemed all right.' He doesn't expand, tell me their names, ask me about them. He does have something more to say to me though, something that I didn't expect him to come out with: 'I saw you and your boyfriend. Josh, isn't it?'

'Yeah.' *Where's this going?* 'I saw you looking at me.'

'I just couldn't help noticing. You weren't exactly secreted away behind a closed door.'

I wait a second or so to see if he'll go on. 'What about it?' I ask when he doesn't.

'Do you always let him treat you like that?'

A frown pulls at my forehead, scrunching my eyebrows together. I would turn and look at him, but I'm driving. 'I don't know what you mean.'

And Todd says, 'Never mind. Sorry. Forget I said anything. It's not my place.'

And we don't speak the rest of the way home.

*Ah, damn it,* I curse to myself as the tardy bell rings, quickening my pace. I don't get detentions. And I don't plan to start on the second day of the semester.

I don't know what this new teacher is like, but hopefully they'll believe my excuse that my locker's a bit busted and I couldn't get into it. It's true; I need to remember to stop by the front office after school and ask them to get it fixed.

I burst into the classroom – after knocking, of course; I don't want to give this teacher – Ms Langstone, according to my schedule – any cause to dislike me.

'I'm sorry I'm late,' I say, a little breathless. 'I had some trouble with my locker . . .'

'Miss Bennett, is it?' She looks over her glasses at the computer screen, where I can see her class register. 'Ashley?'

'Yes.'

'Mm. Well, take a seat, Miss Bennett, we were just about to get started.'

She starts talking about how we shouldn't expect this to be an 'easy-breezy' class, even though everyone knows it will be, and I scan the room for a seat. The classroom's only small, because Creative Writing has never been a popular elective here at Greendale High, and there are only two seats left. One of those seats is right at the front – so that's out of the equation immediately.

The second seat is in the back corner.

And, naturally, it's right next to *him*. I curse under my breath.

Once I get to the seat in the back, I let my satchel drop to the ground and I fall into the seat beside Todd, crossing my arms. He was doing something – doodling, maybe – in a notebook, but as I sit down he closes it shut smoothly, which draws my attention to it. The midnight blue cover is faded, and it looks like it's real leather. The book is thick, and I can see other bits of paper and what look to be Post-It notes sticking out, making it thick and swollen.

We all stay quiet while Ms Langstone drones on and on, until finally, she shuts up and sits at her desk, handing a pile of file paper to some girl in the front row, telling her to pass it around the class.

We're supposed to write a poem from one of the themes on the board. God, how *boring*.

As if it weren't bad enough already . . . I sigh and run a hand through my hair.

'What's got your panties in a twist?' Todd mumbles

next to me, and I look at him to see his eyes trained calmly on me. They look blue today. Powder blue, and a little bloodshot in the corners, like he had a sleepless night. And now, up close, I can see how long and thick his eyelashes are . . . I know girls who would kill for eyelashes like that. Myself included, I'll admit.

'Don't tell me you chose Creative Writing of your own free will?' I say, trying not to think about his eyelashes.

'I thought that was the point of an elective.'

'Yeah, but nobody *likes* Creative Writing. It's always so wishy-washy.'

'Then why are you here?'

'It was either this or choir,' I tell him bluntly. 'They stopped Latin classes this year because not enough people were signing up.'

I snap my mouth shut. Why was I telling him that? I wasn't supposed to go telling *anybody* that. Latin was the class ranked even lower in likeability than Creative Writing. Last year, only four people signed up. I didn't think they'd stop running it as an elective altogether, though. And by the time I realized that, the only class I could take that wasn't full yet was Creative Writing.

I'd planned on telling Josh and the others that everywhere else was full, that Latin had been the only thing

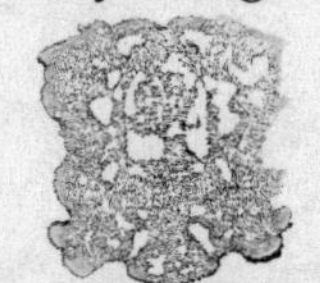

left. They'd have bought it, too – because what kind of loser would actually *choose* Latin?

I don't miss the look of surprise flitting across Todd's face under all that hair. My cheeks burn and I duck my head, hoping my hair hides how humiliated I am.

'I didn't pin you for someone who'd take Latin. I thought the cool kids didn't go for classes like that.'

I shrug. I don't want to reply that I thought it would be a really cool class, that I'd love to learn it. Anybody might overhear.

Some guy on the desk next to us clears his throat. 'Hey, Ashley.' I look over and he's holding out the wad of file paper. I take a sheet and give another one to Todd before passing it on to the desk in front of me.

Todd taps his fingers on his blue notebook in a rhythm I don't recognize.

'What's that?'

He looks at me in confusion, so I point to the book by way of explanation.

'Oh. It's . . .' He clears his throat and lowers his voice a little. 'Do you remember I said to you I write songs?'

'Sure,' I reply. 'So that's where you keep all your songs, huh? That's cool.' He shrugs. 'Can I see?'

His hand flattens possessively over the book, a gesture that I don't miss. 'I don't really like to show people what I write.'

I nod. 'That's okay. I didn't mean to pry.'

'You didn't know.' The corner of his mouth moves up in a smile and then he sits back in his seat, digging his hands into his pocket. A moment later, while I'm thinking which theme will be easiest to write a poem about – fall, or nostalgia, or thunder – I see the flash of that dark gray guitar pick moving around his fingers as he twirls it around.

I wonder if it's a nervous movement, or just more of a habit – like me when I dog-ear books – but I think it might be rude to ask that, in case he's self-conscious, so I say nothing, and we don't really talk much for the rest of the lesson.

Todd gets up as soon as the bell goes, grabbing his blue book and tucking it securely into his bulky back-pack. 'See you later,' he says to me, and then he's weaving his way around the tables and out of the door.

I get up, too, but I'm in no particular rush. I have English Literature next, which is only a few rooms away. But as I stand, I see a pink Post-It note on the floor. It's upside down, but I can see there's writing on it.

Curious, I pick it up. There are a few random letters scribbled down and a couple of lines of writing. It must have fallen out of Todd's notebook.

I don't read it. Instead, I fold it over and tuck it in

the back pocket of my jeans to give it to him later.

I'm tempted to read it; partly out of simple curiosity, and partly because he was so protective of his book and its contents. And he wouldn't know if I had read it or not . . .

No – it wouldn't be fair on him. He wants it kept private, and who am I to disrespect that?

So I don't read it.

My mind continues to drift and think about the pink note in my back pocket, and consequently about Todd O'Connor. News has gotten out that he plays guitar, and the amount of girls I hear talking about how he's 'so hot, with that tortured musician attitude' makes me want to hit my head against a wall. Or vomit. Or both.

At lunch, Eliza says to me, 'Hey, Ashley, I heard someone say that new guy, Todd, was in your Creative Writing class?'

'Oh, yeah.' I snap a block of chocolate off the end of my candy bar, a little startled at the sound of my name. 'He is.'

'What's he like, really?' Naomi asks me. 'He is *totally* hot.'

'Oh, man, not you guys, too,' Neil groans as he drops into his seat at our lunch table with Danielle. 'It's not like he was all that Dan was talking about last period.'

'Guilty as charged,' she jokes, and looks between me and the other girls, waiting for us to continue.

'He's . . . quiet,' I decide to say. For some reason I don't want to use words like 'standoffish' and 'snobby' like I did to my mom. I shift in my seat, uncomfortable with being the center of attention all of a sudden. 'I don't know, really. It's not like he's divulged his life story—'

'You didn't tell me he was in your class,' Josh interrupts.

'I didn't think it was very important.'

'Right.'

I smile at him again and lean in to kiss his cheek. Josh turns his head at the last minute, though, so I catch his lips instead – a gambit I was mostly expecting anyway – and he only pulls away when Naomi says, 'Jeez, you guys, get a freaking room already.'

Later, after school, Todd is already waiting by my car when I get there. He hadn't texted to ask where I was – but then again, I couldn't have been far; my car was still here, after all.

The journey home is pretty quiet. We talk a little about classes.

I start to think maybe Callum was being entirely honest when he told my mom that Todd was shy.

Because I'm no longer getting the impression from his quietness that he thinks he's too good to grace me with his conversation; it's more like he doesn't have an awful lot he wants to say, or he doesn't know what to say.

'Thanks,' he says, unclipping his seatbelt when I pull onto the driveway outside my house. 'I'll see you tomorrow.'

'Yeah.' As we get out of the car, I remember about the Post-It note. 'Oh, hey, wait a second!' I call, and he stops partway down the driveway, turning back to me. I walk up to him, fishing the paper out of my pocket. It's a bit crumpled, so I smooth it out as best I can.

'You dropped this, earlier,' I tell him. 'In class. I haven't read it. I swear.'

His eyes drop from my face to my outstretched hand, and he takes the paper, smoothing it between his long fingers and unfolding it. Then, when he looks back at me, his expression is dubious: he thinks that I read it.

'I haven't read it,' I reiterate. 'You said you didn't like people reading your songs and whatever, so I didn't.'

Todd's eyes search my face for a long moment, and I stare right back at him.

'You could be lying,' he says. 'How would I know if you had read it or not?'

'You don't have to trust me, that's up to you. But I haven't read it. I wouldn't want people to read my private things.' I bite my lip, realizing that I actually do want him to trust me. 'You don't have to believe me.'

He looks at me for what feels like a very long time.

'Thank you.' He's blushing a little bit, but he smiles. One of his teeth is a little crooked. I didn't notice before.

I smile back. 'You're welcome.'

I'm unlocking the front door when I hear him call, 'Ashley,' and I look over my shoulder. Todd gestures awkwardly with the pink Post-It. 'I believe you, that you didn't read it.'

And then he walks away, leaving me standing on the doorstep, key frozen in the lock, wondering what goes on in that mind of his. Sighing, I shake my head, and go into the house.

Maybe those girls at school are right when they say he's mysterious.

## Chapter Four

'I don't mind driving myself to school next week,' Todd says, when I'm taking us home on Friday. 'I mean, you said you'd just drive me for this first week. And I can remember the way.'

But I find myself saying, 'We'll split it. You drive next week, and I'll drive the week after. Makes sense, right? We live next door to each other.'

'I thought you said your boyfriend drives you sometimes?'

I shrug. 'Only sometimes. Just thinking about reducing my carbon footprint here.'

'Of course. And gas money.'

'Exactly.' I pull up on my driveway and kill the engine, smiling at the fuel gauge pointing to 'full' (thank you, Mom). I lean around to the backseat to fumble for the strap of my bag before climbing out of the car. Todd stands just outside the car when I get out.

'I'll pick you up at eight, then, bright and early

Monday morning,' he says. Then he offers up a smile. 'See you around, Ashley.'

I don't expect to see much more of Todd that weekend. At least, I don't expect to see anything other than a glimpse by chance through my bedroom window.

At dinner that night, though, Mom announces, 'We're going over to Callum's tomorrow. He's invited us all to dinner.'

Dad says, 'That's good of him.'

And I say, unable to keep the whine out of my voice, 'But I was supposed to go to the movies with Josh tomorrow.' Mom gives me one of her looks, the kind I bet closes business deals, and I sigh. '*Fine*. I'll call him later to cancel.'

'Thank you.'

I can tell Josh is not exactly very happy that I'm ditching him for dinner with another guy.

'It's a family thing,' I say, for what feels like the billionth time. I rub a hand over my forehead, wondering if the headache I have is from trying hard not to argue with him, or if I'm just really tired. 'I can't get out of it.'

'Sure you can't,' he says, but he doesn't sound very convincing. 'I guess we can always go to the movies another time. It's not like we haven't been planning on this for a couple of weeks, or anything . . .'

I turn the phone away to sigh. I want to yell at him for acting like a child, but I don't – after all, I've just cancelled our date, so how can I blame him for being annoyed at me? I know I would be. And he's been wanting to see this movie since the commercials came out a few weeks back.

'I'm sorry.'

'Sure you are,' he says, but not in a mean way or anything. 'Have fun at your family dinner.'

'It won't be as fun as going to the movies with you.'

'I know it won't.' He sounds irritated now. I gnaw my lip, wondering if he's really mad at me, or if he's being overdramatic. I hope it's the latter.

'I'll call you tomorrow, okay?'

'Love you, babe.'

'Love you, too,' I say, and I smile as I hang up the phone.

Todd opens the door for us, offering up a polite smile, and an equally polite, 'Come on in.' My parents go in before me, and Todd tells them to go on through to the dining room, just down the hallway, dinner is only going to be a couple of minutes. Callum yells from the kitchen to say, 'Hello! Take a seat in the dining room; and Todd, get some drinks.'

'We brought some wine,' Dad says.

'Todd, pour the wine!' his dad shouts then, and my parents laugh. I close the door behind me, and Todd glances back at me with a small half-smile, which I return. After the episode with the Post-It note, he seems to be a little more comfortable around me. Not talkative, exactly, but more *willing* to talk.

Dinner actually isn't so bad. It's relaxed and easy-going, and everyone's laughing and smiling. Callum's gone the whole hog: a bread basket of warm rolls, and then a homemade beef casserole; and dessert is the most delectable strawberry cheesecake I've ever seen (again, made from scratch) and coffee or tea where appropriate. The bottle of wine disappeared during the main course. They poured a glass for me and Todd, too.

I'd pulled a face at my first taste of the wine; it was red, and I'd only ever had white before at Christmas or Thanksgiving when my parents poured me a small glass. Todd noticed and snorted, which sent us both into a fit of giggles.

'Todd tells me you've got a boyfriend, Ashley,' says Callum shortly after he's put dessert in front of us all.

'Um, yes . . .' It sounds a little like a question. I don't mean it to; I just wonder what Todd's said about Josh.

'He's on the baseball team,' Mom says.

'Although they nearly kicked him off because his grades were slipping,' Dad pitches in.

'It was the end of the season anyway,' I point out, 'so it didn't really matter. Besides, he didn't get kicked off. And he's joined the football team this year. He's like on their reserve squad, or whatever they call it.'

'How about you, Todd?' Mom moves the conversation swiftly and expertly onwards. 'Any girls caught your eye here in Greendale yet?'

He shakes his head, and loads some more cheesecake onto his fork. 'Not really.'

'Oh, come on,' I say. 'There are girls swooning when you walk down the hallways. The mysterious Todd O'Connor, with his edgy atmosphere. *And* you play guitar.'

He appears to be fascinated by the sight of the cheesecake on his fork, and shifts in his seat, but I don't miss the bright pink blush spreading over his cheeks. 'They're only interested in me because I'm the new kid.'

I roll my eyes, and put a strawberry in my mouth to shut myself up before I blurt out something incredibly stupid – but, admittedly, kind of true – and say that he's cute, *of course* girls are interested.

I mean, he does have something going for him in the looks department apart from those amazing cheekbones of his . . .

Not that it even matters what I think. He could be the next Adonis for all it matters to me. I've got Josh.

Once we all finish dessert, the adults carry on talking, and they're deep in conversation about their jobs, the state of the economy, and all that stuff. Callum pauses long enough to say, 'Why don't you kids go watch a movie or something? There's some popcorn in the cupboard, if you like. Todd, you know where it is.'

'Okay.'

Todd nods his head at me and I get up to follow him. I say, 'Thanks for dinner, it was amazing. My compliments to the chef.'

'No problem, Ashley,' Callum says with a broad grin, before turning back to my dad and carrying on his sentence. They all start to get up to move this conversation to the lounge, so Todd changes his direction to the staircase and I follow him up.

This time, he doesn't stop on the stairs.

'I would apologize for the quantity of papers on the floor, but I've been trying to catch up on my French grammar – I remember less than I should,' he tells me, without turning. I laugh. He pushes open his bedroom door. 'But I am going to apologize if there are any boxer shorts lying around. Because that's just a bad habit.'

I laugh again. 'Don't worry.'

He kicks a T-shirt that's in a heap on the floor out of

the way of the door and then holds his arm out to me to go on inside.

I've sort of seen Todd's bedroom; I can see it from my window if his drapes aren't shut. Out of the corner of my eye, I see him run to the side of the bed and kick some boxers out of sight.

The wall behind his bed is dark blue, like the carpet, but the others are cream, to keep the room from feeling too closed in and dark. His bedding is a gold sort of color, and there are dozens of posters of bands on the wall. Some are old and torn and some are shiny; some are signed and others are small, like they've been torn out of a magazine. And there are shelves lining the walls, holding so many books and CDs I would lose count if I tried to see how many there are.

'I read a lot,' he says, almost sheepishly, seeing me looking.

'So do I.' I think about the stacks of books leaning haphazardly against the walls in my room, some of which are almost as high as my waist. Dad's always saying he'll put up more shelves for my books, but he's yet to get around to it. And Mom prefers to keep the bookshelves in the lounge for things like recipe books and photo albums, and for displaying a few ornaments and photos.

'I know, I've seen you.' I turn to look at him,

quizzical. He rubs the back of his neck and laughs nervously. 'I mean . . . like the other night, I couldn't sleep, and then I saw your light was still on, so I looked over, and you were sat in your bed reading. It was like, two in the morning. Your shutters were open,' he adds.

Now it's my turn to look guilty.

'You don't read much during the day,' he says. 'At lunch. I've seen you. Sometimes you look bored out of your mind. But you read a lot at night.'

'That's . . .' I can't explain it to him. I wouldn't know how to, or where to start. 'It would be a bit antisocial.'

He nods and says, 'Mm.'

And I say loudly, 'So that's your guitar.' It's one of those acoustic ones, propped up in the corner by the window. His blue book is on the window seat, a black biro lying on top of it, next to a small black cushion.

'You're good,' I tell him. 'I hear you playing sometimes, if my window's open.'

He wavers, like he's not sure how to reply, until he finally says, 'Thanks.'

Todd sits down at the window seat, and I choose the bed, lying across it on my stomach and facing him. He's taken out his guitar pick again. I think he's a bit nervous – I know I am. This whole conversation feels tentative – like it's more personal than anything we've said so far. But I can't help myself from asking about the guitar pick.

'Why do you take that everywhere?'

I hear a soft sigh leaving his lips and his voice is quiet when he finally answers. 'It was my granddad's. He's the reason I got into guitar.' There's a long pause. I can see the struggle in his face – the shadow over his eyes and the frown underneath all that hair, and the contortion of his jaw muscles – and I know he's trying to find the right words to carry on. So I wait, to see if he'll tell me more.

'I was really close to my granddad. See, my mom . . . She left us about three years ago. She and my dad were always arguing, so they got a divorce and she moved to the next town over. I got to see her a lot, but she's back in Idaho. My dad got a job offer he couldn't pass up here, so I decided to move here with him.

'Anyway, my granddad – my mom's dad – he moved closer to us a couple of years ago, just before the divorce, and after my grandma died. Then he died a year ago. My mom's been a little distant since then, and she's got a new guy now. They're engaged.'

'What happened?' I ask before I can stop myself. 'To your granddad, I mean.'

'Heart attack. The hospital called us as soon as they could, and we got there just in time to say goodbye. He couldn't talk, or anything, but he held my hand real tight.'

If I was expecting him to tell me anything, it wasn't that.

I sit quietly for a moment. I still have all of my grandparents, except for my mom's dad, who passed away when I was two or three; and my parents have always had a strong, happy marriage. I can't even begin to relate to Todd's story. I try to think of something to say in reply because I can't stay silent.

Eventually, I manage to say, 'That must've been horrible. I can't even imagine . . .' Trailing off, I shake my head. 'I bet you're sick of condolences.'

'Damn straight.'

There's another long pause that feels like it lasts eons, but it isn't awkward or uncomfortable for once, and I don't think either of us is willing to break that silence for a while.

'That's about when I started writing songs,' he says. 'It helps.'

'I can understand that.'

'They're personal, though. That's why I don't like to share them.' Then he says, 'So do you want to watch a movie?'

And I reply, 'Sure. You pick, I'm good with whatever.'

As Todd sets up one of the *Iron Man* movies in his DVD player and grabs us some popcorn from the kitchen, I sit on his bed and I start to doubt every judgment I've made about him so far.

I don't mean to, but I fall asleep at Todd's house, sometime near the end of the movie. I don't even remember feeling sleepy.

'Ashley!' Mom's voice calling up the stairs wakes me up, and my eyes flash open, disconcerted by the sight of a room that's not mine. A hand shakes my shoulder. 'Are you ready to go?'

I'm lying on my side facing Todd, my knees tucked up and pressed against him. I scramble off the bed hastily, blushing at falling asleep and almost cuddling up to him. God, how humiliating!

Turning away from Todd, I discreetly wipe at the edges of my mouth. I didn't drool, at least – that's something.

'Ashley!' Mom calls again.

'Just a sec!' I yell, then turn to Todd with an awkward smile. 'Sorry, I guess I was more tired than I thought . . .'

'You haven't been asleep long,' he says, 'only about half an hour. I just – um, I didn't know whether to wake you or not.'

I shrug, like it doesn't matter – but I'm still embarrassed. I can hear him gulp, and I shift my weight from one foot to the other. 'I guess I should, um, go. Thanks for the popcorn.'

'Sure.'

He follows me downstairs, and his dad and my parents are laughing at something, and don't seem to notice the uneasiness between Todd and me. Mom has that rosy tint in her cheeks that she usually gets when she's drunk a little bit too much, and she has to hold onto Dad's arm to steady herself.

'What movie did you kids watch?' Callum asks us as I'm putting on my coat and shoes.

'*Iron Man 2*,' we chorus. I wait for Todd to laugh and tell them I fell asleep, but he doesn't.

We thank them again for the meal and the lovely evening, and I glance back at Todd, who's standing on the bottom step of the staircase fiddling with the guitar pick.

'Night,' I say.

'Night, Ashley,' he replies. There's a pause, when I think he might be about to say something else, but then my dad calls my name, and I wave to Todd before hurrying after my parents back home.

# Chapter Five

Neither Todd nor I brought up anything about our after-dinner conversation when we saw each other on Monday morning.

After we'd said hello, I counted to twenty-four before he decided to break the silence.

'I hope it doesn't rain later.' He grimaced, looking up at the dark clouds that were crawling across the sky.

I mumbled an agreement and tried to think of something else to say that wasn't about Saturday night and wasn't about the weather. I managed to make some small talk by asking what classes he had today, and we both complained about the amount of homework we'd already been given from the first week back at school.

Todd drives a lot slower than I do; everything he does is cautious and carefully calculated. He doesn't forget to put his blinkers on even once. But I looked at the clock on his dashboard and thought if he carries on driving like this, we'll have to leave at least five minutes earlier in future.

'You know, if you drive the whole way like this, I'd say we should be at school by . . . oh, maybe Friday. In March. If the traffic isn't too bad.'

He laughed, but didn't go any faster.

Now, it's lunchtime, and Eliza and Naomi are on one side of me discussing an episode of *The Vampire Diaries* that they watched last night, and Josh is talking to the boys on the other side of me.

Danielle comes careering over, slamming her palms down on the lunch table and catching everyone's attention.

'Party at Hunter Smith's house this Friday,' she says. 'Eight o'clock.'

'Cool,' I say along with everyone else, before taking another bite of my sandwich.

'*And* Todd O'Connor is totally going,' she adds. 'I spoke to Reyna who overheard him telling some guys in his French class that he'd go.'

'Wait, are you serious?' Eliza says, eyes bulging.

I roll my eyes.

'Oh, God, you guys aren't talking about the new kid again, are you?' Neil sighs. 'I thought this would've blown over by now.'

'Oh, you're just jealous!' Naomi waves a hand at

him. 'Of course it hasn't blown over. He's hot. And you know he plays guitar.' She addresses that statement more to us girls than to the guys. 'He's totally got that whole brooding musician thing going for him. It's *to die* for.'

'I know, right?' Eliza says.

Danielle says, 'Tell me about it.'

My mouth twists up in a wry smile. 'So I've heard.'

They look to me, perplexed. 'You don't think he's hot?'

I am suddenly very aware that Josh has turned away from his conversation to listen to my answer. I shrug, take another bite of my sandwich, chew deliberately, swallow. I go through the motions carefully, as though it requires a great amount of calculation. Josh is still listening and the girls are still waiting.

Finally, I sigh, 'Sure, I guess, I don't know. I haven't looked at him in that way. We just carpool. That's all.'

Satisfied that I think there's a certain charm about Todd O'Connor too, the girls carry on talking – now about the party.

Josh says to me, 'You just carpool? You had dinner with him.'

Turning to Josh, I place a hand on his knee underneath the table. 'Come on, you know I couldn't have got out of that. It was a family thing. It's not like I had a lot of choice in the matter.'

'Mm.'

Irritated at how much of a big deal he's making out of this, I settle for raising my eyebrows and giving him an unimpressed look.

'Aw, come on, Ashley, don't look at me like that.' He leans forward and gives me a brief kiss and smiles. I don't smile back, and when I reach for my bottle of water, and Josh turns back to the conversation about football, my eyes drift across the cafeteria, bored. Everyone is chatting and laughing and eating and maybe doing a bit of last-minute homework for their afternoon classes.

I start when I catch Todd's eye across the room. I don't know if he's been watching me or if he just happens to look over in my direction when I look in his. There's something in his face I can't quite define, and then he turns to the guy next to him. I shake my head to myself. Todd O'Connor is a very strange boy.

The rain is far heavier than it threatened to be this morning. I should have listened to Mom; I should just keep an umbrella in my bag all the time like she does. I don't even have a coat, just a sweatshirt with a hood. I didn't think it'd get this bad.

From inside the school, you can hear the rain ricocheting off the windows like teeny tiny cannonballs even if you're not near a window. It's ridiculous. The air in the hallways feels muggy, and I am grateful that Greendale High School is all within one large building so I don't need to get drenched going between classes.

Josh is supposed to give me a ride home after school; we were going to go back to his place for a while, and I'd stay for dinner. But he texts me during last period to say that football practice isn't canceled after all, so he won't be able to see me until later this evening.

Mom has to go to a meeting this afternoon, and Dad will be working till at least seven o'clock.

I find myself texting Todd, asking if he can give me a ride home after all.

*'Sure thing. Meet me at my car after school.'*

At least I'm not walking, I think with a sigh of relief.

When the day is over at last, I weave through the throng of students heading the same way as me to the parking lot, and push against those moving the other way to catch their buses.

'Ashley! Hey, Ashley!'

I look around, people bumping into me from all directions. I crane my neck, stretching myself up on my tiptoes. I see Josh waving me over, and I join the crowd of people moving to get their buses until I detach from them to stand in the corner he's lounging in.

He leans against the wall, arms folded across his broad chest. As I step up to him, he opens his arms and folds me into them, and I breathe in the weakened smell of his aftershave. I bury my head into his blue T-shirt for a moment. The fabric softener his mom uses makes it smell of coconut. For those brief seconds, I inhale his smell and I smile, curling my arms around his neck. 'I was sure Coach was going to cancel with this weather,' he tells me. 'Have you got a ride home?'

'Yeah, Todd's going to take me. Give me a call later if you still want me to come over.'

He nods. 'Of course I will. It'll probably be about six.'

'All right.' I reach up and he leans down to meet me for a kiss, a kiss that he draws out and deepens. I pull away first; not because I don't want to kiss him but because I don't want to kiss him like that here, in plain sight. 'I have to get going. I love you.'

'I love you, too,' he replies, kissing me quickly once again. I smile and wrap my hair into a knot at the back of my neck to keep it tucked into my hood as I pull it up.

'See you tonight,' he calls after me.

My sweatshirt is already soaked and my T-shirt

sticking to my skin by the time I reach Todd's car near the back of the student parking lot. I automatically go to open the door, but it's locked – then I notice that Todd's not even in his car yet. I look around, squinting because the rain's getting in my eyes, but I don't see him. I hold my binder over my head, but it offers little protection.

I am left with no other option but to wait here for him in the rain.

He jogs over a minute or two later, holding his hand over his head – *as if that's going to help*, I snort derisively to myself – and by then, my teeth are chattering, and my hands have turned numb.

'Sorry,' he says, almost shouting because the rain is so loud. 'Had to talk to my history teacher.' He unlocks the car and I clamber in, my limbs stiff from the cold.

He cranks up the heating. I'm glad; I'm shivering all over. 'How long were you waiting?'

'Not long.'

He nods. There's no point in either of us making some sort of small-talk comment about how horrible and dreadful this weather is. We can both see it for ourselves.

'Josh's football practice wasn't canceled,' I say. The words sound clipped where my teeth are still chattering.

'Sorry, if I'm being rude or anything. My parents are both in work.'

'No, don't worry about it. You live next door. It's not like it's an inconvenience.' He twists his head slightly to give me a small half-smile, and I smile back.

'Well, thanks.' Then I recognize the song playing on the radio, and, smiling to myself, I turn the volume up slightly, humming along to it because I don't like to sing outside the safety of my bedroom or the shower.

We turn down Maple Drive and Todd parks on the kerb outside his house. I yell a quick, 'Thanks for the ride! See you tomorrow!' and make a run through the rain for my front door.

The rain's gotten even heavier, and it stings my hands. I sigh with relief when I step under my porch. It leaks a little, but it's shelter, so I'm not complaining.

I root through the front pocket of my satchel for my house key, and frown when my fingers can't find it. I pull the bag open, holding it up near my face, and carry on rooting around, but I don't hear the jangle of my keychains. It's not there. My key isn't there.

I hastily check my wallet and pencil case in case I put it there by accident at some point, and dig a hand under my books, groping hopelessly for my key.

It isn't there.

God. Just as this couldn't have gotten *any* worse.

I lean my head against the front door. I remember now: I left it on top of my math homework, on my desk. I'd purposely put it there to remind myself about the homework – which I still forgot about. We don't keep a spare key outside anywhere. I step backwards, out of the protection of the porch and onto the lawn, craning my neck up. My hood falls down before I'm able to catch it, and I squint through the rain, trying to pull my hood back up even though my hair is already wet and sticking to my face and neck.

I've managed to sneak out of the house before, and back in: I can just about climb up the tree in the back garden and onto the strip of roof around the middle of the house, and from there I can get to my window.

But my window is not open and so that plan will not work.

Of course. Mom always makes sure that she closes up all the windows and locks the front and back door whenever we leave the house. So it's no use trying to get in around the back either.

I stand there in the rain, shivering, and wonder what the hell I'm going to do.

'Ashley! Hey!'

I turn my head so sharply that a tendril of hair whips at my cheek and sticks there. Todd waves at me from his porch. He's barefoot, hugging his arms around him now that he's taken off his jacket and is only in a T-shirt and jeans.

'What are you doing?' he yells over to me.

'Wondering how to break in,' I shout back. 'I forgot my key this morning.'

'Come on.' He waves, gesturing for me to go over there.

'What, do you have a crowbar I can use to jiggle open the window in the dining room?' I ask as I jog over.

My pumps aren't made for running on wet surfaces though, which doesn't occur to me until my back smacks with a disgusting wet sound onto Todd's muddy front lawn and the air is slammed out of my lungs. I groan.

I hear a burst of laughter. Moaning, I sit up, and shake some of the mud from my right hand. Gross. I can feel it seeping through my damn jeans and my hair feels heavy with the stuff. I pull a face in disgust.

Then Todd's dashing out toward me, shoes halfway on his feet, helping me up regardless of the sludge on my hands. He ushers me into the house.

'You really need a welcome mat,' I say, and take my shoes off before I step into the hallway. I leave them outside because I don't want to ruin the carpet, and they're soaked anyway – they can't get much wetter out on the porch.

Todd drags me upstairs after him and then pushes me into the bathroom. There are men's grooming products all over the place – razors and electric shavers and a tube of Crest, which has toothpaste all around the cap. Todd rinses his hands, muddy from helping me up, under the faucet quickly and wipes them dry on his jeans.

'I'll find you a towel and something dry to wear,' he says. He takes my satchel from me, and then closes the door behind him.

I sneeze.

I stare at the closed door for a moment before my brain finally begins to process what to do next. I don't exactly feel comfortable about taking a shower at Todd's house. It's kind of weird. But I look in the mirror and see that my hair is dripping mud and my clothes are stuck to me. So until my parents get home, it's not like I have anywhere else to go. And I can hardly sit around Todd's house like this – I mean, I'd ruin the couch.

Stripping off my clothes and stepping into a hot shower, rinsing the rain and dirt from me, feels much better than I'd expected. I don't want to stay there too long, but I lose track of time. There's a bottle of shampoo on the side, so I borrow a little and clean my hair out thoroughly.

I don't know when I started singing, but at some point, I realize that I'm singing the way I always do in the shower, and I clamp my mouth shut in case Todd overhears.

After that, I hastily rinse my hair and pull back the shower curtain. A towel is tucked just inside the door; I didn't even hear the door open. And I'd forgotten to lock it.

I dry myself off, and then . . .

I can't put my wet, muddy clothes back on. Even my bra is soaked.

My underwear's a little damp, but I don't care. I put that back on. Then I secure the towel around me and push open the door only enough to poke my head out and peek around to see if Todd's left any clothes in the hallway for me.

He hasn't.

'Todd?' I call out cautiously. No answer. Where the hell is he? I raise my voice a little more. 'Todd?'

'Just a sec!'

I retreat back into the bathroom, and decide to start scrubbing the mud off my sweatshirt in the sink. The sound of the door opening again makes me jump about a foot in the air, and I drop the sweatshirt, clutching a hand to my chest to hold the towel in place.

'Jeez, Todd, want to try knocking next time? You scared the hell out of me!'

I shift uncomfortably, feeling very exposed in just this towel – which is very small, and only just about covers my boobs and butt at the same time. I put one arm around my chest and hold the towel secure. I feel like I may as well be naked.

I hear a quiet chuckle, and settle for glaring at him.

'Are you going to make seeing me in a towel a habit? I might have to get a restraining order if that's the case.'

'I'm sorry, I didn't think . . . I mean, when you yelled for me, I . . .'

I raise my eyebrows at him, trying to use the glare to divert any attention from glancing downward. But then I realize that his eyes are anywhere but on me – the ceiling, the floor, the dripping faucet in the sink.

'Here,' he says, offering me some clothes. 'They'll probably be too big, but they're the best I could do. If you hand me your clothes, I can throw them in the dryer for you, if you want?'

I shake my head. 'It's okay. I can wash them when I finally get into my house. Do you have a plastic carrier or something I can put them in, though?'

'Sure.' Still not looking at me, he puts down the pile of clothes in his hands and takes the wet ones from me.

I hug the clothes to my chest and he quickly backs out of the bathroom.

I let out a long breath of air and shake my head, turning my attention to the clothes.

He's given me a long-sleeved shirt, and a pair of jeans and a belt. I'm glad he thought to give me the belt – which is the kind you loop through a hook so there are no holes – because the jeans sag to my knees without them. I have to roll up the legs, and also the sleeves of the shirt. But I'm not complaining. This is better than nothing.

I walk out of the bathroom, refreshed, and shout for Todd again.

'In here.'

His voice comes from the end of the hallway, from his bedroom. When I go in, he's sitting cross-legged on his bed reading. I linger, hesitant, in the doorway.

He looks up.

And laughs.

'What?' I scowl. 'What's so funny?'

'You look ridiculous.'

I roll my eyes, but can't think of any sarcastic retort to snap at him. Exasperated, I purse my lips and turn away to look at his bookshelf, only half paying attention as I glance over the book titles he owns. 'Thank you, by the way.'

'I could hardly leave you standing out there in the rain like that.'

'Yeah, but still . . . thanks,' I mumble. I tuck a piece of hair behind my ear.

After a few seconds, Todd says, 'Your hair's red.'

'No it's not,' I snap, looking over my shoulder to scowl at him and glare. 'It's not red. It's *auburn*. It's closer to brown than it is to red. I should know, I see it every day.'

He shakes his head at me, unperturbed by my snappiness. 'No it isn't. It's red. I've been trying to decide, because some days it looks brown, but more often than not it looks red.'

'It's the *lighting*.'

'It's your *perspective*,' he shoots back.

I grind my teeth, not sure how to reply. It would sound childish if I repeated him. So instead, I march up to him and lean close to his face. He leans back, looking a little worried, but I lean forward with him, scrutinizing his eyes. Today they look gray. But yesterday I was so sure they were blue.

I sigh in defeat, and throw my hands up in the air.

'What?' he asks.

'Your eyes. I can't decide what color they are.'

'I usually say that they're blue, it's easier.'

'And I say that my hair is auburn, it's easier,' I retort.

He shrugs. 'That's your choice. I was simply making a statement. I didn't know you'd get so touchy about it.'

I just shrug, then sit at the foot of the bed. I pick up a school textbook to move it out of the way; it's poking into my knee. From the corner of my eye I see Todd sit up straighter, leaning forward. Then I see why – his blue book is under the book I just moved, right next to me.

The book he keeps close to him all the time and never lets people see, with its faded midnight-blue cover made of leather. I pick the book up and see Todd's body jerk reflexively, as though his nervous system is connected to this thing. I place the book in my lap, keeping my eyes on it rather than Todd; but I can see him in my peripheral vision. He looks ready to pounce.

I trail my fingers over the cover. It has that strange softness to it that only leather has, and it's heavy, weighted down by all the loose papers and Post-It notes tucked inside. A ribbon attached to the spine hangs out of the bottom of the book. It's frayed. I wrap it around the tip of my index finger, and then hold the book firmly in both hands, bringing it up to my face. It smells faintly of leather, and of old paper. It's a scent that reminds me of some of my dad's old books from college.

'So,' I say. And I put the book on the bed between us, but closer to Todd. 'Are you going to Hunter's party on Friday?'

A cautious and curious frown tugs at Todd's dark eyebrows, and he cocks his head to the side slightly. The light throws shadows over his face from his sharp cheekbones. 'I pour my entire heart and soul into that book. You don't even try and take a look.'

'You're avoiding my question,' I state simply.

The truth is, I do want to look. I want to see the kind of things that Todd writes in this book, read and feel his emotions and thoughts and see his deepest, darkest ideas. I want to read the book. But he is too protective of it. It's like when I found the Post-It note he dropped in Creative Writing.

The answer I give him when he refuses to answer my question is, 'You don't want me to read it.'

It's true, but it's not enough for him. 'Care to expand on that?'

I mull the words over in my head. 'You're . . . not weird, that's the wrong word. Different. You're *different* and I'm curious. Of course I want to see for myself what you're hiding so badly. The fact that you're so damn protective of that book makes me wonder even more what you don't want anybody to see. But I'm not mean. I don't really know you, but I know that that book means a lot to you.'

He looks at me like he is studying me. His eyes have a calculated look about them, like they are trying to pick me apart.

I don't have anything to add, so I settle for staring right back at him instead.

Finally, he says, 'You aren't mean, Ashley, not at all. Sarcastic, sure, but you aren't mean.'

'I try not to be. But I could've been nicer to you when I met you. I could've tried to introduce you to people at school. I—'

'Just because you aren't the most selfless person in the world doesn't make you a mean person,' he tells me. He picks up the book and holds it lightly in his lap.

I don't have a reply for that, so I settle for looking at my hands, which are folded in my lap now.

A while later, Todd speaks again. 'I got expelled from my last school.'

My head whips up. '*What?*'

He shrugs, a twisted smirk on his face as he leans back against the pillows and props his legs up in a triangle. 'Not exactly like the rumors are saying, don't worry. It was a boarding school, in Idaho,' he adds as an afterthought. 'After my granddad died, we got some money, and I knew he'd always wanted me to go to this boarding school, where my mom had gone. But I . . . I didn't cope well, with him dying. I skipped a lot of classes, and my grades were *abysmal*. And I mean, it was a pretty prestigious sort of school, and they didn't want me ruining their reputation with my bad grades and even worse attitude. They gave me a chance to clean up my act, but when I didn't, they said I could finish up the semester and that I wouldn't be coming back after that. I finished the year at a local high school, and then my dad got the job offer for here, so we moved.'

I realize I'm gnawing on my lip as he tells his story, and I stop.

'After I got kicked out of boarding school, my dad was furious. Said I was risking my entire future. I want to get into a good college, really I do. And I'm willing to bust my ass to get the grades I need. Getting expelled was the reality check I needed, you know?'

'Josh could do with one of those,' I mutter. 'The reality check, I mean. He barely gets a B average, and I keep telling him he could get better grades if he worked harder, but he doesn't listen. He acts like he doesn't care when he fails a test, but then he'll sulk like a little kid outside of school.'

Todd nods, and I notice that his left hand is balled into a fist, resting on his thigh, and his breathing is shallow, like he's upset. I'm not even sure he just heard what I said about Josh. I start to reach out to touch his knee, but my hand hesitates midair and I let it drop back onto my lap.

'Why are you telling me this, anyway?' I ask him quietly, when he doesn't say anything more.

He shrugs. 'I don't know. I . . . I don't find it . . . *easy* . . . to trust people. I believed you when you said you didn't read that Post-It note. You didn't even try to look at my book and read it.' He chews on his lower lip, frowning, and his eyes look up at me from under all that hair flopping over his forehead. 'I don't know.'

I give a small smile. 'I won't tell anybody. The truth, I mean, not if you don't want me to. They can go on believing all those wild rumors about you. Like that you blew up a science lab, or whatever it was.'

'I know you won't. That's not the point.' He puts his legs down and shifts his position.

'Then . . . what is the point, exactly?'

Todd opens his mouth, then closes it, and frowns again. The scrape of pages makes me look at the book in his lap. He's flicking through it. The writing is loopy and slanted on the page.

'That one, right there.' As he hands the book to me, he taps a finger on a torn piece of green paper about the size of the palm of my hand, stapled to the top of a page. Wary, I take it.

*They say the truth will set you free*
*That the lies will drive you crazy*
*Well, truth be told, I don't care for either*
*I'm not looking, I've no desire to see*
*What this crazy little world's hiding from me*

*Keep your truths and I'll keep mine*
*We'll get along just fine*
*Keep your mouth shut*
*And your head down low*
*In our sick little world of lies*

There are a few letters scribbled on the side. I point to them. 'What are they?'

'Chords,' he says, taking the book back from me and closing it. 'I never bothered to finish it. I tend to do that a lot – write half a song and leave it at that.'

I don't ask him why he showed me this particular song, but I let it sink in. I swallow, and say, 'You never answered my question about Hunter's party.'

'Well, damn, I thought I'd done a pretty good job of distracting you from that.' He sighs exaggeratedly in defeat, which makes me laugh. 'Yeah, I'm going. Some guys in my class were talking about it earlier and said I should go, so now I am. I'm not usually one for parties, but what the hell, right?'

'He threw a couple of parties over the summer. They were pretty good.'

'Cool. I'm just going to get a drink, do you want anything?'

'No, I'm good. Thanks.'

'Suit yourself.' He leaves the book on the bed where he was sitting, and I don't touch it. I know I didn't want to 'buddy-up' with this guy purely on principle, but I misjudged him. And, hell, I'll admit it: I'm curious about him. And even though I know Josh is a bit wary (and I think probably a bit jealous) about me hanging out with Todd even just a little bit, I don't care. I really don't care.

# Chapter Six

Josh's hands slip around my waist from behind and he kisses the side of my neck.

I'm surprised to see him here, but smile at him in the mirror we're facing and say, 'I thought I was picking you up from your house? Did you drive here?'

'My parents dropped me off on their way to the grocery store. Your mom sent me up to wait while you finish getting ready.' He kisses my neck again softly.

'Careful,' I say, moving the hair-straighteners away from my head so that I don't burn either of us. I set them down on the heat-proof mat and turn around to slip my arms around Josh's neck.

'You look good,' I tell him. He does, in the white shirt that sets off the tan he got in Cancun when he went at the end of summer, and the dark-wash jeans slung low on his hips, held up by the tan leather belt I bought him last Christmas.

'So do you.'

I laugh. 'I'm not even ready yet.'

'What's your point?'

I giggle again, and kiss him quickly. 'Five minutes, okay? Then I'll be ready to go.'

'All right,' he sighs, stepping back and throwing himself on the bed, turning off the music I had playing before flipping through TV channels and settling on an episode of *Fresh Prince of Bel-Air.* I finish my hair, and smooth out the skirt of my dress. It's navy, with a white peter-pan collar and a white bow on the sash around my waist. I got it a few weeks ago when I went shopping with my mom.

'Is that new?' Josh asks, of the dress.

'Yeah.'

'It's nice. You look gorgeous, Ashley.'

I smile, feeling warm inside. 'Thanks.' I lean into the mirror to top up my mascara and then pick up my shoes. 'Ready to go?'

'Wait till the commercial break,' he says. 'There's no rush.'

He pats the space on the bed next to him, and, still smiling, I lie down beside him, my head cushioned by his arm that wraps around my shoulder. We don't talk, we just watch the show, and I half wish we could stay here like this all night, and that we didn't have to go to the party. Every so often, he kisses my cheek or my forehead, and occasionally I turn my head to kiss him back. 'I love you,' I murmur.

'I love you, too.'

The show cuts to commercial and we stand up, and call goodbye to my parents as we leave. I'm driving tonight, since we decided it was my turn, and I don't mind staying sober too much at these parties, whereas I know Josh likes to have a beer with everyone else.

It doesn't take very long to get to Hunter's house, maybe fifteen minutes at the most. It's nine-fifteen, so I have to park a street away since most people are already here now. His house is pretty big, and I quickly see that this party, like the ones he threw over summer, is no small event.

There are people on the front lawn, and people around the back, and the house is completely full, with people sitting on the stairs and kitchen worktops and coffee tables. The music pounds through the house, filling my body with an adrenalin rush.

'There they are.' Josh has to shout to me because the music is so loud. I let him tug me off in the direction of our friends. Naomi has her arm around Sam's waist, her head on his shoulder, giggling to herself between hiccups, and Eliza looks spaced out, swaying on her feet.

'Hey.' They greet us with nods and hellos.

'Where's Danielle?' I ask.

'Last I saw her she was making out with Neil?' Eliza tells me, looking at me with wide, blank eyes that aren't focused on me at all.

'Again?' I roll my eyes. Neil and Danielle are always making out at parties. But whenever anyone suggests that they actually date rather than play the whole friends-with-benefits game, they look scandalized, like, how could we ever suggest that, they're *friends* for God's sake, jeez.

I'm listening to snatches of conversation going on around me, when I realize just what Josh, Sam and Austin are talking about.

'What movie is that?' I ask, though I already have a good idea.

'That new Marvel movie,' Austin says.

I turn an accusing glance on my boyfriend. 'You mean that one we were going to go see together, and I had to cancel because we were having dinner with Todd and his dad?'

He sniffs, and looks away. 'We went to see it yesterday.'

'So when you told me that you were hanging out with the guys, you went to see the movie we planned on seeing? You didn't think to tell me?'

'I figured we could see it together anyway.'

I shake my head. It's not even worth arguing with him over it. I'm just put out that he didn't bother to tell me about it. I mean, what else doesn't he tell me.

'I'm going to go talk to some of the football guys for a sec,' Josh announces, though I get the feeling he wants to go before I have chance to argue with him any more. He squeezes my arm. 'Catch you in a bit.'

And he disappears, weaving through the crowds, and calling out to someone. I turn back to the others. Danielle and Neil show up not long after and Naomi starts gushing to me about the almost-fight earlier because this guy from Kingsley High made out with Shauna, who everyone knows is only 'on a break' with that guy in Naomi's algebra class . . .

Someone taps my arm, making me look around. I know it's not Josh.

Todd gives me a hesitant smile. 'Hello.'

'Hello,' I reply. 'Having fun?'

'Oh my God?' I hear Eliza say behind me, and Naomi adds, 'Totally.'

'Sure, it's a good party. You?'

'I only just got here a little while ago,' I say.

He nods. 'Um. You look pretty.'

I'm taken aback by the compliment. 'Oh, well . . . thanks.'

'The dress suits your red hair very well.'

'It. Is. Not. *Red!*'

'In fact . . .' He scrunches his face critically at me. 'I'd even say it was ginger.'

I shove his shoulder, scowling, but when he tries to bite back a grin and repress a laugh I find myself fighting off a smile as well.

'Goodbye, Todd.' I turn my back on him and listen to Austin telling Neil and Sam some joke. Naomi leans forward from Sam, stumbling into me, and grabs at Todd over my shoulder before he can get away. Poor guy. He should've left while he had the chance.

'I don't think we've met,' she says, sounding far less drunk than she is. Her sister is twenty-two, and she'll always buy us alcohol for parties if we ask her. She stands up from leaning against me and tosses her hair over her shoulder. 'I'm Naomi. You're Todd, right?'

Half of me wants to get out of there, but I don't – the option of staying and seeing him flounder as Naomi makes a move on him is too funny to pass up.

'Y-yeah,' he stammers. 'Nice to meet you.'

'You haven't got a drink,' she says. 'Come on, we'll go get you something.'

And she puts her hands on Todd's shoulders and steers him away toward the kitchen, not even tottering a little bit in her heels. If nothing else, I have to admit that Naomi is tough, managing to walk in those three-inch stilettos all night without complaining, or toppling, once. Lesser women would cry. I know I would.

Todd glances back to me with one thing written clearly all over his face: *Help!*

Soon enough, Josh finds me when I'm hanging with Austin and Neil who are playing pool with a few other guys. Eliza's somewhere in the lounge dancing, and Naomi . . . well, she's probably trying to make out with Todd. I'm not sure how that's going; not sure I *want* to know.

Josh's arm slips around my waist from nowhere, making me jump and spill some of my soda on the floor. I don't turn in to his kiss, letting him just kiss my cheek instead. I'm still annoyed that he didn't tell me he went to see the movie.

Okay, so it's just a movie, and it's not a big deal. It's just that he didn't *tell* me about it, and after he gave me the cold shoulder for about a day when I cancelled on him like it was a huge deal.

'Hey, again,' I say casually. 'How were the guys?'

He shrugs vaguely. 'All right.' He takes another gulp of his beer, emptying the can.

'How much have you had?' I ask, curious, wondering if that's his second or third.

'Three,' he tells me, setting the empty can on a

cabinet. Then he draws me in close and kisses me deeply. He pulls away first. 'Why don't we go dance?'

'Sure,' I reply, and he smiles, walking with me to the lounge where a writhing tangle of sweaty bodies moves to the music blasting from the speakers.

I love the atmosphere at parties – everyone having a good time, laughing and dancing and talking and occasionally making out. And one of the good parts is, if you ever embarrass yourself, you can just pretend that you were drunk and don't remember. At least, that's what Naomi and the others always say.

I briefly wonder what happened to Todd and Naomi – but again, I'm not sure I really want to think about it.

Josh's lips find mine and I hook my arms around his broad shoulders, losing myself in his kiss, his touch; for a moment, I forget where we are, caught up in the excitement of the party.

Someone bumps into me from behind and yells, 'Sorry!' which makes me remember where I am, and I pull back slightly from Josh's kisses. He slips a hand quickly to pinch my butt and then back onto my hip. He looks away innocently, before laughing and kissing the end of my nose, making me smile.

'Sorry,' he says, a twinkle in his green eyes. 'Guess I just can't keep my hands off you.'

I roll my eyes and go up on my toes to kiss him. At

six foot one, he's five inches taller than me, and he's built like a boulder – or so I tease him – so he makes me feel small in comparison, even when I'm used to being taller than a lot of the girls at school. It's a nice sort of feeling though.

After a while, when Josh is talking to some of the guys in his gym class, I head out to the back yard, where I find Eliza, Austin and a couple of other people. Austin and one of the girls – Charlotte – are holding roll-up cigarettes; they're passing them between each other, taking long, labored drags before letting the smoke ease out. They wave me over, and when I'm a couple of feet away, the smell hits me. I don't even want to ask where they got them from.

I cough a little, and wave a hand in front of my face.

'Hey, there you are,' Eliza says. She takes another drag as one of them is passed to her, and then holds it out to me. 'Want some?'

'Uh, no – no thanks,' I stammer, wondering if I can just back away quickly before the smoke clings to my clothes and makes my hair smell. Although I think it's probably already too late for that.

She shrugs. 'Suit yourself.'

Austin pipes up then, saying, 'C'mon, Ashley, I bet you've never even tried it.'

I frown. 'I don't plan to, either.'

Turning away on my heel , I go swiftly back into the house. I ignore the one shout of 'Prude!' from one of the girls in the circle. I make straight for the bathroom, wanting to go freshen up somehow – maybe find some perfume, or air freshener even, to mask the smell of cigarette smoke that's undoubtedly attached to my clothes now. It's so *disgusting*. And I don't want my parents to think I was the one smoking.

I should be surprised at them, but I'm really not.

I have to step around people on the staircase up to the bathroom. There are a couple of people waiting in front of me to use it though, and I sigh, leaning against the wall behind them. Now I'm here, I realize I need to pee anyway.

'Boo.'

I turn to the person walking up behind me. It's Todd, and I grin at him. 'Hey.'

'Hey yourself.' He sniffs, scrunches his face up, then leans in to sniff around my neck and shoulders. When he stands back up straight, his eyebrows are raised skeptically. 'I never took you for someone who smokes.'

I jut my chin out stubbornly. 'I don't. I made the mistake of standing around some people who did, though.'

'Oh. Sorry. My bad.'

He rubs the back of his neck uncomfortably, like he's

ashamed for having not just asked and made it sound like he was judging me. Wanting to lighten things up a little, I ask with a mischievous smile, 'Where's Naomi?'

He clears his throat. 'I managed to detach myself from her about an hour ago.' He smiles wryly. 'After making it explicitly clear that I was a) not interested, and b) not kissing her anyway.'

'Break the girl's heart, why don't you?'

He gives a breath of laughter. 'She's . . . very determined. Confident.'

My laugh is abrupt and loud enough for a few people to shoot me a strange look. 'That's a nice way of putting it.'

'You and Josh really don't have much of a problem with PDA, do you?'

The question catches me off-guard. He says it in a composed, off-hand tone, looking at the people walking past us instead of me, as though it were more of a statement than a question. My eyebrows pull together of their own accord, and instead of moving up the queue as someone leaves the bathroom, I turn to stare at him.

'What's that supposed to mean?'

He sighs. 'Nothing. Look, forget it. I didn't mean anything by it.'

'No, tell me.' My voice sounds harsher than I

intended, but I don't care. 'What did you mean by that?'

He doesn't answer.

'*Todd.*' I sound pissed as hell now, and a couple of heads turn again, but I'm past caring. I just want to know what he meant by that comment.

'Forget it.' He starts to walk off. 'I'll see you Monday.'

I ignore my bladder and march after him, grabbing his arm. 'Todd, tell me. I'm not going to let it drop.'

With a huff, he stops in his tracks, so suddenly that I walk right into him.

He turns and looks me dead in the eye. 'I just meant that maybe next time you should think about going somewhere a little more private if you're going to get so handsy.'

'I was *not*—'

'No, but *he* was.'

'He was not!' I burst out, but I try and think back and wonder if he was. 'Besides, you've got no right to—'

'I'll see you Monday, Ashley.' And he marches down the stairs and around the corner. I bounce on the balls of my feet agitatedly, torn between following him and dashing back to the bathroom – I do *not* want to let him win this argument – but my bladder wins out, and I let out a noise of frustration. After that, I try to enjoy the rest of the party and not think about it.

But when I'm lying curled up in bed later that night back at home, I scowl at the shadows on my walls, wondering what the hell Todd meant by all that, and what the hell it has to do with him what I do with my boyfriend anyway.

# Chapter Seven

Todd and I don't speak on Monday morning. I'm still a little mad about what he said at the party, even though it feels childish to sulk about it.

He's returned to giving off the aloof, brooding impression I first had of him. He stares out of the window the whole time, mouth pressed in a tight line. I almost want to say something to him – not necessarily about our argument, but just a 'So how was your weekend?' but I don't.

Two can play at this game.

If he's going to be stubborn and not talk to me, then I will be, too.

It's my turn to drive this week though, and my mom told me I was not allowed to cancel on Todd.

'It's stupid. You had a little argument over nothing and it'll blow over,' she said. 'He lives next door, Ashley, it's stupid not to carpool.'

'Mom, you don't get it,' I sighed, but she was going

on again before I could say anything else. And I wasn't about to explain why I was so mad, because I wasn't entirely sure any more myself.

'Ashley. Don't be so silly and stubborn. Drive the guy to school. Don't make me ground you.'

By that point, I wanted to tear my hair out and just go to bed already without any hassle – Mom was already annoyed because I'd missed my curfew and got home late from the party. So I threw my hands in the air and yelled, 'Fine!' and stormed up to my room. And I didn't cancel on Todd.

Wednesday, I'm contemplating how best to cut my next class, Creative Writing. The car rides with Todd have been insufferable. He looks at me sometimes and there's something in his expression – maybe confusion, or pity – that makes me want to snap at him. I don't want to spend the next class with him. I really don't want to.

But I don't do that kind of thing; I don't cut class, I don't get detentions, I don't do anything to make myself stand out too much.

So I go to class and slip silently into my seat next to him and keep my eyes trained on the pen marks on the desk. Todd, for his part, is pretending not to acknowledge my presence.

After Ms Langstone sets us work, a hum of chatter

consumes the room and people start to take out their pens to look productive.

I can't help but steal a glance at Todd, who's tapping his pen in an erratic rhythm on his blue book.

'Something you're working on? The tapping, I mean.' I clamp my mouth shut as soon as the words are out, and twist my head away, letting my hair fall between us. So much for not talking to him . . .

I half expect him to not reply.

'Yeah. Just something I started writing the other night.'

'Oh.'

'Yeah,' he says again, then looks away and bites his lip. There's a pause. 'So we're talking again now?'

I don't answer at first. I feel so stupid for not talking to him all week, but after our silent car ride to school on Monday morning, I felt like it was too late to give in and apologize, and admit I'd been stupid. Feeling humiliated with myself, I mumble, 'I suppose.'

'I'm sorry,' he says. 'For being rude to you at the party. I should've just kept my mouth shut. It wasn't my place.'

'Damn right it wasn't.'

It had been lucky that the people who had been around to see that we'd had an argument (even just a little one) had been too drunk to remember anything about it, or at least, hadn't thought it important enough to gossip about.

Todd pulls his iPod out of his rucksack and, after stealing a glance at Ms Langstone, who is marking papers, he puts an earphone in and presses play. I look at the artwork that comes up on the iPod screen out of curiosity – it's Green Day – and then he hands me the other earphone. I smile, and take it.

We get away with that because we're hidden from sight back here, mostly. The school has a strict policy (at least, most of the time) on no cellphones and no listening to music during class, so I feel like I'm doing something daring and breaking the rules – something I *never* do.

Later that evening, Josh and I sit on my bed. I've pushed my stacks of books out of the way underneath my bed so that my room doesn't look so messy.

We sit cross-legged facing each other, and Josh has plugged his iPod into my docking station; some of his favorite rap songs are playing. I'm looking through college brochures, and even though Josh has one on his lap, he hasn't so much as opened it.

'. . . and Coach reckons there are going to be some college scouts at this game,' he says. 'It's the first game of the season, but he seemed pretty sure of it. And you know what he said to me after practice? He pulled me and Craig aside and said to us, "Now, boys, you listen here, you're going to play the best damn game you've played yet next week on that field, in case there's a scout there." He knows we're two of the best players on the team, really thinks we've got a good shot at a scholarship.'

I don't bother pointing out that he's only playing in the game because one of the guys is off sick with mono, and Josh has been temporarily promoted from reserve. He'd be on the actual team if he could keep his grades up (but he never seems to hear me when I point that out). And the college scout is more likely to be looking for someone who gets good grades alongside being good at football.

'I thought you weren't bothered about a scholarship?' I say. It's not like he can't afford college anyway; his grandfather left him a pretty big inheritance he'll have access to when he's twenty-one, and his parents have a more than comfortable lifestyle. His dad's always saying (loudly and brashly) that they'll pay for Josh to go to a good college and still have money left over to build that extension on the house they want.

'But if I can get one, Ashley, then—'

'What about your grades?' I say then, looking up at

him. 'When you said about the scholarship before, you said they wanted straight A grades, and—'

'Ashley. C'mon. I can pull my grades up for that. Or are you trying to say you don't think I'm smart enough to get into college?'

'I didn't say that.' I repress a sigh as I say the words, and refrain from rolling my eyes. 'I didn't say you weren't smart enough for college, I just meant that you might need to, you know, study a little more if you really want the scholarship.'

'You don't think I know that?' He sighs loudly, aggravated with me. 'Jesus, Ashley, give me some credit.'

'I didn't mean it like that, you know I didn't.' I let out a long breath through my nose and smile. It's no use getting angry and raising my voice: if I ever get really mad over something, Josh just finds it funny. Well, 'adorable' is the word he uses. So I know he won't take me seriously if I get short with him over this. 'You'll be brilliant at the game, I know you will. A college scout would have to be crazy not to look at you.'

*It's just the grades that might affect you*, I add silently. Last year he got mostly B's and C's, not quite meeting the baseball team's A/B grade requirements. This year, I know, he isn't exactly putting all that much effort into studying. He spends his free time playing football or hanging out with the guys, or with me instead.

But what's he going to say if I tell him to study more, to work harder, to stop wasting his time? I'm only thinking about the long-term and what's best for him, but he won't even listen to me, not about this. He'll realize without me soon enough that he can't keep handing in assignments knocked together the night before they're due and putting off homework to play video games.

So I don't say anything. Let him figure it out the hard way.

*God*, I think with a moment of horror, *I sound like my mother*.

'What about you?' he asks. 'Thought any more about college?'

I shrug, one shoulder and then the other. 'I'm thinking about maybe doing a degree in French now. I looked at some courses and I'd get to spend a year studying in France as part of the degree . . .'

'I thought you were going to do English and history?' he says. 'Where's this coming from?'

'I just like the thought of doing French. I could work as an interpreter, or abroad, or something. I hear there's always a demand for that kind of thing. It'd be interesting. I could meet all kinds of people.'

Josh shakes his head slowly, patiently.

'Do you want to watch a movie?' I ask, before he can make some comment and put me down about it. He's always thought that studying languages is stupid, and I've never been able to talk him around to it. 'My dad bought that new Will Smith film on the weekend, we could watch that? You know, that one with him and his son coming back to Earth?'

'Yeah, sure.'

As we lie side by side on my bed watching the movie, Josh plays with my hair, and I can't focus on the movie. I hate that he doesn't listen to me sometimes, when I talk about colleges and school. It's not like he ignores me, it's just that he doesn't seem to really understand that what I have to say might be important, that he should actually pay attention to what I'm saying.

When I was dating Josh at first, it changed my whole high school experience. It's not like I'm just dating him as a way into the more popular crowd – I love him, after all – but now, when I quietly seethe about him not listening to me, I think about how different my life would be without him in it.

And I don't really like the thought of being that lonely.

I think a little more about colleges, running over in my mind where I might apply for a French degree. My parents have taken me on holiday to France twice, and both times I loved it over there.

But I've still got a year left of high school, and I might change my mind by then.

The more I think about college, and leaving high school, the scarier it all becomes, and I start to think that we're all growing up way too fast.

Josh stays over that night – but in the spare room, of course – since his parents are away for the night (the funeral of some uncle Josh hadn't known well a bit further upstate). They didn't want him staying home alone. It wasn't that they felt bad about leaving him on his own, I don't think – the opportunity for him to throw a party was probably their main concern. That's why they'd spoken to my parents before consulting either me or Josh about him staying over, I guess.

Getting dressed for school, I mull over what to wear today. It's bleak and gray outside, the threat of rain looming within those clouds. So I opt for a pair of red skinny jeans and a black sweater over a plain white T-shirt. I run a brush through my hair and tie it up into a ponytail. There's no point in doing anything with it – if it does rain, it's only going to get frizzy, no matter how much product I use.

I throw my drapes open and roll up the shutters, and

see Todd moving about in his room. He's pulling on black jeans over a pair of—

I clap a hand to my mouth and stifle a giggle. No way. No *freaking* way.

I bite hard on my lip and blink, but when I open my eyes, he's just pulling the jeans over his butt – and over a pair of SpongeBob SquarePants underpants.

I shake my head and turn away before I start laughing again. *He will not hear the end of this . . .*

Josh walks in then, dressed and with his hair spiked up just the way it always is. 'What're you smiling about?'

'Just in a good mood,' I say brightly, bouncing over to kiss him. He wraps his arms around me and kisses me back.

'Want some breakfast?' I ask. We've easily got twenty minutes before we need to leave. 'I fancy some pancakes.'

He kisses my nose. 'Sounds good to me.'

Then he looks past me, out of my window, and I see a frown slip onto his face. 'You didn't tell me that his room was that one.'

I step back, rolling my eyes and letting Josh's arms drop back to his sides. 'Does it matter? It's just Todd.'

'But—'

'I'm going to go make pancakes, Josh, but if you

want to stand here and make irrational and irrelevant arguments to thin air, then be my guest.'

He grunts, not quite admitting I'm right and he's being stupid, but close enough. I decide it's probably best not to mention the hilarious sight of Todd in SpongeBob underpants. We go downstairs and I start making pancakes, and he starts talking about the football game again, but sounding much more upbeat today.

When it's time to leave, we both grab our schoolbags and get into my car. I picked Josh up from his place yesterday, since it made it easier for driving to school. Although I have to admit, I didn't think that plan through, and now I'm not so sure about Josh and Todd in the car together.

But, as per usual, I pull off the drive and stop in front of Todd's house, giving the horn two quick beeps. Josh shifts in his seat.

He's out of the house in a minute, and pauses at the passenger door before climbing into the back seat. 'Hey.'

'Hey. Todd, you know Josh, right?'

'Sure.'

'We have gym together,' Josh says.

'And math,' Todd adds.

I never knew that. Neither of them had ever

mentioned it to me. I don't know why it seems like such a shock to me; they're in the same grade, after all, so it's not unusual that they might have classes together.

'Okay, then,' I say, and I drive off without thinking up any end or substance to that sentence. A while later I say, 'I hope it doesn't rain today.'

*God. I've resorted to talking about the weather. Help.*

They both reply at the same time. Their voices overlap.

Josh says, 'Wouldn't want your hair frizzing up, huh?'

Todd says in a conspiratorial tone, 'Sure you've got your house key, then?'

Josh twists in his seat to look at Todd for the first time. I fleetingly glance in my rear-view mirror at Todd, sitting up straight in his seat, not at all intimidated by Josh, who's doing a great job of looking like a jealous boyfriend right now.

'What's that supposed to mean?'

'Josh,' I sigh, because he sounds like he's accusing Todd of something.

'Last week it rained and Ashley forgot her key. She was locked out for a while. We've got a spare key I had to lend her,' Todd carries on before I can say anything. 'I couldn't leave her out there in the rain. Catch pneumonia or something.'

Josh squirms, obviously put out by the innocent answer. 'Oh, right.'

I steal another look at Todd in the mirror. He looks right back at me.

I don't know why he covered for me.

I didn't tell Josh about it because I didn't want him to take it the wrong way. He's the jealous type, and saying 'I took a shower at Todd's house and wore his clothes and hung with him for a while' sounded worse than it really was, and it wasn't like I'd had anything to feel guilty about – so I didn't tell him.

But . . . why did Todd lie for me?

We don't talk again the rest of the way. Josh reaches over to put his hand on my knee, squeezing it lightly, and I smile at him, squeezing his hand back before I reach for the gear stick.

Later, at school, I say to Josh when we're hanging out by my locker between classes, 'You never thought to mention you had classes with Todd?'

He shrugs. 'I don't associate with the kid. We just happen to be in the same class. We don't talk or anything.' I wait a second or so, because he seems to want to carry on – his mouth twists up to the side, and he takes a hand from where it's sitting on my waist to rub the back of his neck. 'What he said about giving you the spare key so you weren't out in the rain. He's not all that bad. I guess.'

He's reluctant to admit it, and it's not much, but it's enough. I smile and reach up on my toes to kiss him. 'See, what did I tell you?'

The bell rings then, and Josh leans down to give me a lingering kiss. 'I'll see you at lunch.'

'Yep. See you then.'

I don't know why it's made me so . . . happy? No, relieved – that Josh has stopped thinking Todd is some sort of heinous person. I mean, okay, so maybe he did get expelled from his last school, and cut class, but he isn't a bad person. 'Troubled' is maybe the word I'd use.

But it grates on me every time Josh calls him 'kid' – like he's so much better and wiser and more mature than Todd. They're the same age, for God's sake! It's little things like that that really frustrate me about Josh sometimes. And if I tried to talk to him, I bet he wouldn't understand why calling Todd 'kid' all the time was so bad anyway.

I like Todd. I like the way he's sarcastic and blunt and quiet. I like his company, like how he enjoys similar music to me and doesn't think I'm silly to waste my time reading books.

Part of me that knows Josh should come before any

other guy in my life – but I know that doesn't mean I can't have guy friends, like Todd. I've already lost a best friend because of my relationship with Josh. Maybe it's time I found a new one.

Allie and I used to do everything together, back when she was my best friend. We learned to ride a bike at the same time. We used to have sleepovers and paint each other's nails and gossip about the boys we had crushes on all the time. And when we got older, we used to go to Denny's for milkshakes after school on a Friday. She was my other half.

People use that phrase a lot: 'other half'. Like they're incomplete without someone to kiss them and hold their hand, or something. Usually, they're talking about a boyfriend or girlfriend.

But losing my best friend was like losing half of myself.

We'd argued over stuff before, like all friends do, but we'd never stopped talking or hanging out because of it. We'd patch things up almost immediately. The conflict over my relationship with Josh was so different – so *final*.

It's not that I don't like the people I hang out with now. It's not that at all. They're pretty nice people, and they're funny, and all-right company. But they're Josh's friends, they were never really mine.

I'd been with Josh about five or six weeks when Allie and I had the fight. She got mad because I spent so much – apparently, too much – time with him, and didn't make time for her or anyone else any more. I'd snapped in reply that she was just jealous because now I got to hang out with some of the cool kids, and she was still a nobody.

And then we just didn't talk again.

She didn't text me, and I didn't go up to her in school. We've had classes together since, but there's barely even any acknowledgement between us: just a wall of resentment, at least from her side. We've both moved on, and that's okay, really, because people change, and grow apart.

That's what I told myself, anyway. But it never made me feel any better about it.

After that, I sort of just integrated into Josh's group of friends permanently.

It doesn't surprise me that I don't really click with them, that we don't have all that much in common, because frankly, Josh and I don't have a hell of a lot in common. But they say opposites attract, right?

I don't know how things have worked out so well between us, but I love him. And he loves me. We're happy. And we don't need to have everything in common or similar tastes because being happy and in love is more than enough and we appreciate each other's differences.

I don't know why I'm reminiscing about all this as I walk to class and take my seat in biology. I begin to feel nostalgic, thinking about how easy my friendship with Allie used to be – we'd known each other since middle school and had been all but joined at the hip for years.

Then my mind drifts away from nostalgia and the presentation on mitosis and meiosis, and I think of Todd.

Todd O'Connor, with his mess of floppy brown hair that always looks ruffled and wild, and those eyes that can penetrate right through you. The way his head cocks to the side and his forehead crinkles and he bites on the inside of his cheek when he's thinking hard. The way he's always fiddling with his guitar pick; the sound of his voice and the guitar, barely there if both our windows are shut, but soft and clear if both windows are open; the careful, cautious manner in which he drives.

I shake myself. I shouldn't be thinking about Todd. If I am daydreaming about any boy when I'm in class, it should be Josh, my boyfriend, not the guy next door.

'Ashley?' the teacher calls for me, and I look up to answer his question.

'Mitosis leads to growth or cell replacement. The

four daughter cells are all clones of each other and identical to the original cell. Meiosis is used in the production of gametes and there are only two new cells produced from the single mother cell, each with half the required chromosomes to create an embryo.'

'Good.' The teacher carries on talking and has successfully distracted me from my thoughts, and I slump forward on my elbow, listening carefully to him even though I know I look mildly uninterested.

# Chapter Eight

'Where's Dad?'

'His conference got pushed back a day,' Mom tells me with a small, kind of sad, smile. 'He'll be back tomorrow night. There were flight delays from the people getting in from New York and they couldn't start without them, so they had to push the whole thing back.'

'Oh, that sucks.'

'I know. But your dad says the catering at the hotel's great. And the company's paying for it all, so they're not having too bad a time waiting.'

I laugh with Mom and offer, 'Do you want any help? I'll peel the carrots, if you want.'

'I've been waiting for you to ask,' she laughs, and points toward the bag of carrots she bought earlier. 'I've got too much now that your father won't be here, but we'll cook it all anyway. One of us can reheat it tomorrow. I'm sure he'll want a good home-cooked meal when he gets in late.'

'Yeah.' I pick up the peeler and start working. 'What time are they coming around?'

'Seven thirty.'

I glance at the clock on the wall to my right, near the door. We have an hour and a half, but dinner won't take that long to cook. The lamb is already in the oven and Mom is preparing the broccoli and potatoes. Oh, and there's the red wine sauce to do, but Mom's a pro at sauces, it'll take no time. Or so she assures me.

I take over the vegetables while she turns to the sauce.

'Why didn't you ask Josh if he wanted to join us?' Mom asks. She'd told me I could, but I'd decided against it.

I shrug. 'He and Todd don't really hang out or anything, I figured it would just be a little forced for the two of them. Besides, all the guys are going over to Austin's tonight. His parents are visiting relatives and won't be back till late, so they're having a boys' night in or something.'

'Pizza, beer, video games?' Mom clarifies, giving me a knowing look.

'Probably,' I say with a smile.

'Todd's made a few friends – Callum was telling me the other day. They sound like nice boys.'

'Mm.' I've seen him with them sometimes in

corridors between classes, or at lunch, or before school. I don't know them all that well, though. 'Yeah, good for him.'

'Callum says he has a hard time making friends.' Then she adds, 'Maybe you should try to spend some more time with him, out of school. Go see a movie or something.'

'Maybe.'

Mom asks how school is going, and I tell her about how gym class is an even bigger waste of time than creative writing, and how I'm enjoying math and biology and how chemistry is hard, but in a good way, and I tell her about the book we're studying right now in English – The Great Gatsby – which is great, because I first read it when I was about thirteen, and a few times since then.

It doesn't take long to finish preparing the vegetables.

'Go on, go get ready,' Mom tells me, glancing at the clock. Forty minutes until they'll be here. 'Thanks.'

'No problem, Mom.' I smile and head upstairs to take a shower. I don't spend too long there, though I'm loath to leave the hot water that pounds on my body and relaxes my muscles.

I towel dry my hair and braid it, because it's so thick, it will take far too long to dry. I do, however, apply some anti-frizz serum first to ensure it goes wavy rather than frizzy. I put on some make-up to cover up my freckles, too.

As for clothes, I don't make any special effort, not like Mom asked me to do when we went to dinner at Callum and Todd's. A pair of comfortable skinny jeans, and a Mayday Parade T-shirt that is too big and obscures most of my figure, but is one of my favorites because it's so damn soft.

When I head back downstairs, Mom is re-heating the sauce on the stove. She's changed into a pair of jeans and a nice pink blouse. She glances over at me, in my band T-shirt and bare feet, and just rolls her eyes.

'Lay the table, please.'

'Okay.'

I've just put down the last fork when the doorbell rings, and I call, 'I'll get it,' even though Mom knows I will anyway.

Callum stands there with a covered dish in his hands. He's wearing a blue shirt and slacks, and smiles amicably at me. Todd stands slightly behind him, and offers me a small smile.

'Come on in.' I smile back politely and step aside so that they can come in.

'I brought dessert,' Callum says, holding up the dish

awkwardly as he shrugs out of his coat and hangs it on a peg on the wall.

I take the dish from him and say, 'Awesome! I'll pass it on to the chef. Uh, come sit down.'

I gesture for them to go on into the dining room and then take the dish in to Mom. She takes the lid off. 'Ooh!' It smells gorgeous. I peek and see that it's a trifle which looks even more tantalizing than it smells.

Mom tells me to get the pitcher of water from the fridge and says she'll bring the food through in a moment.

I invite Todd and Callum to sit at the dining table. It's large enough to fit six, maybe eight if you used the ends. We don't use the dining room much because Mom likes to keep it for special occasions. We usually eat in the kitchen. But for things like Thanksgiving and Easter, and when there are guests (other than Josh) or family over, we use the dining room.

The carpet is dark red and the walls are cream, the table and chairs made of a dark wood I don't know the name of, and the lights are soft, making everything feel cozy and warm.

'Now I'm not all that much of a cook, unlike some people,' Mom announces, her arms laden with plates, 'so there's only a main course from me.'

'Just as well, really,' I say. 'Keep some room for dessert.'

'This looks great, Isabelle,' Callum says as she puts a plate in front of him. And it does look great. Mom is a good cook – but not quite the cook that Callum is. While we eat, they ask Todd and me questions about school, or talk about other things between themselves.

'Oh, you're studying *Gatsby*, too?' Mom says when Todd mentions it. 'How do you like it?'

'It's good. I don't like Carraway as a narrator, but it's a good book. And the quote from Daisy at the start—'

*'That's the best thing a girl can be in this world, a beautiful little fool,'* I quote it quietly, looking up from under my eyelashes across the table at Todd, who catches my eye.

'Yeah,' he says, 'that one.'

'It's my favorite quote in the entire book,' I tell him.

He cocks his head and bites the inside of his cheek. I can't see his forehead but I bet it's crinkled. He's thinking hard, but doesn't say anything. He doesn't invite me to elaborate on why I love that quote so much, and I don't want to bore them all with an extensive analysis of it, so I say nothing.

There is silence, a heavy one; I count seven heartbeats.

'It's supposed to be absolutely horrendous weather

coming in next week,' Mom says. *God*. Now I know where I get it from. I smile down at my meat and vegetables and shake my head a little.

We finish dinner not long after, and then conversation is easy as we all fill the empty places in our stomachs with the trifle, which, for the record, tastes even better than it looks and smells.

We all sit a while longer and carry on talking lazily. Eventually, Callum says, 'I think I'd best be heading home. I have to be up early in the morning, so an early night's on the cards for me I think. Thank you for the meal, it was wonderful.' He lays a hand on Todd's shoulder then, and they exchange a glance, an unspoken conversation.

Mom bumps her foot against me under the table. When I look at her, she gives me a prompting look in return. I understand immediately. She wants me to spend more time with Todd, be his friend, like she said earlier.

'Do you want to stay and watch a movie?' I ask Todd. I don't have a problem hanging out with him. I'm just unsure of myself around him, because he knows a different side of me than I usually show, the side I like to keep behind closed doors so people can't judge it.

'Uh . . .' He looks at his dad, who gives him an encouraging smile. 'Sure, why not?',' he says, nodding and giving me a tiny half-smile. I smile back, and help my mom to clear away the dishes. Callum tries to help, but we're too quick for him, and refuse to let guests help tidy up.

'Are you going to go upstairs?' Mom asks me.

I shrug. 'I guess so. Unless you mind, particularly.'

She shakes her head. 'That's all right. There's a movie I recorded on the TV in the lounge anyway I'm going to watch. Oh, and your grandmother called earlier, remind me to call her back tomorrow.'

'OK.'

I go back into the dining room, and we say goodbye to Callum, who's already yawning, let him out, and then I start up the stairs. 'Come on,' I say over my shoulder to Todd when he doesn't follow.

'Are you sure your mom doesn't want some help doing the dishes?' he says. 'I feel kind of bad.'

I shake my head. 'She'll put it in the dishwasher. Don't worry about it.'

'Okay.'

In my room, he hesitates by the doorway, taking it all in. He looks at the photo frames on the chest of drawers and the stacks of books piled around my room in an efficiently organized mess; and he looks at the CD tower in the corner of my room – it's mostly filled with the back-up copies of albums I've downloaded online so I can play them in my car.

'It's nice,' is all he says. I laugh, and bend down by my CD tower to the small collection of movies at the bottom.

'How about *Toy Story*?' I ask, picking up the first one I see.

He lets out a breath of laughter. 'Sure.'

He perches on the edge of the foot of my bed. I laugh at him, but not in a mean way. 'The bed doesn't bite, you know. Lie down, if you want. I don't mind.'

'I'll sit,' he says, moving more comfortably onto the bed and tucking a leg beneath him, and then he takes out his guitar pick, and his eyes roam my books as restlessly as his fingers fidget with the pick.

I set up the DVD and wait patiently for it to load. Dad offered to get me a new DVD player for Christmas, but this one works fine – it's just slow.

'I didn't know you were such a *Gatsby* fan,' I say.

'I could say the same for you,' he replies. Then, 'Your favorite quote.'

'Yeah?' I turn my head to look at him.

'Why that one? I mean, it's the kind of book kids all over the country study in English class. There's a lot of quotes in it. So why do you like that one best?'

'Do you want the essay answer, or . . .?' He gives me a look and I laugh. 'I just think it's a great quote for the society in those days. It's a good one to analyze themes and characters for class. Does it really matter?'

'I think it matters,' he says, looking me dead in the eye. 'People say that a person's interests and dreams and likes can define them, but so can the things they read, and the quotes they like.'

Then he gives me one of his rare, proper smiles, this one fuller, and sadder, than any I've seen before. 'Music is what feelings sound like; and art is what feelings look like; and quotes are the things we might've felt and thought and said if some other bugger hadn't got there first.'

I frown quizzically, but then I smile. 'Who said that?'

'My granddad,' he says, with a short bark of laughter. 'It seemed appropriate.'

'Entirely so,' I agree gravely, and we both laugh again. Then I press play on the movie and I go to lie on my bed, and we don't really speak about anything particularly important the rest of the evening – just things about school, and classes, and amusing stories that aren't very personal at all.

Well, nothing very personal until I remember his SpongeBob underpants, at which point I start laughing helplessly.

'What?'

When I control my giggling I bite my lip and look at

him. 'The other day – I forgot to say to you – but I opened my curtains and saw you getting changed for school . . . and . . .' I'm laughing again and the next words come out in a rush. 'You had SpongeBob undies.'

There's a brief moment where my words register in his brain; when it begins to sink in, his eyes (currently a soft blue) bulge from their sockets, his mouth falls open.

'Oh, God, you didn't.'

I nod, still laughing – not so much at the mental image, but at the concept of this moody, secretive, seventeen-year-old guy wearing such childish underwear.

He shakes his head, horrified. 'You didn't tell anyone.'

'Not yet. I make no promises.'

'God. Don't. I'd never live it down. I have a reputation to uphold. Remember, I apparently went to juvie?'

'It's cute.'

'No it's not. Don't tell anybody.'

'Or else what?' I open my eyes wide, as if daring him, the tone of my voice ominous but strained as I rein in a laugh.

He hesitates before saying, 'You have a Wonder Woman bra.'

My cheeks flare red, and I glower at him. I must've forgotten to close the shutters when I got dressed one morning or something, and he'd seen it. Oh, *brilliant*.

We're at a stalemate.

'What if I don't care that people know I have a Wonder Woman bra?'

He raises his eyebrows at me, and I look away, faltering.

'Fine.'

'Fine.'

'Good.'

'Okay.'

'Glad to see we're in agreement on that.'

There is a still moment between us, the film continuing in the background, and then we exchange a cool glance, and he cracks into a wide smile, and I start to laugh again. I collapse back onto my pillows and the both of us are laughing, suddenly unable to stop, and even though my stomach aches from it, I can't help but laugh.

It's just nice being there with Todd. Easy. Like it's the most natural thing in the world.

And not once do I think of Josh.

# Chapter Nine

Before I know it, it's already October.

The leaves are starting to turn shades of mustard yellow, burned umber, watered-down red, sunset orange. As the days progress, a few leaves begin to drop, scattering the ground.

I love fall. It looks so beautiful. My favorite days are those when the sun is bright but it's not too warm out, and it's early in the morning, when nobody else is awake, and the world seems more alive somehow. There are few people, and no cars; the leaves crunch beneath your feet with each step you take, each one producing a sharp melody; and the birds and squirrels rustling in the trees make everything feel almost like a fairyland.

The weather gets colder, though, and the wind picks up a little.

The glowing green numbers on my digital alarm read 06:03. I don't need to be up for school for an hour, but I'm wide awake. I wish it was the weekend. Instead, it's Friday – so close, yet so far.

I showered last night so there's no point killing time by taking another, so for a few minutes, I lie staring at the ceiling and not doing anything at all. It's deathly quiet outside – nobody's leaving for school or work yet. There's a breeze though – I know because I can hear the leaves rustling, crisp against the road.

I decide that today I'll wear the black skinny jeans I bought last week when I went to the mall with Mom, with an orange sweater. Getting up, I turn off my alarms. I sit on my bed and stare at the curtains before I go and open them.

There is soft morning sunshine and the old man who lives at number eighteen is out walking his Labrador. At least I'm not the only one up so early.

I go lie back down, snuggle under the covers and into my cool pillow, and relish the heavy feeling of my comforter wrapped around me.

Then I remember: it's Todd's birthday.

I've got him a present, of course. I only know it's his birthday because Callum mentioned it in passing to my dad a couple of days ago. Todd never mentioned it, but then again, I never asked.

I've got him a copy of *The Perks of Being a Wallflower*, after he told me he hasn't ever read it, and a T-shirt, and a jumbo pack of Post-It notes, which I'd seen in the supermarket and thought appropriate.

He was surprisingly easy to buy for.

Josh's birthday isn't until March. He's so difficult to buy for. I should start thinking what I'll get him for Christmas.

With a sigh, I get up. I have time to straighten my hair for a change. But by the time I'm ready, it's still only 06:39. So I have breakfast, making sure to be quiet so as not to wake Mom and Dad, but it's barely seven o'clock by then.

After a few more minutes, when I hear my parents begin to move about upstairs, I decide to go outside and sit on the swing for a while.

We put the swing up when I was about six or seven, something like that. The metal poles used to be red; now they are flecked with rust and the red has faded. The ropes are frayed and weathered with age – but it's still a pretty strong swing for all that.

I sit down and spin myself around in a circle, the ropes twisting above me. I keep going and going and going until the ropes have coiled around each other all the way down to the back of my neck, and then I pick my feet up and spin madly around with the swing. I throw my head back and smile.

'Still five years old at heart, huh?'

I jump at the voice, and have to wait until the world stops spinning in a blur of fall colors. My eyes flit first to the door to the house, then the patio, and then towards the house next door. Todd leans over the five-foot tall wooden fence that divides our houses, his arms folded lazily on the top of it.

'You scared me.'

'Sorry.'

'Happy birthday,' I remember to say.

He grimaces – although it's so fleeting, maybe I imagine it. 'Thanks. My dad told you, huh?' I nod; Todd lets out a long sigh. 'I don't like a lot of fuss on my birthdays. That's why I don't make it a well-known fact.'

'Why don't you like a lot of fuss?' I ask, and then I bite my lip. 'Sorry; was that a bit too personal?'

'Just a little.'

I press the balls of my feet into the ground, moving backwards and forwards on the swing without taking my feet off the ground.

'I have your present inside,' I tell him. 'Stay there, okay?'

I got up and rushed up to my room to get his presents. If he didn't want people knowing it was his birthday then he might not appreciate carting presents around school.

'Happy birthday,' I said with a smile when I return, passing the gift bag over the fence to him. He gave me a tiny smile and a quiet, 'Thank you,' in return. I'm grinning eagerly as he sets the bag down, taking out the T-shirt. I love watching people open presents. I just hope he likes them.

He chuckles at the T-shirt when he opens it. 'No way. I looked at this just last week.'

'Really? It seemed like the kind of thing you'd wear.' It wasn't anything special, just a blue T-shirt with the Captain America logo on. He'd mentioned he loved those comics once.

'Thanks,' he says, and smiles a little wider to me. He opens the Post-Its and chuckles again, and seems to like the book. Then he lifts his arms, dithers, and leans forward as if he's about to grab me for a hug, but steps back. 'Thank you.'

'Oh, don't be so silly,' I laugh, and pull him forward for an awkward hug over the fence. Close up like this, he smells like Old Spice. 'Happy birthday.' I have to pull away because my boobs are squashed up uncomfortably at the top of the fence, but I smile at Todd.

'I have to go have breakfast,' he says. 'I'll see you in a while.'

'Okay.'

He walks back to the house but stops by the door

and says, 'Ashley.' I turn around and look at him. 'My dad's away tomorrow night. I was going to ask some of the guys over for beers and whatever, but if you wanted, um, you know . . .' He shifts his weight from one foot to the other. 'Not a fully fledged party. Just a few people.'

'Sure,' I say brightly, although I can't say why I'm so happy. 'Sounds great.'

It's Todd's party tonight. Well, I say *party*. There aren't all that many people going, he said, maybe twenty at the most.

He said I could bring Josh, if I wanted.

But . . . I didn't really want to ask him. I can't explain why, not in so many words. It's not just because I know they don't get on too well. When I thought about asking him, I got that same feeling that you get when you've just read the most magnificent book but you feel like you'd be betraying the book if you told other people about it. I guess I just wanted to hang out with Todd for the night.

It's selfish, when I think about it like that, but it's true.

I pat some more powder over my freckles, and let out a sharp breath through my mouth, trying to think about something else so I don't feel guilty for not inviting Josh. I didn't mention about the party to him; and it wasn't like he spoke to anybody Todd hung out with, so likelihood was that he wouldn't find out. But given how he'd turn suddenly grumpy and act all moody with me whenever I talk about Todd or mention hanging out with Todd, I thought maybe he just didn't need to know about the party. There was no harm in simply not telling him, right?

I'm kind of worried about the party. I'm not exactly popular, except by association, and Todd's friends aren't the sort of people I hang out with any more. I've seen him at lunch with some people I used to be friends with, people Allie is still friends with.

God, I hope she's not there tonight. Maybe Todd doesn't know her. I mean, I've never seen them at the same lunch table, so that's a good sign . . .

I cross my fingers that I don't have to trail about after Todd all night because nobody there will talk to me.

Once I'm sure my freckles are concealed, I stand up and survey myself in my full-length mirror.

A pair of thick brown tights and a blue sweater dress make up my party outfit. My hair is a bit too unruly today to straighten (I knew I should've blow dried it after my shower) so I've pulled it into a bun and fixed it in place with some pins.

I didn't want to dress up too much, like I might for any other party, because Todd said it wasn't really a proper party, just a few of us hanging out.

I don't call out goodbye as I leave; my parents have gone to the theater and dinner an hour's drive away, so they won't be back till midnight at the earliest.

Todd's front door is unlocked, and as I walk inside, I hear music and the buzz of conversation, but it's not as in-your-face as the parties I'm used to. The atmosphere isn't so big and flamboyant, it's softer, friendlier. Much more my kind of thing.

I go into the lounge, where most of the noise is coming from. The furniture has been pushed out to the walls and people are sitting or standing around. Todd was right about there only being twenty or so people. A couple of heads turn to look at me when I walk in, but then they go back to talking. I put an arm across my body to hold onto my elbow, nervous and uncomfortable already.

'Hey,' says a voice behind me, making me jump at least a foot in the air.

'Jesus, Todd! Are you in a habit of giving girls heart attacks?'

He chuckles. 'It's a pastime of mine, I'm afraid. Beer?'

'Um . . . okay.'

'Here, you can have this one, I'll grab another.' He hands me the beer he's holding, and I take it cautiously. 'Relax, it's only beer. I haven't even drunk any of it yet. Scout's honor.'

I laugh. 'Okay.'

He lowers his voice and says, 'Don't mention it was my birthday yesterday.'

I nod, not asking questions, though I'm still wondering why he has such a problem with his birthday.

I take a sip of the beer and turn back to the lounge. Sucking in a deep breath to steel myself, I say to a guy sitting on the edge of the couch nearest to me, 'Hey, you're in my history class, right?'

And as it turns out, the party isn't so bad. At least not for the first half hour, when I sit talking to a couple of people – mostly about music. Lucky for me, I chose to talk to the guy who put himself in charge of the stereo, so we all argue playfully over songs and artists. Then someone over by the window calls, 'Allie, c'mon,' and I freeze for a moment.

Slowly, I turn my head round, but I already know.

I just need the visual confirmation.

Her hair is deep jet black, not soft brown any more. She's dyed it. It's still curly though, but shorter, only to her chin. Where she's got her hair tucked behind her left ear, I can see a metal bar going through the top of her ear.

Almost like she knows I'm looking at her, Allie's eyes flicker in my direction, away from the girl she's talking to, and she stops talking. The girl looks over her shoulder at me, and rolls her eyes as she turns back to Allie, saying something. There's a steely glint in Allie's eyes and I look away first.

I feel a wave of nostalgia and guilt wash over me, and I turn quickly back to my conversation, ignoring the glare I can feel cutting into my skin. I begin to gnaw on my nails and pull at a loose thread in my tights and bounce my foot agitatedly.

It was pretty much an unspoken mutual decision that we stopped being friends. One day we just didn't meet up at the front of the school, before homeroom. And then we stopped hanging out at lunch and talking by the lockers in between classes. It wasn't just my choice to ditch her.

But it was my fault that we stopped being friends.

*No. No, she was the one being horrible about me dating Josh, and that was why we argued. I'm free to date whoever I wish.*

I gulp down the last third of my beer in one and say, 'I have to go to the bathroom.'

I should just go. I don't want to make everything

weird. She's got more right to be here than I have.

Locked in the bathroom, I sit on the edge of the tub feeling queasy, and put my head between my knees. I'm debating what to do, when I hear voices outside.

'What's she doing here?' It's a girl, someone I don't know well enough to recognize by their voice.

'I know, right? Like I know Todd invited her just because she's his neighbor, but she didn't have to come. I just feel so bad for Allie.' It's another girl, someone with a higher-pitched voice, but again, I can't name her. I gulp, and will my heart to slow down so the blood stops roaring in my ears and I can listen to them.

'Tell me about it.'

'And did you see the way she just swanned in here acting like she was friends with everyone? She's not really wanted here, can't she see that? Jeez.'

'I thought she looked a bit awkward, though.' There's more sympathy in the first girl's voice now. 'I feel kind of bad for her.'

'I don't. She's such a bitch to Allie.'

'Yeah . . .' The first girl sighs.

The other one says, 'Come on. Let's just go back downstairs.'

I hold my breath, waiting to see if one of them will try the bathroom door at all before going back downstairs, but they don't. I'm shaking all over, and my palms are so sweaty I have to wash them and run cold water on my wrists to try and cool down. They were talking about me, I know they were.

Nobody wants me here.

I should go.

But then again, why am I made out to be the bad guy here? Allie was just as much to blame as me. She started the whole argument in the first place. We're both at fault and we're both victims in this. It's not just her.

And Todd wanted me here, it wasn't a pity invitation. He wouldn't do that. I have just as much right to be here as Allie does. And if she thinks she can drive me out, she can think again. I'm staying.

Someone knocks on the door of the bathroom, jolting me back to my senses. I stand up and unlock the door, and Kelly, from my history class, smiles at me as I leave the bathroom and she goes in.

I can't help but wonder if it's a pity smile, or if maybe she's thinking how big of a bitch I am.

I start to walk down the stairs, but then I hear movement from Todd's room; I re-route, pushing open his door, which isn't fully shut anyway.

I'm not sure what I expected to see. Maybe people making out. Some people sat around playing spin-the-bottle. I just thought that Todd probably wouldn't want people in his room, especially with his guitar, and his blue book possibly there for somebody to see.

The room is dark, and the drapes are billowing wildly – the window is open and the wind is really bad tonight, howling above the distant sound of the music up here. Todd's silhouette is outlined, hunched on the window seat, arms wrapped around his legs, his head turned away.

The door creaks slightly as I push it further open to step inside, and he looks over.

I hesitate in the doorway before taking a couple of steps into the room. 'Are you all right?'

He doesn't answer. I see him shrug, so I push the door closed and walk over to him. He pulls his legs closer into his body to make more space, which I take as an invitation to sit down. The wind pulls at my hair, and Todd's is windswept, even messier than usual. I note that he's wearing the T-shirt I gave him. I lean past and shut the window before settling on the window seat.

'Nice shirt.'

'Thanks. I know somebody with good taste.'

I nod.

After a while he says, 'It was just getting a bit too loud.'

I'm not sure what he means. It's a small party, and up here, you can barely hear the music – especially with the wind – and none of the guests are being too raucous.

'I'm not following,' I confess apologetically.

'I don't suppose you would,' he says softly, still looking out of the window. There isn't much to look at, but he doesn't actually seem to be paying attention to anything out there. 'I just . . . don't like my birthday. It's . . . not . . . the easiest time of year for me.' Then he blurts out words so fast that they run into each other, vomiting them as though he doesn't want to keep them in and if he doesn't say them now he never will: 'My parents always made a huge deal about birthdays. It was the only time of year they didn't seem to argue. Since they got divorced, everything's been weird. I don't like birthdays so much any more. I know it sounds stupid, so don't laugh at me. And I've been thinking about my granddad a lot, too, lately. I just needed to get away from the party for a bit.'

I don't say anything for a moment, because I'm not sure how to respond. He takes a long, deep, shaking breath. I see his fingers fidgeting with the guitar pick again. I put a hand on his free hand because it's the only thing I can think to do.

'My granddad was really there for me after they divorced. And my birthday, yesterday, it just made me think about him a lot, and . . .'

'I don't think anybody could get over something like that,' I say quietly. 'You know . . . it's okay . . . to get upset about that kind of thing.'

He gives a snort of empty laughter. 'It's dumb. I don't know. And it's really stupid to feel this sad when there is a bunch of awesome people downstairs and . . .' He shakes his head. Then he reaches to pick up a bottle of beer that is on the floor beside him, and takes a swig.

'It's not dumb.' Tentatively, I pry the bottle out of his hands, in case he's planning on getting wasted just to try to feel better. 'Do you . . . do you mind if I ask you something?'

'Sure, go ahead.' He sniffs loudly, and rubs at his eyes with his knuckles.

'I didn't realize you were friends with Allie.'

He gives me a wry smile, looking a little less sad now. 'That wasn't a question.'

'Right. Sorry. I mean – how do you know her? Are you guys, um, you know . . . good friends?' I'm too scared to ask him directly if she's been badmouthing me to him behind my back, telling him I'm horrible and shallow and self-centered or something.

'I wouldn't say we're that close,' he tells me easily. 'The guys I made friends with in my French class invited me to sit with them for lunch, and she was there, along with a bunch of other people, who are all downstairs now. She's nice.'

My stomach churns, and not from the one bottle of beer I've had. 'Yeah, she is.' At least, she was. I don't know her any more. For all I know, she bitches about me constantly behind my back and is the reason those other girls don't like me.

'She told me you guys used to be friends.'

'Oh?' My heart starts racing again and I sit up straighter. 'What did she say about me?'

'Just that you used to be friends, like I said, before you got together with Josh.'

'Did she say anything else about me? Todd, tell me. Even if it was really horrible. I'm a big girl, I can handle it.' I give him what I hope is a convincing smile.

'Honestly, that was all she said about you. I tried to ask her more about what you were like – because this was still the first few days of school and I didn't know you that well – and she refused to talk about you.'

'Oh.' I'm not sure how I feel about that; mostly I feel agitated.

'I saw her glaring at you earlier. What happened between you two?'

Todd's gray-blue eyes hold mine. They're filled with gentle concern, and I avert my gaze. 'We, uh, had a fight. That's all. It happens, you know?'

'Was it about you and Josh?'

I wince. 'Maybe another time, Todd, yeah?'

If I tell him, he's going to think I'm a bitch, and he's going to take Allie's side because he's her friend too, and he's going to hate me. I don't want that. I can't tell him all the details.

'Okay.' He doesn't even try to press me for more answers because he knows I wouldn't do that to him.

I twirl the ends of my hair around a fingertip. I don't want to tell him all the gory details of how I lost my best friend, but I do confess, 'I heard a couple of the girls talking earlier, about me. They said that nobody really wants me here, because of the fight me and Allie had.' I peek up at him from under my eyelashes.

'Bullshit. I want you here. And so do most of the others. They're nice people, and they'll give you a chance. Just because some girls were gossiping about you—'

'Yeah, but—'

'Do you know who it was? Because I'll go talk to them and find out what's going on.'

I laugh nervously and put a hand on his shoulder as he starts to stand. But it makes me feel warm all over that he'd defend me like that. 'That's okay.'

'You'll stay though, won't you?'

'I'll give it a half hour, at least.'

He smiles. 'Deal. And thanks, by the way. For distracting me.'

'Any time.'

'Ready to go back downstairs?' He stands now, and offers me a hand.

I draw in a deep breath and hesitate before taking it. 'Well, it is *your* party, you're being rude staying holed away like this, you know.'

He laughs and as we start downstairs, I notice that he looks a little unsteady; I'm not sure how well he holds his alcohol, or how much he's had.

'How much have you had to drink?'

'A few.'

'Yeah, well, I think maybe that's enough,' I say firmly.

'You sound like your mother.'

I grimace melodramatically, which makes him laugh again.

Todd slings an arm around me as we make our way back downstairs, but he doesn't lean on me like I expected; I don't push his arm away though. It feels comfortable. And a little bit like a piece of armor to protect me from any glares as we go back into the lounge.

'How about truth or dare?' he announces as we get into the room. His words don't slur, but he stumbles slightly as he walks through the doorway.

One of the boys, Will, calls out laughingly, 'Where did you two sneak away to?' He winks, with a pointed look, and I raise a hand to my hair, which I feel is a bit messy from the wind. I bite my lip to keep from making a sarcastic comment back.

But people are making noises of agreement about truth or dare, and gather into an awkward almost-circle on the floor. Todd takes an empty beer bottle from a nearby nesting table and lurches to put it in the center, spinning it.

The people who choose 'truth' usually get asked about their crush, or their boyfriend/girlfriend and how far they've gone with them, or their most embarrassing story. The people who choose 'dare' – and they are few and far between – usually get dared to kiss someone, or to do a striptease in the case of one guy (though he keeps his underpants on, thank God).

I start to think that maybe we'll all get bored of the game before the bottle can land on me; it's been about half an hour and so far I've been safe. The girl next to me, Amanda, gets up to go to the kitchen for another drink, and the bottle slows to a stop, pointing between me and the empty space.

Since Amanda's no longer here, it's all on me.

'Um . . .' I weigh up which could be worse. 'Truth.'

'What's your biggest regret?' It's the girl who was

outside the bathroom, I recognize the high-pitched voice. I can see the devious gleam in her eyes, like she's so proud of herself for being subtly vindictive.

Everybody gives a big 'Ooh' and I roll my eyes, laughing like this question is no big deal and like I don't know what she was saying about me earlier.

My biggest regret – easy. She's sat right across the circle from me, blanking me, like I don't exist. I regret that I let my friendship with Allie fall apart to nothing so easily and I didn't try and talk to her about Josh and explain.

But I don't want to say that. I won't give this girl the satisfaction of humiliating me, and I won't embarrass Allie by saying it either.

So what else can I say, that they'll believe is a truth?

'Um . . . okay, that's a toughie . . . Uh . . . Oh, okay! My biggest regret is that I never learned to play the piano. I always really wanted to be able to play.' Then I lean forward and spin the bottle, and I ask Kelly (who picks truth) if she ever had a crush on someone a friend was dating.

As the game continues, we begin to grow bored, and some people peel away, until sometime after ten we give up on the game altogether. I end up sitting talking to a few people, until I decide to slip away to the kitchen for a few minutes. It's not that they're all not nice people. They are surprisingly easy to talk to. It's just that I don't normally hang out with them, and I've never really spoken to any of them properly before, so I feel a bit awkward, like I might be intruding.

And, you know, there's the whole maybe they all secretly hate me but are pretending to get along with me for a big joke issue.

Nobody is in the kitchen, at least.

I pour myself a glass of cold water then sink onto a stool at the little breakfast bar, resting my elbows on the cool counter with my head in my hands. Maybe I'd be better off just going home.

A hand on my shoulder makes me almost fall off the stool.

'I swear one of these days, Todd, I am going to start to carry a frying pan around with me, and every time you sneak up on me, I'll end up hitting you over the head.'

He laughs. He's loosened up a lot. 'I did say your name. You didn't hear?'

'Obviously not.'

'Lost in your own little world. Is my party really that bad?'

I smile, shake my head slightly. 'No, it's a good party.'

'Then why do you look like you're far away?'

A frown tugs at my eyebrows before I compose my expression. 'I'm not far away. I'm right here, talking to you, aren't I? I think all that beer's gone to your head.'

He shakes his head then. 'That's not what I meant.' I pause, waiting to see if he'll carry on. He says, 'Your boyfriend not showing up?'

'Not so far as I know. He's busy.'

Todd nods and then says. 'So, you and Josh . . .' I raise an eyebrow at him. Is this related to our vague conversation about what happened between me and Allie? 'I mean, he sounds like an okay guy. But do you really have that much in common with him?'

The question catches me off-guard.

He waits.

I think.

'I didn't think so. I've heard, uh, a fair bit about you two. I don't know, I just thought he didn't seem like the kind of guy I could picture you with.'

I pull a face, curious. 'Then what kind of guy would you picture me with?'

He scratches the back of his neck and shifts from one foot to the other, then goes and gets himself a glass of water. 'I just thought you'd be with someone smarter than him.'

'Someone smarter,' I repeat slowly.

'Yeah. I'm just surprised.'

'Josh isn't stupid.'

'I didn't say that. I'm just saying he's not the sharpest tool in the box.'

'So what? I've been with him since April of sophomore year. I love him, and—'

'All I'm saying is, from what I've heard and seen, I'd have thought you could do better.'

I scowl. 'What's so bad about Josh? Please, tell me, Todd, don't spare me the details.'

Todd huffs and narrows his eyes, looking more than irritated and on his way to angry. 'What, you don't think he's just a little bit too obnoxious at times? That he doesn't put people down and throw his weight around? And the way he talks about you, like you're—'

'You've been here about a month, Todd, and you don't even talk to Josh. Do you really think you're in the best position to talk about him? You don't know him.'

Todd scoffs and gives me a smirk, his expression almost pitying in the way it's so condescending. 'Oh, come on, Ashley, like you don't know the sort of things he goes around saying about you?'

I waver. 'I don't know what you mean.'

And honestly, I don't know that I do want him to tell me. What if it's lies and rumors blown out of proportion? What if it's not, and it's all true?

I gave up a lot to be with Josh.

'Yeah, I guess you wouldn't. Maybe you are as shallow and vapid as he says you are.'

My stomach churns. 'You're lying. He wouldn't say something like that about me.'

The smirk Todd gives me is so self-righteous and so high-and-mighty that I want to slap the look right off his face. 'Sure he wouldn't. Because we all know what a great guy Josh Parker is, don't we? All that stuff he says about you, I don't know what he sees in you. I mean,' he scoffs, 'everybody knows what he *doesn't* see in you.'

The last comment is punctuated with an arch of his eyebrows and his eyes skim over me critically. I clench my jaw so tightly it hurts, and feel my cheeks burning. Todd's making stuff up now, he has to be. He's drunk and for some reason he's lying.

I can't bring myself to believe that any of what he's saying is true.

Josh doesn't say I'm vapid and shallow. He knows I get good grades at school. And what Todd's insinuating . . . I can only assume he's talking about how I haven't had sex with Josh yet.

But how does he know that? It's between me and

Josh . . . and sure, our friends know, but what's it got to do with Todd, or anybody else?

I shake my head. No, I won't ask him. I'm walking away. Josh loves me; he wouldn't say things like that about me.

'I'm sorry I ever asked. Maybe when you've sobered up you'll stop being so arrogant you'll talk to me a little more reasonably. And you think Josh is the obnoxious one? Like you're so much better than him. Jesus, Todd, it's . . .' I'm still shaking my head as I stand up. 'Never mind. I'm out of here.'

'You're leaving?' He seems genuinely shocked.

'It's not like anybody wants me here anyway. And I'm not having this conversation with you.'

'You just don't want to listen, do you? Maybe you are as shallow as he says you are. Maybe you know what he says about you, and you don't care. Everyone thinks he's only interested in you for one thing and he's just waiting around to get it, but maybe it works both ways. Maybe you're only interested in being popular.'

'I'll see you Monday,' I say, not turning to face him and making my way to the door. I find my shoes in the hall and push my feet into them. I pull the front door behind me in an attempt to close it but I don't hear it shut; instead, there are soft footsteps, and I know that Todd is following me.

'When are you going to stop being so stupid and realize he's no good for you?' he calls after me. That makes me stop.

I twist sharply to glare at him.

'What the hell is that even supposed to mean?'

'You know exactly what it's supposed to mean.' He stands up straighter, looking me dead in the eye.

'And you think that *you're* better for me, is that it?' I snap. 'Is that what this is about?'

Todd's jaw clenches, then he smirks. 'Don't flatter yourself.'

I feel heat creeping over my entire face, not just my cheeks, and I whip around and storm back to my house, slamming the front door closed behind me. I don't know if I'm more angry or humiliated at the last comment.

And now part of me wishes I'd stayed to hear him tell me everything Josh says about me and how he talks about me. But it can't be anything bad, can it? Todd's just being . . . Well, it's just some misunderstanding. Yeah, that's all it is.

I go through the house slamming doors to let my frustration out, and by the time I make it to my bedroom, I get a text from Josh, asking if I'm still awake, and is it okay if he comes over for a little while, he wants to see me.

I tell him that I'm going to bed and not to come over. I scrub my make-up off angrily, making my face blotchy and bright, and throw myself underneath the covers, breathing through my nostrils sharply until I get tired enough that drowsiness drowns out my anger, and I somehow manage to fall asleep.

# Chapter Ten

Sunday evening, after dinner. I'm finishing off some history homework I'd forgotten about, and then something clatters through my window, onto my carpet.

I look up, and there's a pen on the floor. A black biro with a chewed-up cap. I look up and see Todd crouched on his window seat grinning at me through the open window.

I'm still mad at him.

So I grab the pen and launch it back, hoping to hit him in the chest or something – but my aim has never been good; the pen sails over his head, into his room. I move to go slam my window shut and he speaks to me.

'Ashley, come on, please. You haven't answered any of my texts.'

'There's this wondrous invention that they call a front door, Todd, maybe you should learn to use it.'

'You wouldn't have answered the door if you knew it was me.'

'I would, I would at least have the satisfaction of slamming it in your face. Now, I have to settle for a window. *Goodbye*, Todd.'

'Hang on a sec, just listen to me a moment,' he says, leaning forwards, as if that will somehow put a physical stop to me closing my window. As it is, I pause, my fingers on the bottom of the window.

I don't want to keep being angry with him. So I give him a chance to explain.

His tense expression eases, his scrunched-up face smoothing out slightly. 'I'm sorry. I was a real jackass last night. I shouldn't have said those things to you. And I'm sorry I was so rude, especially about Josh.'

I wait to hear him blame it on the beer and say that he was drunk, he didn't know what he was saying, I can't stay mad at him for that.

He doesn't.

I think that's why I'm so quick to forgive him.

Although I'd be lying if I said that the fact I like him and hate fighting with him has nothing to do with it.

'I'm sorry,' he reiterates, my silence making him visibly nervous.

I take a breath and say, 'That's okay.'

His eyebrows disappear under his hair. It's shorter, I notice; he must have had it cut today. It still looks unruly, though. 'Really?'

'You don't have to sound so shocked.'

'You can be very stubborn when you want to be.'

My mouth twists up into a grudging smile. 'Yeah, well.'

We both sit unmoving on our window seats for a long moment which I don't think will ever end; he's looking steadily at me, and I am half-smiling back at him. It's as if we're both waiting for the other to say something, but neither of us has anything to say. It isn't uncomfortable – more hesitant.

Eventually, he says, 'Um.'

And I reply, 'So.'

There's another pause, but it's not that awkward, which surprises me.

'I'll see you in the morning then.'

'Yep.'

'All right.'

Todd gives me a small smile. 'Thanks.'

'For what?'

'For accepting my apology. Shocking as it may be, I am beginning to tolerate your company. Wouldn't want all that work on putting up with you to be for nothing.' There's a twinkle in his eyes though, and a hint of a smirk in his smile, and I laugh.

'Of course. I should probably say thanks, too, though.'

'Why?'

'For not blaming it on the alcohol,' I reply simply, and then I go back to my desk to finish writing my essay about Nazi Germany in the 1930s.

After a while – I'm not sure how long exactly – I hear the familiar sound of Todd's guitar. The notes and the melody are harsh, and I move closer to my window so that I can hear him better. He sits with his back to the window, like always, and his words are soft and strong. The contrast of his voice and the music from his guitar shouldn't work this well, but it's beautiful.

*'I need some place to hide away,*
*Where I can feel safe*
*I need to hold you in my arms*
*Just to prove I'm not alone*

*I don't need someone to talk to*
*Who can comfort me with lies*
*I need to feel your heartbeat against mine*
*Cause I can't get through this on my own*

*A place that's safe, somewhere*
*To close the door on all the*
*Troubles in the world*
*Sanctuary*

*Sanctuary*
*You are my sanctuary.'*

The lyrics are haunting and tug at something in the pit of my stomach. He carries on playing the guitar for a little bit, then he scribbles in his book, amending something maybe, and then tries out the same tune again, without singing, changing a note or a beat here and there.

I start smiling to myself, and bury my head back in my homework.

The earphone in my left ear is pulled out, and I turn my head at Todd, who is now hunched over the table, writing furiously in his precious blue book, the pen scratching on the thick paper. I roll my eyes and pick up the earphone, putting it back in. He often starts writing lyrics midway through class; he's told me it's not just in Creative Writing. I also tend to digress from whatever wishy-washy creative writing assignment we've been given to do some homework, and I know I'm not the only one.

I don't think Ms Langstone even really cares all that much, as long as we're handing in the work she asks for. She's given up trying to be strict by this point. Besides, the 'creative' part of this class does imply a certain leniency, after all, as I pointed out when I wrote a haiku as a 'description piece' about a beach, which wasn't exactly what she was after, but it's not like she specified how we should write the description . . .

I surreptitiously reply to Josh's last text and put my phone in front of my pencil case on my desk to keep it hidden, and so I'll see when he replies.

'You'll see him soon enough,' Todd says suddenly, looking at me now. I didn't even notice him stop writing.

I shake my head. 'He's sick today.'

Todd raises an eyebrow, noticing the way I said 'sick' like Josh is anything but. 'Oh.'

'Well. He twisted his ankle yesterday and Coach told him to stay home and rest it because there's a game on Friday night,' I explain.

Todd laughs under his breath, rolls his eyes. 'Of course.'

'Are you going to the game?'

'I don't know. Maybe. I think some of the guys were planning to go, so . . .' He shrugs.

'Not much of a football fan?'

'My dad is, and my uncle on my mom's side. It was never really my thing. We watch a game together sometimes.'

'I watch football with my dad sometimes, too. Ever

since I was little, we'd sit down every year and watch the Super Bowl, and after a while we watched other games together, too.'

'That's cool.'

'What're you writing?'

I always ask, whenever I see him at it.

He never shows me.

Today is no exception: he taps his nose and says, 'Sorry, but that's confidential information. If I told you, I'd have to kill you.'

We both go back to our own writing, but there's a question buzzing in my head that I half don't want to ask, but can't help it.

'You know how in some of your songs, you're always talking about a girl? Or, a significant other,' I amend, because maybe I've assumed wrongly all along, and he's gay.

He hesitates for a moment and closes the book. 'What's your question?'

'Who is she? Or he,' I add quickly.

'I'm straight,' he tells me with a small smile, a note of laughter in his voice when he notices my nervous smile.

'I thought you were,' I say. 'It was a just-in-case.' I hold up my hands, palms out. 'Not judging.'

He nods. 'Well, to be honest, there . . . there isn't

really any "she". It's more that there's the idea of a "she" sometime in my future who will fit those songs.' His mouth twists. 'I mean, there isn't anyone now, but I remain hopeful that someday there will be a girl I fall in love with and she'll be the kind of girl I would want those songs to be about.'

I nod. 'I guess that makes sense. I thought maybe there was someone you'd left behind somewhere.'

He shrugs. 'No. No one.'

'Come on then, since we're on the subject.' I turn my chair toward him, scoot closer, and put my chin in my palms, resting on my elbows. 'Let's hear all about the girlfriends you've had.'

He smiles wryly at me. 'Never had one.'

My eyebrows go up. I make a conscious effort to return my expression to neutral. 'Really? You're more of a guy for flings and random hook-ups? No judgments, again.'

He shakes his head. 'Nope,' he says, popping the 'p'. 'I've kissed a couple of girls, at parties – the prom I went to last year, but that's it. I don't think I'm exactly the best candidate for a boyfriend.'

I let out a stifled snort of derisive laughter. 'Yeah, okay, *sure*.' I lay the sarcasm on thick in my words. 'I can *totally* see why girls have never wanted to date you.'

He sighs, but there's a hint of a bitter smile on his lips. His eyes are gray in this light, and they make him look more melancholy. 'Come on. I'm the quiet guy with a troubled mind who likes to read books. Doesn't exactly put me at the top of the list. The movies romanticize it, but in real life, girls avoid me like the plague.'

'Oh, but the whole cutting classes, getting expelled thing, on top of the brooding image, that doesn't have any appeal for girls. You know, loads of them go for the bad-boy thing. Not me, so much, but others do.'

'Quiet,' he says, eyes flitting around us. 'Those aren't exactly things I want broadcast.'

'Sorry.'

After a pause he carries on. 'Besides, I don't want to go dating a girl who only likes me for what she's seen on the surface, and doesn't know the rest of me, because in the end, it's me who'd get hurt, and it's not worth it.'

'But how are you going to know if she's worth it, if you don't open up to her? She can only like you at first for what she sees on the surface and then as she gets to know you more and more, that's when she'll start to fall for you. So how do you know it's not worth it if you won't let anybody in, in the first place?'

His eyes study my face, holding my gaze.

'How well did you know Josh when you started dating?'

'He sat next to me in English class in freshman year; our teacher decided on a seating chart for the class. At first, I felt awkward around him because I was quiet and he wasn't, and he played sports while I liked books. And he was popular, so I didn't think he'd really notice me that much. We'd just talk in lessons, and sometimes he'd walk with me to my next class, and after a couple of months, he asked me on a date. I got to know him bit by bit over time and then once we started dating, we got to know more about each other.'

I smile down at the table, watching my fingers twirling my pen around. 'When he first asked me out, I couldn't believe it, because I'd started to really like him, but I didn't think he saw me that way. I figured it was a one-sided crush, you know? Then being with him, he just – he made me happy.'

He doesn't say anything. When I look over out of the corner of my eye, he's rolling that gray guitar pick between his fingers again.

'The problem with you is that you're scared to let people in,' I say.

He looks up to meet my eyes. 'And the problem with you is that you don't like to know the worst in people.'

I don't reply; I'm not sure how to. I'm not even entirely sure if he meant that in a bad way. So I just sit and stare blankly at him for a few moments, and then Ms Langstone's voice rings out, 'Okay everyone, I want you to work on this for next lesson, to be handed in on Friday. The bell will go in a few minutes; you may as well leave.'

There's instant movement throughout our small class as people scrape back their chairs on the rough carpet, and sweep books and pens into bags. I take the earphone from Todd, wrapping the wire around my iPod. He gives me a smile and says, 'See you later,' as I leave.

Lunch is long without Josh there, but not altogether unbearable. Mostly, though, I'm thinking about my conversation with Todd. I usually end up replaying our conversations in my head – a lot of the things he says are vague and ambiguous and leave me wondering what the hell he meant. And it is times like this when I smile because even if we do have our arguments, and half the time I can't quite figure him out, I really do like Todd O'Connor.

'Hello-o-o-o-o? Earth to Ashley?'

'Huh?' I look up from my lunch and see Austin waving a hand in front of my face. 'What?'

'How's Josh's ankle? Think he'll be up for the game on Friday?'

'Oh, yeah, sure he will. It's not that bad, really. He just needed to rest it a little.'

'As long as he's okay to kick butt at the football game, right?' Neil adds, nudging Austin, and they both laugh. I'm not sure what's so funny, but the girls join in as well. I force a chuckle just to participate.

I look past the boys to Todd's table. I can see Allie there today, doing what I assume is some homework. Naomi sees me looking and lowers her voice to mutter in my ear, 'God, she's so pretentious, don't you think?'

'What?'

'Allie Lewitt. You guys used to hang out, didn't you?'

'Um, yeah, I – well, I guess . . .'

'Was she always so stuck-up? She's in my English class,' Naomi carries on, 'and she's such a know-it-all and she thinks she's so much better than everybody else, just because she edits the school paper and wears plaid skirts with sneakers like she doesn't care if she looks like a walking fashion disaster. I just hate people like that. Don't you?'

I nod, not because I agree with her, but because I don't want to disagree.

She smiles at me, with her perfect magenta lipstick and immaculately straight teeth that have never seen braces. 'You're so lucky you ditched her when you had the chance.'

* * *

I place the fresh ice-pack I got from the freezer on Josh's ankle, which is still looking a little swollen, but it's not bruised and it should be fine by the game on Friday.

'Thanks, babe,' he says, sitting up and leaning toward me. I lean the rest of the way to kiss him, and he smiles against my lips. He leans back on his pillows and taps at his Xbox controller to get rid of the pause menu and carry on playing. It's some war game; I forget the name of it.

I lie beside him on my stomach and open the poetry book we're studying in English to the page where I dog-eared it last. I pick my pencil back up and chew on the end of it thoughtfully, wondering about all the different implications of the poem I'm looking at now.

'Are you coming back to school tomorrow?' I ask him after a while.

'Probably. I don't think my teachers are going to be exactly happy if I hand in any more homework late, and I can't afford any detentions right now, what with all the football practice.'

I nod. 'Okay. It was really quiet without you at lunch today.'

He wraps his uninjured right leg around both of mine and then mutters to himself, 'Aw, damn it,' over something on his video game.

A while later, when I've finished analyzing a couple of poems for my homework and Josh has reached a new level in his game, he stops playing and finds a channel showing reruns of *Friends* and I snuggle into him.

We don't talk much for a while; we just watch TV and make out.

At one point I start to tell him about something I liked in one of the poems I just looked at, but I instantly stop myself; he wouldn't be interested, so there's no point in boring him.

But that makes me think – about what Todd said both at his party and today in creative writing, about Josh and I not really having much in common. I love him, I really do, and even though we're not talking right now, it's so nice and peaceful just being cuddled up with him.

But . . . well, wouldn't it be a bit nicer if we did have more to talk about? If we had more things in common and could have a proper conversation about things other than colleges and school and Josh's football; wouldn't that just make everything that little bit better between us?

I suppress a sigh.

I'm being stupid. I wouldn't even be thinking those things if Todd hadn't brought them up.

Things are great between me and Josh. I want to shake my head at myself, scold myself for thinking like this, because it's only making me doubt things, and there is nothing to doubt.

I'm happy with Josh.

'I love you,' I say out loud.

'I love you too,' Josh says softly, and leans to kiss me. When we kiss, I look at the shadow the light from the TV screen throws over the one half of his face, and how it makes his cheekbone look sharper, and how thick his blond eyebrows are. I don't want to be thinking about even those things, though; I just want to kiss him and lose myself in the feeling of that and just be in love with him.

I close my eyes, but that doesn't really help erase my thoughts.

We're in love, right? Isn't love when you're just happy being with someone, like I am with Josh? I shouldn't be thinking about how things might be better between us, or persuading myself how good things are with us. It shouldn't be an issue.

I break the kiss and snuggle my head into the crook of his neck. 'I should get going, it's late.'

'You can stay another five minutes.'

I shake my head and sit up, swinging my legs off the side of the bed. 'I need to stop by the gas station on the way home.'

'Five more minutes, Ashley, c'mon, it won't hurt.'

I waver, but then I stand up, picking up my poetry book and my pencil, putting them into my purse. 'I'm sorry. I really need to get going.'

Josh sighs. 'All right, then.' He sighs again and sits up, making to take the ice-pack off his ankle, but I catch his wrist.

'Stay here, don't worry about it.'

'Are you okay?' He squints up at me, his mouth turned down. 'Is everything okay, Ashley?'

I nod, putting on a smile for him. 'It's fine. I'm fine. I just lost track of time, that's all. I'm fine. You stay here, though, you need to rest your ankle.'

'Yeah, I guess so.' He leans back into the pillows without arguing; I kneel with one knee on the bed to give him another kiss goodbye, and then I sling my purse onto my shoulder and head downstairs. I say goodbye to his mom when she pops her head out of the lounge, and I go to the gas station even though I don't need to just yet.

I drive around for a while before I actually get home, trying to clear my head.

It doesn't really work.

# Chapter Eleven

Almost tripping over my own feet, I bolt down the steps of the bleachers and run up to Josh, launching myself into his arms. His arms curl around me and twirl me around, and I kiss him, giggling helplessly, holding his face in my hands. He smells of sweat and victory.

'Didn't I tell you that you'd be amazing?'

He rolls his eyes, but he's smiling. 'Yeah, yeah.'

I give him another kiss, this one a little longer. 'I'll let you go shower.'

'Are you telling me I stink?'

I laugh. 'Go on. I'll meet you at the car.'

He presses his lips briefly to the tip of my nose and then jogs backwards to catch up with the rest of the team who are currently making their way rowdily back to the locker rooms. The losing team, Harrison Prep, drift back in the direction of their bus with their cheerleaders, visibly dejected. People start to get up and make their way down from the bleachers, buzzing with excitement. It stinks of popcorn and hotdogs; sickly-sweet and potent, and the floodlights are blindingly bright against the inky blue sky.

A hand claps on my shoulder.

Austin says, 'We're going to head on back to Sam and Neil's.'

He's with Sam, Danielle, Eliza and Naomi. 'Sure,' I say. 'We'll meet you there in a bit.'

They file past me and I walk with them to the parking lot. Sam and Austin are discussing intricate details of the game, talking about how the other team might've scored if they'd only done this, or how we might've got another touchdown if Neil had passed the ball a little earlier.

'. . . Todd O'Connor to come hang with us,' Naomi is saying. The name catches my attention and I turn to her.

'What's that?'

'Oh, I asked Todd to hang with us,' she repeats, 'but he said no. Can you believe that?' I think she's taken his rejection personally. She's even *pouting*.

'He's probably already got plans or something,' I offer.

'I can never tell what he's thinking, he's always so mysterious. I bet he does it on purpose.'

'Sexy, though, right?' Eliza pitches in with a laugh.

'Oh, hell yeah,' Naomi agrees, giggling. 'But he's barely given any girl a second glance. It's like he's not even interested in hooking up or anything.'

'Well not all guys are like that,' I say. 'It may shock you to hear this, but some guys are actually looking for a committed relationship.'

'He has a date. A date! And not with me. That's why he wouldn't hang out with us. I mean, I've used every trick in the book, I've even asked him to tutor me in French—'

'You don't take French, though?' Eliza cuts in.

'Yeah, that's why he wouldn't. Anyway, not the point. He has a date with someone. Ugh. I'm so jealous of whoever it is.' She huffs dramatically for emphasis.

'A date?' I say, feeling shell-shocked, and delayed in responding. 'Like, an actual date?'

'Well, that's what he told me. Some girl in his math class asked him out, and he said yes. He said they're going for dinner now, after the game.'

My heart feels like it's got a fist squeezed around it, and I can't wrap my head around the fact that Todd has a date. Well, good for him, getting out there, right?

But I don't feel happy for him.

I don't know what I feel, actually.

But it's not jealousy. Definitely not jealousy.

I say, 'I'll see you later,' and slip away to where Josh's car is parked, too distracted now to even try and join in their conversation.

Josh gave me the keys earlier, so I rifle through my purse for them so I can sit inside; I'm a little worried it's going to rain.

'Hey.'

I turn around. 'Oh, hi.'

Todd turns to his friends, saying, 'I'll catch you guys up in a sec.'

They shrug and carry on walking without him, their conversation uninterrupted. I lower my purse so that it hangs at my side.

'Good game, huh?' I can't think of anything else to say.

He nods. 'Yeah, it was. Your boyfriend plays well.' He pauses, thinking, and then says, 'Your friend Naomi asked me to come hang out with you.'

'She told me. I think she's almost convinced that you're not attracted to her. She took it very personally when you said no.'

The corner of his mouth twitches into a smirk and he lets out a soft breath of laughter. He has a very full lower lip, I notice. His upper lip is thin, but with a very defined cupid's-bow. They're a very soft shade of pink, and chapped.

'I didn't think I would be very welcome,' he admits, looking up from under his mess of hair. 'I mean . . . I don't know your friends very well. No offence.'

'That's okay. She, um, she said you had a date?'

His mouth twists and he looks away, ruffling his hair with one hand. 'Yeah, um . . .' He clears his throat. 'It seemed like the only way to make her back off.'

'Oh.'

Definitely not relieved. Why should I be? It's not like it matters to me if he dates someone or not.

I rock back and forth on the heels of my worn-out red Converse. Todd scuffs his feet on the concrete, drawing my attention to the dirty toes of his sneakers.

'You should probably get going,' I say. 'Catch up with your friends.'

'Yeah.' He doesn't move. 'Um. I'll, uh, I'll see you around. Oh, and if you could maybe avoid mentioning to Naomi that I lied about the date—'

'Got you covered.' I smile at him, and I think he returns it, but I can't be sure; he turns and walks off too quickly. I watch him leave for a few seconds before I look back at my purse and dig my hand in for Josh's keys. My fingers close around them just as another pair of hands closes over my eyes, making me jump with a shriek of surprise.

'Guess who.'

I laugh, turning, 'Don't sneak up on me like that. You scared the crap out of me.'

'Sorry, babe, couldn't resist.' Josh laughs, grinning easily at me. He smells less like sweat now and more like cheap soap. His hair is wet, his skin still damp. Neil's with him, too, and both of them toss their dirty football kits into the trunk before we climb into the car.

The others are already there when we get to the twins' house. I sit on Josh's lap on the armchair and the others crowd onto the couches. Sam brings out a box of cold beers from the kitchen and Josh reaches across me to take one from him.

I push his hand away. 'You're driving, remember?'

'Yeah, I know.' He pulls his hand from mine and takes the beer from Sam. 'And we'll be here for a few hours. One won't hurt.'

I give him a look that blatantly says I'm not happy with him.

He opens the can, takes a gulp of the beer and I sigh, but it doesn't stop him drinking it. And it doesn't stop him having another three over the course of the next hour.

When he's about to crack open a fifth can, I cover his hand with mine to stop him. 'Maybe one wouldn't hurt if you're driving, but five?'

'Don't be so uptight all the time, Ashley.' I hear the others stifle laughs and clench my jaw.

'I'm not being uptight,' I say, bristling, and admittedly a little upset by the others laughing at me. 'You can't drive home like this.'

He nudges my hand off and opens the can. 'If it bothers you that much, call your mom for a ride home.'

My mouth drops open and I let out a noise of complete disbelief. 'Why are you acting like this?'

'Like what?'

'Like . . .' I flounder, unable to find the right word. 'Obnoxious.'

He rolls his eyes. 'I'm just trying to have a good time.' I sigh, rubbing a hand across my forehead. What the hell is wrong with him, thinking that this is okay? Like he can drive home later after drinking this much (and I know he's not planning on stopping at five). And like he can make me out to be the bad guy in all this, the party-pooper, ruining his fun!

He must see how angry I am, because he laughs again, like it's all a joke to him and I just haven't seen the punch line yet.

'Oh, c'mon, Ashley. I'm not a lightweight. Unlike some people.'

He gives me a look that makes me sure the lightweight comment was a slight dig at me, but then his face breaks out into an easy grin and he wraps his arm tighter around me, pulling me closer, and they all start talking about the game again.

I push his arms off me, and storm out of the room to the bathroom upstairs.

'Ashley?' Naomi calls after me.

I lock myself in the bathroom for a couple of minutes, breathing deeply in and out to calm down. He's being a jerk, and that's a generous term for how he's acting right now.

There's no way I'm letting him drive me home, and there's no way I'm letting him drive himself home, either.

When I unlock the door to go back downstairs and announce I'm calling for a ride home immediately, Josh is leaning against the wall opposite.

I step aside, holding the door for him, but he shakes his head and I let the door swing back. 'Ashley . . .' He tries to draw me into his arms, his hands on my elbows, but I shake my head and push away, backing into the wall.

With a loud sigh, he steps closer so that he's right up against me, and his index finger pushes my chin up to get me to look at him.

'Don't you trust me, Ashley?' he says. 'C'mon, you know I wouldn't do anything stupid and get wasted. I'm not an idiot.'

'It's a little late for that,' I snap irritably. 'I'm calling my mom and I'm going home.'

He leans down to kiss me, but I narrow my eyes at him; he knows he's not getting out of this that easily. He hesitates before kissing my cheek instead. 'You know I love you.'

'Yeah. Sure.'

'You mean everything to me, Ashley, you know I wouldn't do anything stupid like that. Look, if it makes you feel better, then call your mom for a ride home and I'll crash here. Sam and Neil won't care. I won't even drive *myself* home. Okay?'

Great, now that makes me sound like the bad guy, and like he's being so understanding by making some kind of compromise.

I make a grunt of agreement, but that's the best he's getting. Josh sighs, and I can see he doesn't know what else he can do; he thinks he's done everything he can to make me stop being mad at him.

He kisses me softly, and his hands slide under my tank top and sit on my waist. They start to slide higher, but that's when I pull away. I feel him sigh against my lips as his hands move back down. I know that our friends are always asking when we're going to finally have sex, and they make a joke of it, but Josh knows I'm still not comfortable with anything like that. He leans his forehead to mine.

'You okay?' he asks me softly. He knows I'm not, but right now, I'm not in the mood to talk to him. I just want to go home.

'I'm fine.'

'Are you sure? I don't just mean after tonight, Ashley. You seem to be acting kind of weird lately. Really quiet.'

'I'm just tired. I've had a lot of homework.'

'Oh. Are you sure that's all it is? I can see you're mad about tonight, but did I do something else to make you mad?'

I nod. 'Yeah. Everything's fine.'

He looks dubious, but seems happy enough to believe me. His lips meet mine again and this time I kiss him back for all of three seconds before stepping away and pushing him away so he's at arm's length. He gets the message, and starts to head back downstairs, pausing when he realizes I'm not following.

'Are you coming back downstairs?'

I nod. 'Yeah. I'll just call my mom, and I'll be right there.'

'Okay.' He smiles at me again and heads back downstairs with his heavy-footed tread. I hear voices floating up from the lounge.

'. . . your own house, dude, not here,' I hear Neil say with a laugh.

'Don't worry,' Josh replies, probably not realizing how loudly he's talking or that his voice is carrying upstairs to where I can hear, 'she still doesn't want to.'

'You guys have been together for ages,' Danielle says. I'm straining to hear her, she doesn't talk as loudly as the boys. I tiptoe to the top of the staircase to hear better. 'I don't see what her problem is. It's just sex. Isn't it kind of weird that you haven't done it yet?'

'It's a big deal for her,' Naomi says, and I'm actually surprised that she, of all of them, is defending me. 'Not everyone wants to put out. If Ashley doesn't want to have sex, then she doesn't have to have sex. I know we tease both of you about it sometimes, but it's no big deal if she doesn't want to. Josh respects that, don't you?'

He grunts, like he's not so sure. 'Yeah, but . . .' He sighs. 'I just wish she wasn't so uptight about it.'

For a second I manage to forget all about how mad I am at him for drinking those beers when he's supposed to be driving, and I stand there in a state of shock, unable to tune out their voices. Why hadn't he ever talked to me about this?

Then they're talking about the rumor of one of the football guys being on steroids, and there's nothing more to overhear on the subject.

I step back from the top of the stairs and lean my head back against the wall for a moment. Do they all think it's so weird that I don't want to – to be that intimate with Josh yet? Well, all of them except Naomi, apparently.

I pull my cell from the front pocket of my jeans and dial my mom's number.

'Hello?' Her voice is drowsy, like she's just woken up. I pull the phone away from my ear to look at the time. It's just before eleven. I hadn't realized it was so late already. 'Ashley? Is everything okay?'

'Hi, Mom. Do you think you could come pick me up, from Neil and Sam's?' My voice sounds guilty; I think I woke her up.

She yawns as if to confirm my thoughts. 'Oh, I thought Josh was bringing you home?'

'He – he was, but . . . he had a drink so he's crashing here.'

'Oh. I see. Well, I suppose, but you'll have to give me ten minutes to get dressed. I was already asleep.'

'Sorry, Mom.'

'No, it's not your fault.' Despite the tiredness in her voice, she sounds almost as annoyed about Josh being too inebriated to drive me home as I am.

'I can, um . . . I can call Todd? He'll still be up.' I'm usually asleep around eleven on school nights, but whenever I'm up late reading or something, I never see Todd's bedroom lights go out until midnight at the earliest.

'He'll still be up,' I repeat. 'Sorry, I guess I should've called him first. You can go back to sleep.'

'Are you sure?' Mom's words are muffled by another yawn.

'Yeah. It's fine, Mom, I'll call Todd for a ride. Sorry I woke you up.'

'That's okay. Call me back if he can't help. Try and be quiet when you get in.'

I promise I will, and I say goodbye and hang up, then I dial Todd's number. He picks up on the second ring, and sounds wide awake when he says, 'Hey, what's up?'

'Hi. I'm sorry but I really need a huge favor.'

'Sure, what?'

'Could you, um . . . Would you please give me a ride home from Sam and Neil's house? I'll give you gas money, I swear.'

He doesn't ask questions, which I expect him to, except for, 'What's the address?' and, 'What time do you want me to come pick you up?'

'Whenever is most convenient for you,' I reply, not wanting to put him even more out of his way.

'Well I'm not doing anything for the next couple

of hours aside from playing Xbox, so you tell me.'

I consider staying until past midnight, but if I'm being totally honest, I'm not even having that much of a good time here. I bite my lip before answering.

'Is now okay?'

My cell buzzes and flashes up with a text message from Todd not fifteen minutes later.

*'Parked at the end of the street when you're ready.'*

'That's my cue to leave,' I announce, and stand up from my spot on the couch next to Danielle.

'See you guys.'

They say goodbye and continue their conversation. Josh stands up and walks me to the front door, despite me giving him the cold shoulder since coming back downstairs. 'I'll call you tomorrow,' he says. 'Maybe we can go see a movie or something?'

'Sure,' I reply quietly, and when he leans to kiss me I duck my head away, so he settles for kissing the side of my head instead.

'I love you.'

'Enjoy the rest of the night.' I unlock the door and start down the path. I get about halfway when he closes the door. Once I'm on the sidewalk, I look down the street both ways, and see the glow of car brake lights on my left, so I head that way. It's dark even with the streetlights, so only when I'm about halfway down the street do I recognize Todd's car.

I slide into the passenger seat. 'Thanks for this.'

'No problem.' He starts up the engine and pulls off.

After a moment that feels so endless I can hardly bear the silence any more, I hear myself blurting out, 'You're not going to ask why I needed a ride? Or make some sort of comment about Josh?'

He shrugs. 'I thought you two might've had a fight, in which case, it's really not my place. And you might not want to talk about it.'

'Oh.' His answer doesn't surprise me, which is weird, but a good kind of weird. 'We didn't,' I say. 'Well, not really. It wasn't exactly a fight.'

'Good for you, I guess.'

'He had some beers, earlier, so I refused to get in the car with him.' I don't know why I'm telling Todd this. He didn't ask, and there's no reason I should tell him. But I can't help myself.

'Hold on,' he says slowly, his voice lowering. 'So you're telling me he was going to drive you home after he'd had a drink?'

'He didn't think he was that drunk, and made me out to be the bad guy when I said he shouldn't drive. I don't know. He was just being a – a jerk.'

'Not one for strong language?' Todd sends me a smile, and I laugh.

'Okay, so that's a pretty weak term considering how I feel about him right now. It's just . . . I don't why he had to act like it was okay for him to do something like that.'

'Josh thinks he can get away with all his crap because for guys like him, they're invincible. They can get the girls they want, they can fail classes and it's no big deal, they can do what they like and nothing can touch them.'

'Those are some deep observations for a Friday night.'

'Nah, they're just me being bitter and jealous because I'm not one of those guys, and I'd like to be.'

'You're jealous of Josh?' I say incredulously.

'I'm jealous of guys like him,' he corrects me. 'Because they live in this perfect world, and I'm stuck here in reality with the other losers.'

I look over at Todd, expecting to see him scowling and looking upset, but he's smiling a little, his face lit up a greenish shade from the dash. 'Thank you,' I say again. 'For the ride home.'

'It's okay. What're friends for?'

I'm shocked for a moment at his words, but only for a moment. I never really thought about it before. He's just Todd. Just the guy next door. Just Todd. But I guess we really are friends.

'Still,' I say. 'I really appreciate it. And I should probably profusely apologize for interrupting your video games. I mean, it's a rare occurrence when you get the chance to play them.'

I earn a chuckle for my sarcasm, which makes my smile widen. It starts to rain a bit, so he turns on the wipers, and we sit in companionable silence the rest of the way home.

When he pulls onto his driveway and parks, I start to take a few dollars from my purse – gas money, like I promised him – but as soon as he sees them, his hand closes over mine.

'Really,' he says, 'it's okay.'

'I owe you.'

Todd shakes his head. 'Honestly, it's okay. Look, I'd rather drag out at nearly midnight to give you a ride than let you go home with Josh after he's had a drink. It's not like I was doing anything before, anyway. You don't owe me anything.'

I'm about to argue again, but he gets out of the car and I have no choice but to follow suit. 'Todd . . .'

He cuts me off again. 'You don't owe me anything, Ashley, really.'

'Five dollars, at least. Please.'

'You really don't like to feel like you're indebted to someone, do you?'

'I . . .' I blink rain out of my eyes, distractedly thinking I'm glad I forgot mascara earlier. But his question catches me off guard enough that he changes topic: 'Goodnight, Ashley.'

He starts toward his house, and with a sigh, I walk back down the driveway to go around the fence to my own front door.

'Ashley,' I hear him call after me when I'm at the end of the drive. I turn, holding my purse over my head in an attempt to keep the rain out of my face. 'Are you okay?'

'I'm fine,' I reply. 'Everything's fine.'

## Chapter Twelve

'How very unhealthy of you,' a voice says behind me as I thank the lady behind the counter at the lunch queue the following Monday. I look over my shoulder and Todd puts down his two candy bars and can of full-fat soda.

'I can see your diet is just top-notch,' I reply, rolling my apple over in my hand. 'Remind me to get the number of your dietician.'

His lips tweak in a half smirk and he mumbles a 'Thanks,' as the dinner lady hands over his change and he takes his stuff. I wait for him, and we fall in step beside each other, both of us heading down the corridors to the field around the side of the school. It's an athletics track in summer, but the students tend to use it to hang out in fall, if the weather's nice.

'How's your day been?' I ask him.

'All right, for a Tuesday.'

'What's wrong with Tuesdays?'

He grimaces. 'Never mind.'

I don't press him for an answer. Maybe it's just that he has really bad subjects, or something. Maybe it's something personal. We carry on walking, turning to make our way toward the doors.

'My granddad died on a Tuesday.' Todd's voice is so quiet I barely even notice he said anything at all. 'Crazy, right? Associating something like a Tuesday with missing him.'

'Oh. I don't think that's crazy,' I reply, after a long pause as we go outside. I feel like I ought to say something – comfort him, console him, tell him I'm sorry, but I feel like all that would be useless. So, at a loss for words, I bump him with my shoulder and brush the back of my hand against his.

Todd bumps my hip in return, and the tiniest hint of a smile pulls at the left corner of his mouth. I move to bump him again, and he jumps forward, causing me to stumble past him. I laugh, and jog a few steps to catch him up.

'So, any plans for tonight?' he asks me amiably.

'I offered to babysit for Mr and Mrs Freeman, at number eighteen. Josh has got football practice again.'

'Does your whole life revolve around him, Ashley?' Todd stops walking, and after the step it takes me to realize this, I stop too, and turn to face him. His eyebrows are knitted together, furrowed low over his pale blue eyes. His mouth is set in a grim line.

'I'm sorry?' I somehow manage to keep my voice steady and calm; I'm still mentally tossing up whether I should be incredulous or offended.

'If you aren't doing something with Josh, you just stay at home – doing your homework or reading a book, or whatever. You don't hang out with people, except me, unless he's there. Your whole life revolves around him. And don't try and deny it,' he adds brusquely when I start to object, 'because you know it's true.'

I settle for glaring at him while I decide how to reply.

My life doesn't revolve around him. It doesn't. Josh is just a huge part of my life – he's my boyfriend . . . But . . . Todd's *right*: when I'm not with Josh, I mostly do just stay home.

How do I explain that one to Todd, though? I don't go out much without Josh because the girls in the group we hang out with aren't really great friends of mine. They're nice people, sure, I'm not saying otherwise – but we're different, have different outlooks and views and hobbies. I just feel so out of tune with them.

I'll tag along on a shopping trip or something occasionally, but I find I never have an awful lot to *talk* to them about. I haven't really had any really close friends since Allie – and it seems that I've been totally alienated from our old group of friends now, given what it was like at Todd's party.

Since I've taken just that little bit too long to reply, Todd's decided to carry on shooting his mouth off.

'You don't even have any real friends. They're all his friends. And don't tell me I don't know that, because I've heard it from a lot of people who've known you for years. You hang out with his friends, but you don't treat them like they're your friends. I've seen you sitting at that lunch table with them for weeks and you hardly ever join in their conversations. It's crazy.'

'You don't know any—'

'Would you stop that already?' he snaps at me, narrowing his eyes.

I shove him.

I don't know what else to do. So I shove him, and he stumbles back a step. For the slightest second, we stand there looking at each other. His eyes are softer now, pitying, even. I narrow mine to slits, and the sight of him starts to blur.

I'm not crying, though – I can't be crying, not over *this*. It's stupid.

I'm not going to argue with him again.

So I take a deep breath and let it out shakily, rolling

my apple between my hands. 'I'm sorry. You're right, okay?'

He doesn't reply, just looks astounded that I'm not arguing.

'Have you got any plans tonight?' I say.

'No,' he says, albeit hesitantly.

'Great.' I grin at him, even though it feels a little bit forced, more like a grimace. 'You've just got roped in to helping me babysit the Freeman twins.'

He laughs, and runs a hand through his hair, messing it up even more than it already is. 'Sure. What time?'

'I'm heading over there for five thirty.'

'I'll meet you outside your house?' I nod, and he smiles again. 'Do you, um . . . Do you wanna eat lunch with us?'

I glance over to where he jerks a thumb, to the same group of people he invited to his house party. Allie's there. I can only see the back of her head, but I know it's her.

'No, that's okay.'

'You sure? I swear, they don't hate you or anything, if that's what you're worried about.'

I nod. 'Yeah, I'm sure. I'll see you later.' We wave goodbye and head off in opposite directions, him to his friends and me to . . . well, Josh's.

'Hey guys,' I say casually, dropping down next to Josh. After I'd ignored his texts and calls all of Saturday after the football game, he dropped by my house on Sunday afternoon to apologize. He hadn't apologized for anything specific, but I was so scared of losing him that I'd relented and told him that it was okay. I couldn't risk breaking up with him, because I couldn't imagine what I'd do without him. I'd be left with nobody.

'Is everything okay?' he asks.

'Sure, why?'

'You and O'Connor – it looked like you were having an argument.'

'Oh, it was nothing.' I smile. 'Just a misunderstanding.'

'Are you sure?' His brow furrows with concern for me, and for a second I consider telling him. Everything Todd said was true, I know that, and I have known since I stopped being friends with Allie. But hearing someone else say it made it feel a lot more real, and a lot worse; now, it weighs heavily on my chest and I have the words on the tip of my tongue to confide in Josh, but . . .

I don't.

Josh leans a little closer. 'You know you can talk to me about anything, right?'

I just smile and say, 'Sure. Everything's fine.'

He kisses me on the temple, and I lean against him, listening to them all talk about a movie I've never seen but apparently everyone else has at some point. The sun is warm on my face and arms, and I look over the field at Todd. He's laughing at something, head thrown back.

And I realize that it's been a long time since my so-called friends have made me laugh like that.

'You're babysitting the Freeman twins tonight, aren't you?' Dad says, buttering some toast. He's still dressed in his suit from work, even though he's been home all afternoon. We had to get a plumber in to fix the leak in the kitchen sink, so Dad said he could work from home while the plumber was here.

'Yeah,' I say, pouring myself a glass of apple juice.

'So you don't want dinner with us?'

'Nah, Mrs Freeman said I could help myself to something over at their place. She said there's plenty of leftover meatloaf.'

Dad nods.

'I, um, I asked Todd to come babysit with me.'

His eyebrows shoot up. 'And here I thought you were just carpooling with the guy to save gas money. You two are pretty good friends, then, huh?'

'I guess so. I mean . . .' I sigh. 'I don't know. We argue, sometimes, but . . .' But only when he's being brutally honest. '. . . I like him.'

'What does Josh think of him?'

I tilt my head to the side. 'Does it matter?'

Dad shrugs. Then he says, 'We haven't seen Josh for a while. Is everything okay with you two?'

I start to say of course it is, but I stop myself. 'I don't know.'

'Have you guys had a fight? I thought you forgave him when he came to apologize for Friday night.'

'It's not that simple . . .'

'Let me guess: the boy next door has stolen your heart?'

I laugh. 'Not quite. Things have just felt weird lately between me and Josh. Like, I don't miss him when I'm not with him. Is that bad?' I don't add the bit about how since last Friday I've been stressing out that he thinks I'm a prude and weird and frigid. Not the sort of thing I want to bring up in conversation with either one of my parents.

'You both need your space,' he says, probably repeating something he's heard women say on TV.

'Shouldn't I miss him all the time when I'm not with him, though? Shouldn't I want to be with him all the time?'

Dad takes a long, thoughtful bite of toast, chewing carefully. 'Well . . .' His cell starts vibrating violently on the kitchen counter, and he mutters, 'Damn, I have to take this. Sorry, Ashley. Hello? Yes – yes, hi, great to hear from you . . . No, everything's great – ha-ha, yes . . .' Balancing the cellphone between his ear and shoulder, carrying his toast in one hand and coffee in the other, he heads back to the office.

I sigh, and down the last of my apple juice, putting the empty glass by the sink. Maybe I'm just thinking too much about this . . .

I go to my room to gather some calculus homework to take to the Freemans', in case I get chance to work on it, and change into a sweater from my thin T-shirt. By then, it's close to five thirty, so I call goodbye to my dad, who's still on the phone so shouts back a quick, 'Bye, Ashley!' through the door.

I go out to wait on the sidewalk, rocking back and forth on my feet with the crisp autumn air blowing some loose hair from my braid around my face. I tuck the strands behind my ear, out of the way.

I'm not waiting long for Todd.

The sound of his front door opening, and the creak of a footstep on the porch makes me look up. I raise a hand in greeting. 'Hey.'

He shoulders his backpack, which is looking a lot less bulky than usual. 'Hey. Ready to go?'

'Yep.'

'You weren't waiting long, were you?' he says, as we start to head off in the direction of number eighteen.

'Nah, only a minute or so.'

He nods, and starts telling me about how unfair his geography teacher is, setting them a midterm next Monday – 'It's not even the middle of the semester yet!' – and how geography is his worst subject – 'I mean, what do I care about rock formations?'

'Geography's not that bad,' I say. 'I'll help you make some flash cards. It's easy.'

'Thanks,' he says, looking genuinely grateful. 'I appreciate it.'

'But only if you help me with my calculus homework.'

'Ah, calculus. The bane of my life.'

I laugh, and we turn up the drive of number eighteen. I ring the doorbell, and there's some shouting inside as they debate who's best positioned to answer the door, and then it's thrown open by Mrs Freeman. In the corner of my eye, I can see Todd twirling his guitar pick between his fingers.

'Oh, Ashley, hi!' She smiles, stressed, fixing an

earring into place. Her eyes flit to Todd. 'Is this your boyfriend?'

'No!' I say quickly. 'No, this is my next-door neighbor, Todd. Is it okay for him to keep me company? I—'

'Are you trying to tell me my precious monsters are too much of a handful for one person?' Arching an eyebrow at me, she plants her hands on her hips with that stern look that only moms seem to be able to do. Then she drops the facade and laughs. 'I can't say I blame you for bringing reinforcements. It's very nice to meet you, Todd.'

They shake hands and she steps back to let us inside, where we both start taking our shoes off while trying to listen to her instructions.

'Now, they've both had a bath, and there's plenty of meatloaf and mashed potatoes in the refrigerator for dinner, and some peas in the freezer. Ethan will try and convince you he's allergic to peas – he did with the last two babysitters – but don't pay him any attention. Bedtime at eight thirty, and Alice likes to have the nightlight kept on.'

It's nothing she didn't tell me the last time I babysat, about a month ago, but I pretend like this is all new information I'm absorbing carefully.

'Roger that.'

'Are you almost ready?' Mr Freeman calls from upstairs. 'We have to leave in ten minutes, Julie!'

'Yes, yes!' Turning back to me, she adds strictly, 'And no sugar before dinner!'

'Got it, Mrs Freeman.'

'And our numbers are on the refrigerator door, if you need us, but if you can't get hold of us, then their grandparents' numbers are on there too, and—'

I laugh. 'It'll be fine, really. I've babysat them before, remember?'

'Okay. Well, go on in the lounge and make yourself at home. The kids are in there watching a movie.'

Todd and I head into the lounge, and I say brightly, 'Hey, kids!'

Alice's head spins around and she grins at me. 'Ashley! Hi!' Her eyes fall on Todd and widen a little. 'Is this your boyfriend?'

'No,' I say hastily.

'We're just friends,' Todd pitches in.

'He's not my boyfriend,' I reiterate. 'This is Todd, he lives next door to me.'

'Oh.' Her smile droops with disappointment. 'Look, Ashley, I got ninety per cent on my homework.' She runs to the cabinet, snatches up some paper, and thrusts it in my face, smiling widely at me with her front tooth missing.

'That's great, sweetie!' I gush, crouching next to her. 'What about you, Ethan, how did you do on your homework?'

He mumbles, and Alice says, 'He only got seventy because I told him he wasn't allowed to copy me.'

'Seventy is still really good, Ethan,' I tell him. The twins look very similar, both with button noses and the same shade of sandy blond hair, both with narrow shoulders and slight frames. But they're as different as night and day; it's a struggle to get Alice to shut up sometimes, and you have to be really patient to get Ethan to talk to you.

'Thanks,' he mumbles.

'What movie are we watching?' Todd asks, sitting down on the floor with his back against the couch, near where Ethan is lying on his stomach. He is drawing the vase of flowers on the cabinet, his tongue poking out a little as he concentrates.

'*Kung Fu Panda,*' Alice replies. 'It's one of Ethan's favorites. Have you seen it?'

'No,' Todd says. 'Is it good, Ethan?'

Ethan just nods.

'Is that art homework?' I ask Ethan.

He nods again. Todd gives me a curious look, and I just smile and shrug as if to say 'What can you do?' and he lets it drop.

Mr and Mrs Freeman leave only three minutes behind schedule (pointed out a little irritably by Mr Freeman as he stands by the car and his wife talks me once again through the kids' schedule and the numbers on the refrigerator door.

'It'll be fine, Mrs Freeman, really.' I smile widely, confident. 'Trust me.'

# Chapter Thirteen

'I can't have peas,' Ethan tells me, peering into the pan of boiling water where the peas are cooking. He tilts his head to look me in the eye. 'I'm allergic to peas.'

'No, you're not.'

'How do you know?'

'Because I can read minds,' I tell him gravely. 'So I know you're lying to me.'

He scowls at me, not believing a word of what I just said. 'My mom told you, didn't she?'

'Yep.'

His shoulders sag and he slumps away back to the table to sit opposite his twin. Todd takes the meatloaf out of the oven while I plate up the peas, and the microwave beeps shrilly for the third time in the last minute to remind me that the potato is reheated. I divide it out, having to dodge past Todd as he turns around with a hot baking tray in his hands.

The twins don't talk much over dinner, and Ethan

pouts the whole time, poking his peas around the plate and sighing like, every thirty seconds. I'm tempted to tell him to stop sulking and eat the damn peas, but I hold my tongue.

There's ice cream and chocolate sauce for dessert. Once we all finish dinner, I start doing the dishes, Todd on drying duty, while the twins eat dessert.

'Sorry for dragging you into this,' I say, feeling only a little bit guilty. 'I know you probably had better things to do with your evening than this.'

'It's okay.' He smiles, meeting my eyes briefly before turning to put away a glass. 'I don't mind hanging out with you.'

'Well, thanks. It's nice to have some company.'

'Doesn't Josh ever come with you?'

I snort, loudly. 'As if. Josh would hate babysitting, and the only time I did ask him, he said he'd do some homework. That's how desperate he was for an excuse not to come along – *homework*.'

'And we all know Josh isn't the greatest advocate of homework.'

'Yep.' I scrub a little more vigorously at some meat-loaf burned onto the baking tray.

'Ashley . . .' I glance over and see Todd bite his lip briefly. 'Tell me if this is out of line, I don't mean for it to be, but . . . what do you see in him? I mean, really.'

'Well . . .'

'If you tell me it's all down to his cute butt, I might puke.'

I laugh. 'Not *all* down to the cute butt. He's good to me, you know? And I'd never had anybody like Josh interested in me before. He sort of swept me off my feet.'

*He made me feel like I mattered*, I add silently, *like I wasn't invisible any more.*

'And, uh . . . about what you said earlier, at lunch. About me not having my own friends. Truth is, I lost all my friends when I lost Allie, and they don't want me back now. Why should they? I dropped them like that' – I snap my fingers, spraying a little water into the air – 'for some popularity and a boyfriend. I haven't got friends because I pushed them away, and I hang out with Josh's friends because I'm scared of being alone.'

I don't know how I manage to say it all with such a steady voice, but I'm glad that I do.

He nods, and if he's going to say anything else, he doesn't get a chance as he's interrupted by Alice jumping down from the table, declaring that she needs to use the bathroom. I take the opportunity to change the topic of conversation. All this talking about my relationship with Josh and my lack of friends is making me uncomfortable; my stomach is knotting itself up.

'So I figure we put a movie on for the twins and get on with some homework?'

I can see the flash of annoyance on Todd's face, but he doesn't say anything except a muttered, 'Sure, whatever.'

Alice picks *Monsters University* for us to watch, and she sits at one end of the couch, playing Angry Birds on her mom's iPad. Ethan sits at the other end, alternating between playing Pokémon on his Nintendo, and watching the movie.

Todd and I sit on the other couch, binders and notebooks propped on our laps as we work quietly through my calculus homework.

'See?' he says, tapping the page lightly with his fingertip. 'It's easy.'

I run a hand over my neck, grimacing. 'Yeah, sure, maybe for you . . .'

'I thought you were good at math? And pretty much everything else.' I raise an eyebrow at him. 'You leave your assignments on the backseat of the car, sometimes. You get As in almost everything,' he continues.

I feel my cheeks warming a little. 'Calculus has never been my strong point.'

'Have you always been good at school?' he asks, leaning back to rest his elbow on the arm of the couch and his head in his hand.

'I guess so . . .'

'You don't have to look so embarrassed,' he tells me, smiling softly. 'What, do you not want to be called a nerd, or something? It's not like there's anyone around to hear.'

'No, I don't care about that, so much, it's just . . . I don't know. I like learning, that's all. I always have. And if I do my best in school, I can get into a really good college. Hopefully, try and get an academic scholarship, too.'

Todd nods, and his smile drops a little, and his eyes turn to the TV screen. 'I'm trying hard this year. I almost had to redo the whole year, did I tell you that? My dad managed to convince the principal here that I'd knuckle down and do well. And I'm trying, you know? It doesn't come as easy to me as it does to you, though, I don't think.'

'You're good at calculus,' I offer.

'I'm good at math, but not much else – not naturally, at least. I like reading and I like finding out new things, but school . . .' He shakes his head and blows air upwards, making his hair flutter away from his forehead. 'I just want to get into a decent college, but B-plus average might not get that.'

'You'll be fine,' I reassure him. 'Seriously, a B-plus average is good. And there's plenty of time to make that an A, if you want. It's only, like, halfway through October.'

He grunts in response, reminding me of Josh for a moment.

'Ashley?' Alice asks, dragging my name out to about five syllables.

'Yeah?'

'If Todd's not your boyfriend, then who is?'

I smile, setting my binder on the floor with my pen. 'A boy called Josh, from school.'

'Oh. Do you love him?'

'Yes, I do,' I tell her.

'Do you love Todd as well?'

I grit my teeth to suppress a groan. Alice and Ethan are seven years old, so I guess I should've expected Alice to pester me with questions like this when I brought Todd along.

'No, I don't.'

'Don't you like him?'

'Well – well, yes, I do like Todd.'

I can feel Todd shaking with repressed laughter next to me, his leg quivering against mine. I also know that I'm blushing, probably horrendously, judging by how hot my cheeks feel. I smack Todd's thigh lightly, a signal for him to shut up.

'Then why isn't Todd your boyfriend?'

'Because – because Todd's my friend, and Josh is my boyfriend.'

She huffs, not satisfied with this answer. 'But why don't you want Todd to be your boyfriend? I think Todd's very nice.'

'Josh is very nice as well, Alice.'

She decides to turn her attention to Todd, and I feel him stiffen a little under the sudden scrutiny of a pouting, scowling, seven-year-old. 'Have *you* got a girlfriend?'

'Noooo . . .' He says it like he's almost terrified of answering, and that's when *I* start having to try not to laugh.

'Why don't you want Ashley to be your girlfriend, then?'

'Ashley has a boyfriend,' he says, patiently. 'And you should only have one at a time.'

'Oh. Do you like her?'

'Yes.'

'I think you should ask her out on a date.' It's like Alice has almost forgotten I'm here. All the years of middle school and high school, and I don't think I've ever felt more awkward than I do right now. Not even when I spilled grape soda down my white top in ninth grade, and had to walk around with a purple stain on my shirt the rest of the day, with everyone snickering at me.

'I'll think about it,' Todd tells her, seriously. Finally satisfied, she turns back to the movie.

I get up and leave the room. Todd isn't far behind me. His footsteps are heavy on the carpet as he trails after me to the kitchen. I lean against the counter when he stops in the doorway.

'Sorry you got dragged into that,' I mumble. I press a hand to my cheeks. They're still hot. 'I, um . . .'

'It's okay. She's seven. What're you gonna do?'

I nod. 'Tell me about it.' Turning away from him, I put the coffee maker on, and get out two mugs, and the sugar. My stomach is flipping over and tying into tangles again, like after dinner, and my palms are clammy.

Todd doesn't say anything, but he doesn't leave. Like he knows I want to say something.

And I do, but I don't know *how* to say it.

I pour the coffee, adding sugar to mine. When I turn around, I jump, seeing that Todd's suddenly a lot closer than I expected him to be, only about a foot away from me. I wet my lips.

The way he's looking at me right now . . . Josh has never looked at me like that.

I can feel my heart skitter in my chest, and whatever sentence I might have said suddenly becomes a jumble of words on the tip of my tongue. I swallow, hard, as Todd lifts a hand and brushes some hair off my warm cheek, leaving his hand against my jaw and tilting up my head.

His eyes look bright blue in this light, like summer sky. They flicker down to my lips, and slide shut as he leans in closer. My eyelids flutter, too.

I shouldn't want to kiss him this much.

His nose presses against mine, his breath mingles with mine, and then—

I push him back as hard as I can, glaring at him. 'What the hell, Todd?'

He blinks, disorientated. 'I—'

'You can't just – just – just—' Words fail me, and I settle for a high-pitched grunt of frustration instead. 'What the hell?'

I'm angry at myself for wanting to kiss him, and for almost kissing him – but I'm equally mad at him, for initiating it in the first place. What was he thinking? I have a boyfriend!

I don't realize I've said that last part out loud until he responds.

'I wasn't thinking!' he exclaims, careful not to raise his voice too much in case the twins overhear us. 'I just – I don't know, I—'

'You can't just go around doing things like that! Especially with girls who have a boyfriend! Jesus, Todd . . .'

'I'm sorry, okay?' He does look sincere, but I don't care. 'I didn't think. I'm sorry, Ashley, I didn't mean . . .'

'Go home,' I tell him, when he trails off. 'Maybe I gave you the wrong impression by asking you to come babysit with me, somehow. I didn't realize that my friendship gave you a signal to try making out with me.'

'It didn't. You didn't – I mean, I just . . .'

*'Go home.'* I turn back to the mugs of coffee, pouring his down the sink.

He lingers a moment longer, and I keep my back to him, breathing heavily, and wait until I hear the door open and close behind him. I grip the counter, letting out a long, shaky sigh.

I shouldn't have wanted to kiss him at all. I shouldn't have goose bumps all over my skin, and shouldn't still feel his hand on my face, brushing my hair back.

Taking my coffee back into the lounge, Ethan asks where Todd went.

'He's gone home,' I say, forcing a smile I hope looks easy and not tense. 'He couldn't stay any longer.'

# Chapter Fourteen

The rest of the week, I drive myself to school (sending Todd a blunt text to let him know I wouldn't be wanting a lift when I get home from the Freemans'). I see him a few times in the corridors, but he seems to be avoiding me – he's always disappeared down a different hallway before I can even catch his eye.

He doesn't turn up to Creative Writing class, either. Part of me wants to see him and talk to him about what happened on Tuesday, but for the most part, I'm relieved when I don't see him and we don't have that conversation.

I don't think I overreacted – well, not that much, at least. Maybe I shouldn't have told him to go home; things might have been better if he'd stayed and we'd talked through it. Truth is, I want to forgive him; I miss him.

I keep looking over to his room, hoping to catch his eye – maybe throw something at the window to catch his attention, since he hasn't answered his phone the few times I have rung. But he keeps the drapes permanently closed.

And it carries on like that.

Having pushed Todd away, I find myself spending more time with Josh, and realizing exactly how lonely I am now that I don't have Todd. Before he moved in, I hadn't ever noticed how alone I was; and now it's like I have this gaping hole in my life. Almost exactly like when I stopped being friends with Allie.

Friday evening of the second week of not speaking to Todd, my parents have noticed.

We're sitting down to dinner, and Mom sighs all of a sudden, putting down her knife and fork. I look up, and so does my dad; things have suddenly gotten serious. I wonder if maybe one of my grandparents is sick, and gulp.

'So I spoke to Callum earlier.'

*Oh, God, here we go . . .*

At least nobody's sick.

'He said he's worried about Todd. You two haven't been talking lately. You don't even carpool. What's that all about?'

'I haven't done anything,' I sigh. 'Todd's just being . . .' I trail off, not knowing which adjective best describes him at this moment. There are a lot of appropriate ones. 'Todd's just being Todd.'

'What happened with you two?'

'Nothing! God, nothing happened, okay? He won't talk to me, or answer my calls. I don't know.'

'I thought you two were pretty close,' Dad comments, shoveling more mashed potato onto his fork.

'We weren't *that* close . . .' I shift in my seat. The subtle look that Dad gives me tells me he knows I'm lying. Not that it matters now, anyway. Todd won't even look at me.

'I know you two have your disputes,' Mom says, 'but you always seem quite happy around Todd.'

'And I'm not happy the rest of the time?'

'No, I only mean that . . . well, it's like you come out of your shell around him.'

'Look, it doesn't even matter now anyway, all right? We aren't friends any more.'

'You should try and talk to him,' Mom says gently. 'Go over there and try and make amends. I don't know what happened between you but whenever you've argued with him before, you've always made up. I don't see why this time has to be any different.'

'He's had a rough time of it, Ashley,' Dad pitches in. 'The least you can do is try. He could probably use a good friend.'

I shake my head. I could tell them that we almost

kissed, but knowing my mom, she'll make an even bigger deal out of it than me.

'Ashley,' Mom says, adopting her stern-parent voice.

I put my knife and fork together on my plate and stand up. 'I'm not hungry any more. I'm going out for a drive somewhere. I'll see you later.'

I pull on my shoes and grab my coat and purse, taking my keys from their hook.

'Ashley, get back here now,' my mother calls. 'Sit back down and talk to us. Ashley!'

'Ashley, come back and listen to your mother. Don't make us ground you, young lady—'

I shut the door, abruptly cutting off their voices. I climb into my car and reverse off the driveway.

I hesitate near the sidewalk, looking over at Todd's front door. The lights are on, and I know he's in, but I can't make myself get out of the car to go talk to him. To be honest, I'm scared. I don't want to lose him, but it's already too late for that.

The only place I can think to go is Josh's.

So I grind my teeth and drive past Todd's house, turning at the end of the road to go to see my boyfriend.

I groan quietly, rubbing a hand over my face as I park outside Josh's house; Austin's and Neil's cars are here. I totally forgot they were having one of their guys' nights. But I'm here now. And I need to see Josh.

I didn't tell him about the almost-kiss, obviously, since nothing did actually happen, and as he doesn't really like Todd as it is, I figured that was best. I'm not lying to him, exactly . . .

I ring the doorbell and wait. When there is no reply I ring again, then knock.

Finally, Josh opens the door with a slight frown of confusion, which disappears when he sees it's me.

'Ashley,' he says quietly, stepping outside and closing the door behind him. 'Is everything okay? What's wrong?'

'I just . . .' I take a deep breath. My voice sounded shaky. 'I just needed to see you.'

He pulls me into a hug, holding me gently around the waist. 'Hey, hey, calm down. What's wrong?'

'My parents were stressing me out, because I haven't been talking to Todd since we – we had a fight, and . . .' I trail off. It sounds so stupid, trying to explain it without telling him the vital detail of what almost happened.

'Hold on, you had a fight with O'Connor?' he says. Josh's expression is less concerned now; his features are pulled taut, back into a frown. 'Since when?'

'A couple of weeks ago. It's just that we were really good friends, and I miss him, but I don't know how to make things right. He won't so much as *acknowledge* me in school, and he keeps skipping creative writing, and—'

'Hey, shush, calm down,' Josh says softly, kissing my forehead. I'm getting flustered – I can't tell him the truth, he'd get really mad at Todd and that's not the point here. I just want him to hug me and tell me everything's okay. That's all. I don't want to make any drama.

'There's something wrong with that O'Connor guy,' he mutters, which is not what I want to hear.

'There's nothing wrong with Todd,' I snap.

'Whose side are you on here, Ashley? From the sound of things, the guy's being a total jackass to you. Why are you defending him?'

I open my mouth; then I look away, and close it again.

Josh sighs, and then pulls me closer again. 'So what's up with your parents?'

'They want me to patch things up with Todd, but it's really not that easy, and they wouldn't understand.' I shake my head. 'I'm sorry. I just needed to get out for a bit.'

Josh nods. 'Well, you know you can't stay long, right? I mean, the guys are here, and . . .' He rubs the side of his neck.

I nod. 'Yeah, I get it. Sorry for interrupting,' I tell him. Then I go on my toes and give him a kiss. 'Thanks, though. I'll get going now, let you enjoy the rest of your night.'

'Thanks, Ashley. I love you.'

'I love you, too,' I reply automatically, giving him a smile. But it feels so forced. We kiss once more, and then he goes back inside, and I get back in my car. I don't want to go home just yet though, so I drive to the gas station, buy a smoothie, and sit in the parking lot slurping it up slowly. I wish Josh had said that he'd tell the guys to go home so he could spend time with me, but we've spent practically every evening together the last two weeks and they'd been planning tonight for a while.

Todd's voice bounces around my head, with everything he's ever said about Josh and me as a couple. Everything was fine with us before he came along. Before he started saying things, making me doubt things, making me feel like something was just off.

I thought I loved Josh. I was so sure, before.

But maybe I was wrong. Maybe I don't love him, not really.

The last two weeks we've spent every spare moment together, and it was a great distraction from the situation with Todd. Most of the time, I'm happy when I'm with him. Sometimes, he bugs me – when he doesn't listen to me trying to encourage him to work harder at school, and stuff like that. I think about how I can't really talk to him about anything and everything. I can't even really be myself around him, can I?

I don't know what to do with that information.

I think about the conversation I'd overheard that night of the football game. And I think about how much he annoyed me that night drinking all those beers.

The same thoughts go round and round my head, until I feel like I'm going crazy.

I lean forward, pressing my head into the steering wheel so hard it hurts. I sit up and rub my fingertips into my closed eyelids. After a while I stop thinking, and I drive home. I don't speak to my parents when I get in. They try to talk to me, but I just look at them blankly, their words washing around me, and I go up to bed.

Mom sets a mug of cocoa on my nightstand, and I look warily at her. It's a peace offering, but why? Last night she was ready to ground me for a month, at least. So what's with the cocoa?

She snaps off the bedroom light and draws my curtains, and opens up my window. I see her looking across into Todd's room.

'Well, that's better.'

'Mom . . . They were shut for a reason.'

'Don't be silly, honey. The sun's out, it's a lovely day, and you're holed up in this room with the drapes shut and the light on.'

'For a *reason*, Mom.'

She sits on the foot of my bed. With a sigh, I dog-ear my book and put it down on my lap, sitting up straighter to look at her.

'Is everything all right, Ashley?'

'Yes, Mom. I'm fine. Everything's fine.'

She shakes her head. 'No, it's not, Ashley. Something's been wrong for a while, and don't think I haven't noticed. You've been quieter than usual, even when Josh comes over. And apart from these last few days since you and Todd stopped talking, you haven't even been seeing him all that much outside of school. Ashley, sweetie, just *talk* to me. I'm your mother; you can tell me anything, you know that.'

I fan the pages of my book between my fingers so that they make a sharp, snapping noise.

'Oh, God, don't tell me you're pregnant?' There's no joke in her tone; she is entirely serious and undoubtedly horrified for me.

I shake my head immediately. 'No! God, no. Definitely not. We haven't, *you know*.'

Mom lets out a huge breath of relief. 'Okay. So what is it that's eating you?'

I squirm a little. I'd tell her, if I had any idea what to tell her. I don't even know what's wrong with me, lately. I'm just so confused about Josh, but worried that if I break up with him that'll be the wrong thing and I'll feel even worse; and I miss Todd so much.

'It's nothing,' I say eventually. 'I'm just getting stressed about school, and colleges, and Josh is stressed too with the football scholarship; and Todd and I aren't speaking . . . It's fine, really. It'll blow over.'

'What *did* happen with you and Todd?'

'It's . . . complicated.'

'Oh, no, I've heard that one before.' She laughs breezily, trying to make me feel a little more at ease with a tender smile.

'I'd rather not talk about it, Mom. But he's been avoiding me ever since.'

She sighs again. There's so much sighing. I sigh in reply to her, and then we're both laughing.

'I really think you should try and talk to Todd,' she says after a pause, when we've both stopped laughing. 'He likes you a lot, Ashley. Callum said you're the first person he's really been friends with in a while. He's so shy. And your dad and I know how close you two were before "complicated" happened.'

'He's got plenty of friends here,' I point out.

Mom shakes her head. 'Well, yes, he does, but that's not what I mean. You're the first person Todd's really opened up to in a long time.'

'Callum told you this?'

'Yeah. He's worried about Todd, and I can't say I blame him. That boy's gone through a lot. It's hard for kids when their parents divorce, and he doesn't get to see his mom any more . . . And you know about his grandfather. Callum told me that Todd actually seems to be doing better here. Not just better grades, but he's happier, especially because of you.'

'I doubt it.'

'Would you please just go over there and try and talk to him? Just try. If he's really that adamant that he won't see you or hear you out, then fine, but at least you tried. I raised you to be a good person, Ashley. Would you please just do this one little thing?'

I look at my mom, and how desperate she looks for me to give it a shot at patching things up with Todd.

'Why do you care so much?'

'Well for one thing, you're my daughter, and this has all clearly upset you. And Todd hasn't got a mother around right now, Ashley. Yes, he's got Callum, but that's not the same. Call it a mother's instinct, all right? But I feel like I should try and look out for him a little.'

'Okay,' I breathe, caving in at last. 'All right, I'll do it. After I drink my cocoa.'

Mom grins and places a hand on my leg. She knew she'd get me to give in eventually by pulling the guilt card. 'Thank you.'

'I'm only doing this because you asked so nicely and you're my mother.'

'Oh, of course. Not because deep down, you really care about Todd, or anything.' She's biting back a smile.

'Exactly.'

# Chapter Fifteen

'Ashley!' Callum looks almost ecstatic to see me. His whole face is stretched into a giant grin and he looks like a five-year-old at Disney World. 'Come on in!'

I follow him inside and through to the kitchen.

'Would you like a drink?'

'Orange juice would be great, please.'

'Sure thing, no problem. How have things been with you?'

'Good. School's going all right.' I shrug and give him a sheepish smile, not knowing what else to do. 'Um. Is, uh, is Todd here?'

'He's not, actually, he went to the music shop in town. He said he needed some new strings for his guitar.'

'Oh, okay. Well I can come back later, or something . . .' I sip my orange juice. 'I don't want to intrude.'

'It's fine, don't worry about it, really. He'll be back in a few minutes. Sit down.'

He looks at me as if he expects me to say something.

'I know he doesn't want to see me, but . . .' I trail off. I caved when my mom asked me to come see him; and I hadn't actually been reluctant to come over here and apologize and explain. I was just nervous. But hey – at least Todd hadn't answered, and I hadn't had the door slammed in my face.

Callum sighs, and leans on the breakfast bar opposite me. 'Look. I don't know what happened with you two, but I want you guys to work things out. You've been so good for Todd. He's been doing so much better since you two started being friends.'

I don't say or do anything. I just mull over that for a minute.

I swallow some more OJ.

Callum opens his mouth to say something more to me, but there's the sound of a car outside. We hear a car door slam, and a few seconds later the scrape of keys in the door. Every muscle in my body tenses up; the door opens and there's a shout of, 'I'm back.' I gnaw on my lip before downing the rest of my drink.

'In the kitchen,' Callum calls back. I stand up and turn to face the door as Todd walks in. When he catches sight of me, he stops walking and stares at me like he's just seen a ghost.

Todd looks just the same as ever. He's wearing a white, loose fitting T-shirt, and a pair of faded jeans, held up by a black belt. His hair is falling over his eyes. Some earphones hang out of the neck of his T-shirt, emitting a slightly tinny noise because he's got music playing. He draws his cell from his pocket, pressing a button to stop the music, and tugs on the wire of the earphones where they're attached to the phone, pulling them from under his T-shirt.There's a seemingly endless silence between us all.

'Long time no see,' I say quietly. My voice catches as I try and keep the nervousness from my voice.

'Yeah.' His voice is quiet and strained.

'Cup of coffee, anyone?' Callum offers.

'Sure,' Todd says, wrapping the earphones around his cell, but he doesn't take his eyes off me. I shake my head in answer to his dad. We wait in silence, looking at each other – me, shyly, and Todd, incredulously. Callum hands Todd a mug of coffee, and he cups his hands around it.

There seems to be an unspoken agreement when he turns around that we'll go to his room to talk, where it's more private, because when he starts to walk, I follow him up the stairs.

I shut the bedroom door behind me. Todd sets his mug down on the nightstand, takes a packet of guitar strings and his wallet from the pockets of his jeans, and then sits on his bed, propped up against his pillows with one leg bent over the other. I hesitate before sitting on the window seat; I don't know if he wants me to sit near him.

Todd clears his throat, but doesn't speak.

The silence continues for a couple of minutes. I know I have to say something, but I don't know where to start. Todd surprises me by shooting to his feet, and pacing up and down. He laces his fingers together and places his hands behind his head.

'Do you hate me?'

He blurts the words so quickly that I almost don't understand him.

My eyes flash to Todd's face, and I watch him with a steady expression. My voice is calm and quiet: 'You've been avoiding me for the past two weeks, and I'm not sure I understand why. Of course I don't hate you. I was angry for a while, that's all. I'm sure you can understand that.'

It's a while before he responds.

'I figured . . . you probably hated me. Why wouldn't you? I was completely out of line, I put you in a position you shouldn't have been in, and you didn't deserve that.' He lets out a huge gush of air, closing his eyes for a moment. He looks like a wounded animal when he opens his eyes again. 'It's been so – hard to deal with everything, and when I messed everything up between us, I freaked out.'

'Why?'

'I don't open up to people easily, you know that. I opened up to you and I wrecked everything, and I couldn't face you afterward. I was *scared* of losing my best friend, but I messed up and I didn't know how to apologize when I knew you'd hate me.'

'You should've just talked to me,' I say, standing up. 'I didn't – don't – hate you, like I said. But when you were avoiding me, I guessed you didn't want to talk to me, and I didn't know what to do once I stopped being mad at you. I thought that we just – you know, stopped being friends.'

'It's not that easy to stop being friends with someone,' he mumbles.

'No, I know. I still miss Allie, but it's too late to do anything about that now.'

He nods.

'Wait – did you say . . . I'm your best friend?'

Todd stops pacing and looks at me innocently, his now-gray eyes wide. 'Of course you are.'

The way he says it, like it's so obvious, makes my

face split with a smile, and my heart swells. It's been a long time since I've had a best friend, since I've *been* anyone's best friend.

Maybe it's not precisely the right thing to do, but I close the distance between us to hug him. I hesitate just before I do, and stand an inch or so away from him; he looks down at me warily.

Then I move the rest of the way and wrap my arms around his torso. His face is buried in my hair and my nose is a little squashed against his collarbone but I don't care. We just hold on, our arms tight around each other.

'I missed you,' he mumbles.

'I missed you, too.' Then I say to him, 'You're coffee's getting cold.'

And Todd replies, 'Oh, shit,' and lunges over his bed to gulp down his drink before it gets too cold. I start laughing, unable to stop, and when I look back at Todd, I find him cracking a smile at me over the top of his mug, which only makes me smile wider.

We put his TV on – reruns of *Judge Judy* are playing quietly in the background now, and we sit on his bed, side by side, half watching them, occasionally talking about something.

After a while, Todd says, 'Do you mind if I play you something on my guitar?'

So surprised I'm momentarily speechless, I nod. He gets off the bed to go pick up his guitar, and after he's finished checking the tuning, I manage to find my voice again: 'Is it something you wrote yourself?'

He nods. 'It's, ah, actually something I wrote about you. A couple of days after what – what happened at the Freemans'.'

'Does it have a name?'

'It's called "Stay". It's – it isn't finished, or anything, and it's still pretty rough, because I'm still working on it, but—'

'Todd,' I interrupt, smiling, 'just play the song.'

He draws in a deep breath and then starts plucking at the strings with his gray guitar pick before he begins to sing.

*'Sometimes I think*
*I should let it go,*
*Forget about it,*
*And forget about you,*
*Because some days it feels like*
*I don't have the strength to move.*

*Some nights I lie in bed*
*Just waiting for the daybreak*
*Just waiting for a sign from you*
*That you won't leave me all alone*

*But the nights blur into days*
*Blur into nights blur into weeks*

*Don't leave me now, I need you,*
*Don't listen when I say*
*I never, never, never wanna see you again,*
*Stay here with me*
*Don't leave me now, I need you,*
*There's an empty space left in my heart*
*That's reserved just for you*
*If you'll stay.'*

I don't want him to stop. I'm completely captivated by his voice, the music, the lyrics, knowing that it's all just for me – but the magic is broken when my cellphone rings, and I fumble to get it from my back pocket. Todd strikes a discordant note and stops.

'Hey,' I answer.

'Hey,' Josh says. 'Where are you? You haven't answered my texts.'

'Sorry, I didn't know you'd texted . . . I wasn't looking at my cell. Sorry.'

'Where are you?'

'I'm at Todd's.'

There's a pause. 'What?'

'I'm at Todd's,' I repeat.

'What the hell are you doing there?' His voice is a little louder now, but he's not shouting or anything. Just shocked, by the sound of it. 'You told me you two'd had a big fight.'

'Well, we did. I came over to talk to him, you know, sort things out.'

'After the way he treated you? Ashley,' he sighs my name. I can imagine the look on his face right now – resigned, his blond eyebrows pulled together tightly.

'Yes. We did the adult thing and talked about it, patched things up.'

'Ashley,' he sighs again. But right now, I don't want to hear what he's got to say against Todd.

So I say, 'I'm sorry Josh, I've got to go. My dad's on the other line. I'll call you later, okay?'

'All right,' he says eventually. 'Fine. I love you.'

'I love you, too,' I tell him, and hang up. I put my cell on Todd's chest of drawers and go back to sitting on the bed. I look at him and snap, 'Don't even . . .'

'Okay.'

He comes to sit back on the bed, the guitar pick pinched between his long, thin fingers.

'Sorry he interrupted your song,' I say.

'It's okay. So . . . what – what did you think of it?'

I reach out and put my hand over his, feeling the guitar pick bite into my palm. 'I'm not going anywhere, Todd. I'm staying. I promise.'

## Chapter Sixteen

The Christmas decorations are up in the stores in anticipation of the holidays as November begins. Mom starts fretting about Thanksgiving, and Dad mutters under his breath whenever she tells him to oil the hinges on the door to the dining room ready for when family come to visit.

It's a Wednesday, and one of the girls in my Calculus class, Carly, is throwing a birthday party tonight. She's invited practically the whole junior year class, not to mention a handful of seniors and some college kids she knows – plus a couple of friends she has from nearby schools . . .

A few people threw small Halloween parties last weekend, but they'll have nothing on Carly's 'birthday bash', as she's calling it. Everyone's looking forward to it – everyone except me, it seems.

I finally manage to tame my hair into being straight, and pull on my shoes ready to leave. My outfit for this party is a silky camisole in a bright cobalt blue, a pair of black shorts and some tights. Josh is ready to go, lying on my bed flipping through TV channels as he waits for me.

'Okay, I'm ready. Let me just send Todd a text to meet us at your car . . .'

'I'm sure O'Connor can make his own way there,' he grumbles for something like the hundredth time in the past forty minutes. I ignore him, deciding it's not worth arguing over. I just want to go to this party and get the night over with so I can curl back up in my bed and sleep.

I lean over to give Josh a quick kiss, an arm either side of him to support me. 'You don't have to look so grumpy about it. It's just a ride.'

'I do if I don't like him.'

I sigh. 'I'd ask what's so bad about him, but . . .'

'Let's see, he's arrogant, tries to do that whole "strong, silent type" thing Danielle is always talking about and it just makes him look like a loner and a total loser, but he still acts like he's so much better than the rest of us.'

'Josh, can we maybe not talk about Todd?'

'Why, do you have something else on your mind?' He grins, the grumpy frown disappearing suddenly, and his arms close around my waist, pulling me down onto the bed, and he rolls over so that he's on top of me. I can't help but laugh, and he kisses my neck.

'Josh, come on, we have to go . . .'

One of his hands runs up my thigh before he kisses me full on the mouth, and I kiss him back.

'We have time to kill,' he murmurs, kissing my neck again, 'we don't need to leave for a while . . .'

I mumble incoherently in agreement, but when he starts to slide a hand up under my top and around to the clasp on my bra, I push him off and pull my mouth away from his, sitting up to straighten my camisole.

He sighs. 'Ashley . . .'

'I didn't realize that was what you meant, Josh.'

He sits up as well, and pushes my hair over my shoulder, running his fingers through it slowly. 'We've been together almost two years. When do you think you will be ready for this?'

'I don't know. It's not something I've got planned out to the moment,' I snap. 'I thought we talked about this over the summer.'

'I'm sorry, babe. I didn't mean to upset you.'

He does sound genuinely apologetic, and gives me a small, hesitant smile, so I lean in to kiss him briefly so he knows I'm not too annoyed at him. Then he stands up, pulls me to my feet and says, 'Come on then, let's go.'

Josh slings an arm around me as we head downstairs, and we call goodbye to my parents before going outside to his car. Since he has to be up at seven tomorrow to get to football practice before school starts, he can't afford the slightest hangover. Before we part ways to get in the car, I crane my neck to give him a quick kiss, but he holds my face in his hands.

'Ah-ah, you don't get away that easy,' he teases, and pulls me back for a deeper kiss. And I try to let all my troubled thoughts melt away, but I can't do it. I just kiss him back, trying to work out what I feel, until we break apart and get in the car. Todd comes out a second later, climbing into the backseat with a mild, 'Hey, guys.'

Once we arrive, after a car ride that was deathly silent, the party's already in full swing, and Todd slips away from us quickly to some guys he hangs out with, and we find our own group of friends.

After talking for a few minutes, Eliza says, 'I think I need another drink?' and I say, 'I'll go with you.'

I don't intend to drink much tonight. In fact, I wasn't really going to drink at all.

But Eliza doesn't know that. She hands me a plastic cup of beer, and I down it in one without a second thought, filling it again before we leave.

It's maybe an hour later – perhaps longer, and time is just passing quickly – and I've had about half a dozen more cups of beer. I no longer have the aching desire to curl up in bed and sleep. A boozy adrenalin is pumping through me and the buzz of the beer is making this party turn out to be quite enjoyable. Everything's just so *bright*!

'Come on,' I say in a low voice in Josh's ear, pulling at the front of his shirt. 'Let's just go somewhere quieter.' I tug at his shirt again, walking backwards so that he'll follow me up the stairs. I gulp down the rest of my beer. I don't know how many I've had now. I've lost count.

It's just so *loud*. Everything's very loud and the music is very noisy and maybe the neighbors will complain about it to Carly's parents in the morning, but maybe they won't because they understand that teenagers will do these things and they would too if they were teenagers right now and—

We get to the landing and I stumble sideways into a door, and since it's not shut properly it opens with my weight against it. 'Oops!'

The bedroom on the other side of the door is empty, and the world starts spinning. I stagger toward the bed, and it feels like I'm walking on a waterbed because the floor seems to move beneath my feet, and I fall against the bed, giggling as I slump to the floor.

Josh sits beside me, putting an arm around me, and

I turn in to kiss him. We kiss for a long time, and at some point I splay my fingers out on his bare chest, wondering when his shirt came off. The world is spinning again, and I close my eyes to steady myself.

'Ashley?'

'Mm-hmm?' I drag my eyelids back open, blinking at him and feeling surprisingly drowsy all of a sudden. I lean forward and kiss him again before he gets the chance to say what he wanted to say. I lean with too much gusto, though, knocking him off-balance. I laugh again at the look of surprise on his face when his back hits the floor and I fall on top of him.

'Oh. Um, sorry . . .'

I recognize that voice. I push myself up from leaning over Josh to look who's at the door.

Naomi giggles. 'Oh, sorry! Carry on, we'll find somewhere else . . .' She drags the guy, someone I don't think I know, away to find somewhere else private for them to make out. Josh sits up and I stand up, stumbling into the bed again on unsteady legs.

'Where are you going?' he asks. 'Ashley, you don't look so great. Are you gonna be sick?'

I shake my head slowly.

He stands up and holds one of my arms by the elbow. 'Come on, let's get you a drink of water, and you can sit down.'

Josh holds onto my arm so I don't trip down the stairs, and shoulders through the throngs of people to get me to the kitchen, dropping me into a seat before giving me a glass of water.

'Thanks.'

'I didn't think you'd drunk that much,' he sighs, straddling the chair next to me.

'Mmph.'

'Do you want me to drive you home? It's only, like, ten thirty, but I don't mind. I should probably get an early night anyway.'

'What about Todd?'

'What about him?'

I scowl, blinking a few times because my brain feels like mush and my eyes won't focus properly on Josh. 'You said you'd drive him home.'

Josh shrugs one shoulder. 'He'll find a ride.'

'*Josh*.'

'All right, all right, fine. I'll go find him.'

Josh disappears, and by the time he comes back with Todd in tow, I've finished my water and the elated buzz I felt not too long ago has now faded away and left me feeling heavy and lethargic, my head drooping and eyes struggling to stay open.

'Is she okay?'

'She's wasted.' Josh hooks a hand under my arm and

pulls me up, slipping an arm around my waist. I drop my head against his forearm, my feet dragging listlessly. 'She shouldn't have drunk so much. She doesn't normally drink much, so she's a total lightweight.'

'How much did she have to drink?'

'One too many,' I joke, but my words slur together so much I don't think either of them understand me. Josh puts me in the backseat of the car, and I fall across the seats like it's a couch.

I guess I fall asleep, because the next thing I know, I'm hauled into a sitting position and thrown over Josh's shoulder.

'I'll take her,' Todd says. 'You can head back home.'

'Her parents are gonna flip when they see her like this,' Josh says, instead of answering him.

Oh, crap, I didn't even think about my parents . . .

I'm *so* busted.

I wriggle around, trying to get to my feet. 'I'm *fine*. I can walk.'

Josh lets me down, but I only stagger back against him. Todd takes my purse from me and fishes around inside for my keys, unlocking the door. 'I'll take her in.'

'She's *my* girlfriend,' Josh snaps, snatching me by the arm.

'And my friend.' I look around to see them glaring at each other in some kind of display of macho anger.

I shove away from Josh, snatch my purse back from Todd and slur, 'Thanks,' before walking inside. They both stand on the porch, and I clutch the banister, dragging myself upstairs very slowly and very clumsily.

'Guess I'll see you tomorrow,' I hear Josh mutter, and when there are footsteps leading away and a car door slamming, I assume he's gone. The front door closes, and footsteps follow me.

Todd takes my free arm, draping it around his shoulders. 'You left your keys in the door.' He shows me them dangling off his finger.

'Oh, thanks. You know, you can go—' I yawn loudly '—home.'

'I'll help you into bed first.'

'Why are you whispering?'

'So we don't wake your parents up.'

'Oh.' I realize I'm not whispering, and try again, more quietly. 'Oh.'

He chuckles, biting his lip. 'It's kind of funny, seeing you drunk.'

'It's not,' I mutter, the words slurring. 'I'm so *stupid*.'

He muffles a snort of laughter when I draw the word 'stupid' out, and I attempt to glare at him, but my eyes don't focus very well on his face.

We sneak into my bedroom, and I fall face-first onto

the bed, groaning when my stomach lurches. Todd takes off my shoes, and moves my legs onto the bed. He yanks the blanket away from the foot of my bed, throwing it over me.

'Thanks, Todd.'

'Anytime.'

'I'm sorry you had to leave the party early.'

'I wasn't having that much fun anyway. You know, Naomi is really hard to dissuade. She spent like, almost an hour trailing after me.'

I'm too tired to make a reply, so I just go 'Mmph,' and hear the smile in his voice when he says, 'Night, Ashley.'

I'm only woken up by my mom shaking me awake. 'Ashley! Come on, you're going to be late!'

'Five more minutes,' I mumble, turning away from the hand on my forehead and burrowing my face into the pillow, scrunching my face up. My stomach hurts, kind of like I need to be sick, and my mouth tastes a little like I tried to swallow sawdust.

Ugh, God, I do not want to go to Calculus first thing with a *hangover*.

Mom yanks off the comforter and shakes my shoulder again. 'Ashley, you need to leave in *five minutes*.'

That wakes me up. I shoot up into a sitting position (regretting it immediately when I feel dizzy) and swing my legs over the side of the bed. I groan.

Mom tries to give me a stern look, crossing her arms over her chest and arching her eyebrows at me, but the effect is lost when she cracks out in a smile, trying not to laugh at me. 'Good night at the party?'

'Uh-huh.'

'A little *too* good from the looks of you.' She takes in the fact I am still wearing my party clothes.

'I feel like crap,' I moan.

'I think trying to function at school today is going to be punishment enough for you for drinking so much. We didn't hear you come in, at least.'

'We left early, because I didn't feel so great.'

Mom nods. 'You might want to sort out all that mascara before you leave,' she calls after me, as I drag my feet to go past her to the bathroom. When I look in the mirror while the shower's heating up, I grimace. There's mascara smudged in wide circles around my eyes and down my cheeks, and my hair is like a bird's nest.

I'm four minutes, max, in the shower – a new record. I wrestle my hair into a braid, and throw on my jeans and the first T-shirt I lay my hands on, moving as quickly as I can without feeling like I'm going to puke.

I grab a banana and granola bar from the kitchen, down some OJ, and run outside, only ten minutes later than usual, hearing my mom shout, 'Good luck dealing with the hangover!'

Todd is waiting for me when I reach his car. 'Hey.'

'Hi.'

'How're you feeling this morning?'

'Like hell.'

He laughs. 'I'm not surprised. You were a wreck last night.'

'Don't remind me. No, seriously, *don't*. And I have calculus first period. This day is a nightmare.'

'Were your parents mad at you for getting drunk?'

'My mom said that facing today in my current state is punishment enough.'

We aren't late to school, at least, making it just in time for homeroom, where we part ways in a corridor, pushed along by floods of students. I check my cell, and my mood drops when I see that Josh hasn't texted.

Why hasn't he texted to ask why I didn't meet him like I usually do, before school?

My stomach flips over, and it's nothing to do with the hangover.

I shove my cell into the back pocket of my jeans. Well, fine. If he doesn't want to talk, then fine.

I think back to last night; I didn't do anything to make him mad at me, did I? It's surely nothing to do with what happened before the party; he can't be mad at me for that. Unless he's mad that he had to leave early because of me. Or is it because I didn't say goodbye properly last night when he was arguing with Todd?

Someone bumps into me, and I clutch onto my satchel to stop it falling to the floor as I right myself. I try and push away thoughts of Josh; he's probably just not had chance to text me, if he was busy with football practice before school started. That's all. Right?

# Chapter Seventeen

I don't see Josh until lunch, when he's laughing with the guys on the football team in the cafeteria.

I march over to him before going to the lunch line. I texted him twice this morning, and I know he always uses his cell during class, so he has to be deliberately ignoring me. 'Hey.'

He looks up, the huge grin on his face dropping a little. 'Oh, so you're talking to me now, are you?'

I grit my teeth. So he's mad at me for the end of the night. 'Can we talk?'

One of the jocks teases, 'Oo-ooh, someone's in trouble,' but I ignore him and all their laughter. Josh sighs, pushes up from the table and walks away from their table with me, so we have a little more privacy.

'Why are you ignoring my texts?'

'I thought we weren't talking, after you stormed off last night.'

I roll my eyes. 'You've got to be kidding me. You're

– sulking like a child, because of a little thing like that? From what I remember, you and Todd were arguing, and I went inside and left you two to it, before you woke my parents up.'

He scoffs, shaking his head but not really responding.

'What?'

'You're ridiculous.'

'I'm ridiculous?' I gape at him, then shake my head. I don't even understand what we're fighting over. 'This whole thing is ridiculous! Why are you acting like I did something horrendous? I was a bit drunk last night, sure, but—'

'O'Connor went in after you,' he says in a tone I can only describe as grumpy. 'I saw him, before I left. You didn't send *him* away.'

I stare at him, mouth hanging open, before composing myself. 'Hold on, so you're not mad because I went inside without saying goodbye, you're mad because Todd followed me and you didn't? He brought my house keys to me, because I'd left them in the door, and then helped me get up the stairs to bed. He just helped me out.'

'I just . . . I feel like you keep choosing him over me.'

'So I'm not allowed to have friends now?' I snap. 'God, Josh, you're acting like a child, you know that?'

'You keep picking him over me, Ashley! I'm your boyfriend; don't you think that makes me feel just a little bit crappy? Especially when I feel like you're pushing me away because you won't do anything more than kiss.'

'Prude!' some guy shouts, and they all start laughing and jeering. My face feels like it's on fire, as I hear more people join in the laughter and Josh doesn't defend me, just smirks along with them.

I make an effort to pretend I'm not totally humiliated, and I scoff. 'I can't believe you brought that up.'

'I'm just saying.'

'That has nothing to do with any of this. And Todd's my friend. If it was Naomi, or Danielle, then you wouldn't be acting like this.'

He sighs through his nose. 'That would be different—'

'No, it really wouldn't. And you know what? I'm not even going to have this conversation with you right now. If you can't see how ridiculous you're being, then I'll just wait until you can, and you can talk rationally and apologize for acting like such an idiot.'

I turn on my heel and walk off, going for the dramatic exit. I grind my teeth, but hold my chin high anyway. I hear Josh shouting my name after me, but I ignore him.

And that's going great, until I slip on some spilt soda, almost losing my balance completely.

I regain my composure, and glance around briefly just to check that everybody isn't laughing at me, before I go stand, by myself, in the lunch queue. I glance over in Josh's direction, and notice that Naomi, Austin, Neil and Sam have joined him – and Danielle and Eliza are heading in their direction now, so they're not an option to sit with . . . I repress the urge to yell at him when I see him laughing bawdily.

I look around the cafeteria, and spot a few people I have classes with – my lab partner from science class, and the girl I sit next to in history – but I don't really have the courage to go sit with them for lack of other company. I don't see Todd, at his usual table – but I do see Allie.

Definitely not sitting there.

I pay for my sandwich and chips, and duck out of the cafeteria. I guess I'll be spending the lunch hour in the library, on my own.

It's only later, during last period, that I remember that Todd left early for a dentist appointment, and I was supposed to get a ride home with Josh.

But he hasn't made any move to talk to me since lunch, not even a text. If he's not adult enough to apologize, I'm not going to put away my pride and get a ride home from him. It sounds childish when I think of it like that, but by then I've already started walking home. It's dark and cloudy with the threat of rain, and when the wind picks up, I do up the buttons on my cardigan for a little extra warmth. If I hadn't been in such a rush this morning, I would've picked up a coat – or at least an umbrella . . .

I'm barely five minutes away from school when it starts drizzling.

Resolute, I clutch my binder closer to my chest and duck my head so the rain doesn't get in my eyes. I'm not going back to school to ask Josh for a ride; I won't. If either of my parents had been home, I might've called them, but they're both working until five at least.

The rain gets heavier gradually, until by the time I'm about halfway home my teeth are chattering and I'm soaked. I hold my binder over my head, but it doesn't do much to keep the rain off.

I'm so preoccupied focusing on not tripping over my loose shoelace (I don't want to risk bending over to fix it and getting soaked by a car driving through a nearby puddle) that I don't even notice the car that has slowed down to a crawl on the road next to me until a voice calls, 'Hey.'

I jump, almost dropping my binder. I turn to the car,

and see Josh's face as he rolls down the window. 'What do you want?'

'Get in the car, Ashley. You'll get sick.'

I carry on walking, my steps longer and brisker than before. He can't act all chivalrous now, not when what he needs to do is just apologize.

'No.'

'Ashley . . .'

'Go away, Josh.'

His car continues to crawl along the road next to me, and he leans across the passenger seat to me. 'Stop being stubborn, and get in the car.'

'No.'

'I'll follow you all the way home like this.'

I scowl at the ground, teeth chattering. I must look so pathetic right now.

About a minute later, Josh sighs, loud enough for me to hear. 'I'm sorry for what I said earlier, about you picking Todd over me. I know you're not, but it's just how it feels, you know? But you're right, I was acting like a kid, and I shouldn't have said anything about you not wanting to have sex, either.'

I nod stiffly.

'I'm sorry, Ashley. Will you please get in the car now?'

'You can't just say sorry and think everything's

okay. You were a complete ass earlier, and I'm still madat you. I'm walking home and if I get sick then I'll just have to deal with it. Now go home.'

'I *am* sorry, though. I mean it.'

'Like hell.'

'Ashley!' He smacks his palm against the wheel, stops the car and gets out, which makes me stop. His lips are pressed into a tight line and the muscles in his jaw work furiously. '*Please*, get in the car. If you're mad at me, then fine, and you can glare at me the whole way back to your house if that's what you want to do, but get in the damn car already.'

I glare at him for a second longer before I yank open the door to the back seat and scramble in, tossing my bag and binder on the floor. I don't sit in the passenger seat like I usually would; I don't want him to try to hold my hand or put a hand on my leg. My wet clothes soak into the fabric upholstery and rain drips down my neck, under my clothes. Loose hair sticks to my neck and face.

Josh doesn't say anything else to me, and I keep my eyes staring out of the window so that I don't accidentally catch his gaze in the rear-view mirror.

When we pull up outside my house, I say a grudging, 'Thanks.'

'You're welcome.'

I gather my satchel and binder, and my fingers just close around the door handle when he speaks again, and I stop.

'Ashley, wait. Can't we – I don't know, can't we talk about this? Please?'

'What do you want to talk about?' I sigh, putting my things on my lap and turning to look at him. Josh has twisted around in his seat and I've never seen him look more like a five-year-old caught sneaking cookies before dinner.

'Us. Everything's so weird lately, ever since you started being friends with *him*. You're acting like a different person. You're . . . quieter. Like you don't want to talk to any of us. It's not just me that's noticed, it's all the guys as well. Naomi said you didn't go to their last girls' night in, when they watched *The Notebook*.'

'Maybe that's because I don't have anything to say – I have next to nothing in common with any of them. I barely have anything in common with you, and—'

'Since when has that ever been a problem?'

'Maybe I just didn't realize it was a problem, before. I lost my best friend after we started dating, and I didn't even try and fix things with her. I hung out with your friends because I didn't have the confidence to go back to my old friends after one stupid fight with Allie, and I was too scared of being left alone to try to make new friends. I don't even really get on with them, and you never even noticed. Hell, I can't even talk to you about most things because I don't think you'll care what I have to say. So you'll excuse me if I can't feel too much sympathy for you feeling left out when I do have a friend.'

I look down at my lap. My hands are sweaty and shaking, and my fingers fiddle with the broken corner of my binder.

'Ashley . . . why didn't you tell me any of this?'

I look up at my boyfriend, who looks genuinely shocked. And for some reason, my hands stop shaking, and everything feels weirdly calm for a moment. The sick feeling in the pit of my stomach has vanished, and I feel like smiling, of all things.

'I didn't want to. If I'm being totally honest with you, Josh, I . . . I was happy that someone like you took an interest in me. You made me feel like I wasn't invisible any more. I was happy to have a boyfriend, and I thought that having a boyfriend was the most important thing that could happen to me. And . . . I was wrong.'

Josh stares at me, eyes flickering between mine, trying to discern my expression, before his forehead puckers into a frown and he pouts a little.

'So what . . . what are you saying?'

The corners of my lips tug up, and even though I know it's really not the right thing to do in this situation, I let myself smile. 'I'm saying that I'm really sorry, Josh, but . . . I don't think I want to be your girlfriend any more.'

I grab the door handle again, and Josh continues to stare at me, his mouth gaping open, rendered utterly speechless.

'Thanks for the ride.'

# Chapter Eighteen

'Ashley?' Mom's voice floats through the house to me as I set my keys down. 'Is that you?'

It takes me a second to find my voice. 'Yeah, it's me. What are you doing home?'

'I left one of my files at home for my meeting – we were doing the meeting over Skype anyway, so I just did it from here. I'm making coffee, do you want one?'

'Sure,' I call back. 'I'm just going to jump in the shower quickly, though.'

'I'll leave it in your room.'

'Thanks, Mom.'

I can hear rainwater dripping from me and falling softly onto the carpet as I make my way up the stairs to my room. My limbs feel stiff from the rain and cold, but I peel my clothes off methodically before wrapping my robe around me to go shower.

It's weird, feeling this elated when I've just broken

up with the guy I thought I loved so much. I had been with him since freshman year, and now . . .

Shouldn't I be crying? Shouldn't I feel just a little bit of remorse over what I've done?

I climb into the shower and let the water rush over me, and then I start to belt out one of my favorite songs at the top of my voice.

And I feel *good*.

As I spend ages washing the rainwater and the remnants of last night's party away from me under the hot water, using my favorite gingerbread body gel.

I think about Josh, too; I think about all the cute dates we had, how he made me smile when he'd kiss me midsentence, just because, how I was happy being with him.

And I think about how he'd get that glazed look in his eyes when I did try and talk to him about a book I'd just finished or something I'd heard on the news, and I'd know he was probably thinking about a football game, or his Xbox. I think about how I'd sit there at lunch listening to them all talk and laugh and feel like a total outsider, but I'd laugh anyway just to pretend to be joining in.

I should feel at least a little bit bad for throwing away such a long-term relationship, but I really can't find it in me.

When I get out of the shower, my skin is pink from all the exfoliating and the hot water. The coffee that Mom made me is lukewarm, but I drink it anyway, throw on some comfortable green sweatpants, and a T-shirt, and head back downstairs.

Mom has moved her work to the kitchen, and looks up when I grab some cookies out of the cupboard.

'I heard you singing,' she says. 'What's put you in such a good mood? I thought that today was supposed to be your punishment day for getting drunk at the party.' She arches her eyebrows and gives me a scolding look.

I take a bite out of a cookie and drop onto the seat opposite her.

'I broke up with Josh.'

Mom's jaw drops, and she blinks at me for a while. 'You . . . broke up with him.'

'Yeah, that's what I said. Why? What's that look for?'

'That's . . . Well, it's very sudden, Ashley. I didn't realize that you were unhappy with him. What happened? Did you guys have a fight?'

I scrunch my nose. 'A little. It was over something really stupid—'

'Oh, sweetie, is this one of those stupid things that'll blow over in a couple of days and then you'll be back together like nothing happened?'

I shake my head, laughing. 'No, Mom. I mean, we did have a stupid fight, and because I was mad at him I started walking home, and then he followed me in the car and drove me the rest of the way – it's complicated – and then before I got out of the car, he said he wanted to talk. He said that I've been acting distant and weird, and . . .'

'Whoa, slow down,' Mom laughs, reaching over to take a cookie from the packet in my hands.

'Sorry. Anyway, he said I've been acting weird, and . . . I said that it was because I didn't have much in common with any of them . . . It was a long conversation, Mom, and to be honest I don't even think I remember most of it – but then I just sort of . . . I don't know, I suddenly felt okay about it, and I said I didn't want to be his girlfriend any more. Then I got out the car.'

'Oh, sweetie . . .' Mom gives me a soft smile. 'Are you okay?'

'I'm great, actually.' I smile before taking another bite out of the cookie. 'Despite all evidence of comfort eating to the contrary.'

We both laugh, and Mom reaches for another cookie. I push the packet so it's halfway between us, and Mom closes the screen on her laptop, pushing it aside. I raise my eyebrows at it, but she shrugs.

'You know what I think, Mom? I think I was settling.

That sounds really stupid, right? I mean, I did love him, but . . . I don't think I really loved him enough, or not in the right way. Not in the kind of way you and Dad love each other. In a kind of "This is great while it lasts but it's not going to last forever" way.'

'Have you been reading some cynical chick-lit lately, Ashley?'

'No, I just—' I break off and laugh again. 'I don't even feel a little bit sad when I think about not being with him. I was happy when I was with him, but I didn't miss him when we weren't together. And sometimes, when we were hanging out, I felt like I'd rather be somewhere else.'

'I didn't realize,' Mom says. 'Why didn't you say anything before? You two have been together for a long time.'

'I didn't realize either.'

'Well, as long as you feel you've done the right thing . . .'

'I'm pretty sure I have.'

She nods. 'How did Josh take it?'

'I don't think he saw it coming, despite how he'd said things had been weird between us for a while. He seemed to take it pretty rough, but I think he'll get over it soon enough. I hope he does, anyway. I didn't mean to hurt him.'

'No, I'm sure you didn't,' Mom says. 'But you had to do what was right for you. I hope he's alright.'

'He will be, even if it's not for a little while.'

She nods. 'How about we order pizza tonight, hmm? Extra pepperoni.'

I grin. 'Sounds great to me.' Mom pulls her laptop back in front of her and opens it. I grab another three cookies to go, taking that as my cue to let her get on with some work.

'Oh, and sweetie?'

'Yeah, Mom?'

'You're grounded for the week for getting drunk at a party.'

'Aww, seriously?' I make a disgruntled sound, and give her my best 'You're being so unfair this sucks' look. 'Come on, it was one time! I won't do it again. I learned my lesson. You told me this morning that the hangover was punishment.'

'Well maybe I decided that wasn't strict enough.' She smiles. 'But if you want, you can ask Todd if he and Callum want to join us for pizza later.'

I roll my eyes, but only after I've turned away. At least if I'm going to be punished, it's not much of a punishment.

Todd answers the phone on the second ring. 'Hello?'

'It's me. How're your teeth?'

'Aside from a severe lack of flossing, they're great. No cavities or anything. So, what's up? Or are you just seriously interested in my dental hygiene?'

'You wanna come over for pizza later? Your dad's welcome, too.'

'Sure. What's the occasion?'

'I, um . . .' I clear my throat. 'It's a long story.'

'Did someone die?'

'No.'

'Oh, phew. Good. Hold on, I'll be over in ten. I don't want your dad to yell at me for an exorbitant phone bill when I'm only next door.'

'We say goodbye, and ten minutes later, the doorbell rings. Mom calls for me to answer it, which I'm already doing anyway; then she calls out to ask who it is.

'It's just Todd. You're working, and I'm in a fragile emotional state. I need some company.'

'That's uncalled for, you know I'm tied up,' she shouts in reply. Then: 'Ashley, ask Todd if he wants a drink – don't be a bad hostess.'

'I'm good, thanks,' Todd tells me. 'What "fragile emotional state" are you in, though? You look pretty okay to me.'

We walk into the lounge, and sit on one of the

couches. I curl my legs beneath me and take a deep breath. 'I broke up with Josh.'

'You did *what*?'

It's just as well he didn't want a drink; he'd have choked on it.

'I broke up with him,' I say, brightly, and launch into telling him everything, including the argument at lunch. I can't remember the conversations word for word; thinking about them now, they seem like a blur.

'Oh my God,' Todd mumbles when I'm finished. 'I can't believe you actually did it.'

'Why is that so hard for you to believe? Do I need to play the whole "I'm a strong, independent woman who doesn't need a man" card?'

He laughs, eyes creasing around the corners. 'No, sorry, it's – it's just that I didn't think you would. I thought you said you loved him?'

'I thought I did, I guess. But not, you know, enough, apparently.'

'Huh. Well, good for you. I'm proud of you.'

'Thanks.'

'He wasn't exactly a great catch, anyway,' Todd says flippantly. 'I mean, when I first arrived, and I asked about you, people would say, 'Oh, yeah, that's Josh's girl', like you belonged to him or something. And in gym, once, a bunch of the guys were trying to get him to say if you two had had sex yet, and he said you were still too frigid.'

The words are like a slap in the face, and I hold out a hand to get Todd to stop talking. 'Wait, he really said that? Why didn't you tell me before?' I realized that he'd thought that sort of thing about me, along with some other people, and I'd been mad he hadn't defended me when that guy called me a prude in the cafeteria earlier; but to hear that he'd actually gone around telling people . . . That was another thing altogether.

'Because I thought you'd get mad at me if I did tell you, and it was just after we'd made up a little while ago. You know, after the babysitting incident?' He clears his throat, shifts awkwardly. 'Anyway, I didn't want to cause another fight with us, so I thought it was better to not say anything. Was that the wrong thing to do?'

'I know I got mad at you for making comments about him being handsy at the party and stuff, but this is a whole other level. You should've told me.'

'I tried. At my party.'

'When I didn't want to listen?'

He nods.

'In that case, I should've listened to you.' I force a smile, but my head is reeling still. Maybe if Todd had told me that before, I might have broken up with Josh a bit sooner. 'I can't believe Josh would say things like that to people. I know we were together a long time, but I never felt ready, and I told him that, and he told me he understood, but . . . Wow. That really stings.'

'I shouldn't have told you,' he murmurs. 'I'm sorry—'

'No, it's – it's fine. It's not like it matters, anyway. So what if people think I'm frigid because I'm a virgin? It's not like that's the worst thing they can call me. I could be a vindictive, shallow bitch, right?'

'You mean you're *not*? I guess I should retract that quote I gave the yearbook committee about you, huh?' He grins, though, to let me know he's only joking; and I start laughing, so hard that my sides ache.

'I wanted to tell you before, what a jerk he is when you're not there to see, but I didn't want you to think I was jealous, or something.'

'Well thanks for letting me know now, at least. But . . . come on, I've got to ask now you mentioned it: were you jealous?'

His cheeks turn bright pink and he looks away. 'Maybe a little. If that doesn't totally ruin our friendship by saying it out loud.'

'Well I'm flattered, Todd, really. But just to clear the air, I'm not interested in you like that.'

'Give me some credit, Ashley,' he says breezily. 'You just got out of a long-term relationship and I'm not going to suddenly jump in and ask you on a date. Besides, I don't want to risk losing you as a friend.'

I smile. 'Friendship sounds pretty good to me right now.'

He smiles back, and reaches over to squeeze my hand. 'Me, too.'

I get up to put the TV on, and we sit arguing over whether to watch *America's Next Top Model* (my choice) or *Family Guy* (his choice), before settling on some Tom Hanks film that's playing on one of the movie channels.

Dad gets home around six, and Callum rings the doorbell not long after, so we order pizza then.

'What's the occasion?' Dad asks. We don't order out much. Both he and Mom prefer to cook, and if work is an issue, then the freezer is well stocked with leftovers and frozen breaded chicken.

'Ashley broke up with Josh,' Mom replies, clicking through the pizza delivery website to work out the best deal for five people.

'Really? You did? Why?'

'I don't think that he was the best thing for me, that's all.'

Dad's eyes flicker between me and Todd, who's leaning on the counter next to me with his forearm and shoulder against mine. But he doesn't say anything. 'I see.'

'Your daughter is in dire need of emotional support at this very difficult time,' Mom continues.

'Not a hangover cure?'

'Ha-ha, very funny,' I mutter, laying the sarcasm on thick.

'She's grounded for a week,' Mom adds.

'Like that's much of a punishment,' Dad retorts with a chuckle and a shake of his head. He scratches at his stubble. 'You know that now she doesn't have a boyfriend to go out with, she'll just stay in her room reading anyway, right? *Out of choice.*'

'You say that like it's a bad thing. I could be a rebel child spending all my time out on the streets doing drugs or something. God forbid I pick up a book to read.'

Dad laughs, and shakes his head again. 'Make sure you order those cheesy dough balls, Isabelle.'

The evening is going well – and I don't think about Josh once.

About eight thirty, the phone rings. Dad's closest to the handset in the hallway, so he goes to answer it.

'Ashley?' He walks back into the lounge, holding the handset out to me. 'It's for you.'

I know it isn't Gran or Grandpa, because he'd have

been on the line longer if it was one of them before handing it over. And Todd's right here, so . . . there's only one person it can be.

I sigh and stand up, taking the phone and walking out into the kitchen for some privacy. I start to say something when he talks first.

'Don't hang up on me, please.'

'What do you want, Josh?'

'I want to talk. I know that things have been weird lately with you, but . . . do we really have to break up over this? I love you. I thought you loved me, too. What happened?'

'I don't feel the same way any more, Josh. That's all. I'm sorry. And after you being such a jackass to me that night we went over to the twins' after the football game, when you had all those beers, I started wondering if I was really happy with you. Maybe I should've said something sooner. But, you know, the fact you think I'm frigid and a prude isn't exactly acting in your favor.'

'I never told you that you were—'

'Not to my face you didn't. I heard you talking with everyone a while ago, when we were over Neil and Sam's after the game, and you said something along those lines. And earlier today, you didn't exactly defend me in front of the entire cafeteria when they were all laughing at me and calling me names.'

'But—'

'I'm sorry, but I don't want to be your girlfriend any more. It's best for us both.'

'Ashley, please. Can't we have another chance?'

'Do you think this was really that sudden? I've been wondering if we should break up for a while, and . . . It's not working, Josh. We don't click.'

'Ashley—'

'Hey,' Todd interrupts, poking his head into the kitchen. 'We're gonna watch a movie, you coming?'

'Sure, I'll be there now,' I tell him. I hold up a finger to signal to give me a minute, and he nods before leaving.

'Who's that?' Josh asks.

'Just Todd, we're watching a movie.'

'O'Connor's there? Now? He's got something to do with all this, hasn't he? What's he been saying to you? Ever since you two started hanging out that's when things—'

'That's when I realized I wasn't really happy with you, Josh,' I interrupt. 'But since you brought it up, he told me that you go around actually telling people I'm frigid. Is that true?' There's silence on the other end, and I plant a hand on my hip, even though he can't see me to know just how annoyed I am. 'Well, is it?'

'It's not how it sounds,' he mumbles, a weak effort at defense.

'Yeah, sure. Josh, please don't call again. We're not together any more. Goodbye.' I hear him protesting, but I hang up the phone anyway, and return it to its cradle on my way back to the lounge, where conversation is suddenly louder than it should be. I think they probably overheard my conversation, but I don't ask.

'What did Josh want?' Mom asks.

'Another chance, I think. I wasn't really in the mood to listen. I told him no, and hung up.'

Mom lets out a loud, short burst of laughter, and I know from the way she doesn't ask how Josh is feeling about all this that she heard what I said to him. 'That's my girl.'

## Chapter Nineteen

The next morning, when Todd parks in the student parking lot and kills the engine, he grabs my hand before I can get out of the car.

'Are you sure you're gonna be okay today?'

'Sure. I mean, I'm the one who broke up with him. It's not going to be that awkward. At least, I hope not.' I was doing my best to be optimistic about that, but then I clench my hands into fists, groaning. 'Damn, I forgot about lunch. I guess I'll just go to the library instead, again.'

'Again?'

'I went there yesterday, after our argument. I didn't want to make it obvious to everyone how much of a loser I was by eating alone in the cafeteria. Everybody was already laughing at me because some guy called me a prude.'

'Why don't you come eat lunch with us? My friends won't mind. They had a great time with you at my party a while ago.'

I grimace. 'Really?'

'Yeah. Come on. It's just lunch.'

I start to agree, but stop myself, and turn away. 'I can't.'

'Why not?'

'Allie's going to be there.'

'So? I know you two don't get on so much, but just don't sit by her or talk to her. Easy.'

'No, you don't understand. I don't want her to think that just because things are over with Josh, I've come crawling back to her. It'll just make her feel crappy. Would you want to be someone's second choice like that? She'll think I'm only hanging out with her because I've got nobody better to go to.'

'But you won't be hanging out with her,' he points out. 'You'll be hanging out with me.'

I shake my head. 'She won't see it like that. I wouldn't, in her shoes. It's fine, don't worry. I'll go to the library. I have some reading to do anyway.'

I get out of the car, closing the door, and Todd has no choice but to head into school with me. We linger in the corridor together for five minutes until we have to go to homeroom, and that's when I start to miss Josh – and realize how pathetic I am, without any friends.

I trudge to homeroom, fall into a desk at the front of the class, and bury my head in a book.

I see Josh a few times throughout the morning because we have a couple of classes together, but I always choose to sit somewhere else, not next to him. I accidentally catch his eye in chemistry, and smile, but he just scowls and looks down at the desk, so I don't try that again.

The bell finally rings for lunch, and a growing sense of dread forms in the pit of my stomach, only making me feel hungrier – the library is closed over today's lunch hour, according to the paper sign taped to the door I saw earlier, so I have little choice but to go to the cafeteria.

I let the swarm of students carry me from class to the cafeteria, and I focus on thinking about whether to go for tacos, or a sandwich, instead of the fact I'll be eating alone.

Hands clap on my shoulders, and I jump, looking over my shoulder but still walking with the tide. 'Oh, it's you. I swear, Todd, you're going to kill me one of these days.'

He shrugs. 'Well, I was going to say that we'll have lunch, just you and me, so you don't have to deal with the Allie situation, but if you're not happy to see me . . .'

I grab his arm, pulling him around to my side. 'That sounds perfect. Are you sure you don't mind?'

He ruffles my hair. 'What are friends for, right?'

We opt for tacos, and I grab some Hershey's Kisses from the counter, too, and find a couple of empty chairs at the end of a busy table to sit at.

'So how's today been? You know, with regard to Josh.'

'On a scale of one to ten, with one being totally fine and ten being the most cripplingly awkward thing I've ever experienced? I'm going to say a six.'

'Ouch.'

'Mm-hmm. I mean, I tried to smile at him in class, but he just got really grumpy and wouldn't look at me. It could be worse, I guess. He could've been crying.'

'Yeah, I'd believe that when I see it.'

I take a bite out of my taco, and try to look as surreptitiously as I can around the cafeteria. Josh is there, staring over at me. When he sees me looking, he turns to Naomi and Sam, and starts talking.

I set my taco down, swallowing past the lump in my throat.

'You starting to feel bad and regret it now?' Todd asks.

'I feel kind of sorry for him. I didn't realize he'd take it this hard.'

'You were dating for a long time. He was in love with you, right? For him, it came out of nowhere.'

'I guess, but . . . I did the right thing, didn't I?'

'You weren't happy,' he says simply. 'So yeah, you did the right thing.' He eats another fry, looks up at me – and smirks a little. 'You have some sauce on your nose.'

'Oh, crap, where?' I look at my hands, but they have grease and sauce over them, and search around desperately for a napkin, but I can't see one anywhere. We didn't pick any up. 'Have you got a Kleenex, or something I can use?'

'Here.' He reaches over and wipes the end of my nose with the pad of his thumb. 'But I'll go find some napkins anyway.'

'Thank you!' I call after him, and pick my taco back up. As I raise it to take a bite, my eyes meet Josh's; this time he doesn't look away. He just scowls and glares, and I have to look away first.

I wait around Todd's car for him to show up. Last bell rang like, fifteen minutes ago. The wind has picked up, and it's freezing out here! I wrap my arms around myself, and lean against the car bonnet carefully. Most of the cars in the parking lot are already gone . . . where the hell is he?

It's Friday, and it's been a hellish week, and I just want to go *home*.

I texted him five minutes ago, but he never replied.

I wait another few minutes, distracting myself with Angry Birds, before closing the app and typing out another text to Todd. I'm about to press 'send' when I hear footsteps approaching, and look up.

It's not Todd, though, just some kid I don't know. I huff, and look at my phone, but I still don't send the text. I'm going to go find him myself.

I know he had gym last, so I head in that direction, toward the boys' locker rooms. I linger outside, wondering whether or not to go in. I probably shouldn't really, but . . .

There's the sound of clanging metal, like someone fell into a locker, and a muffled, 'Oomph!' I frown, trying to listen more, but I can't tell what's going on. So I suck in a breath and push open the door.

It stinks like sweat and feet and the overpowering stench of various deodorants. It's absolutely vile, and I almost gag, and start to breathe through my mouth instead of my nose. I walk around some of the lockers to the sound of bawdy laughter, and muffled grunts.

I stop in my tracks when I see Josh shoving someone, someone with floppy brown hair and headphones around their neck. They drop their backpack, and someone else kicks it, sending papers scattering out across the dirty floor.

'I saw you two at lunch,' Josh is saying, spitting the

words out in anger. 'Don't try and deny it. Come on, how long have you two been sleeping together, huh?' Todd starts to stand back up, only to be pushed again.

'She deserves better than you,' Todd spits.

'Oh, what, like you?' They all laugh. 'Come on; tell me. How long has she been cheating on me, screwing you behind my back?'

I gasp audibly, a hand flying up to cover my mouth. The sound draws their attention: Josh, three guys – Austin included, I notice – and Todd.

'What are you doing?' I all but screech, shoving through them when they don't move aside. I grab at Todd's bony shoulders, but he pushes me away, and ducks his head like he can hide what's happened. But it's too late, I've already seen: his lip is split and swollen, and there's a graze across his cheek – from the lockers or a fist, I don't know.

'Todd—'

'Get off,' he snaps, shoving me backwards, and he rubs the back of his hand across his bloody lip.

A hand sits on my shoulder. 'Aw, come on, Ashley, we were only—'

I shrug Josh's hand off. 'What the hell do you think you're doing? You can't just beat him up for no good reason—'

'I had a reason,' he said, through gritted teeth.

'Oh, what? Thinking he was sleeping with me? Are you kidding me? You really think I'd do something like that? One second I'm frigid, the next I'm sleeping around. Make your mind up already – but don't take it out on Todd.'

'I don't need you to defend me,' Todd snaps, pitching in from behind me with a scowl.

'Tough,' I respond. I can't believe Josh would do something like this. I realized earlier how hard he'd taken our break up, but I hadn't thought he'd take it out on Todd . . .

Todd bends down to scoop up his scattered books and papers, and is about to put a hand on his blue notebook when one of the other guys, Ian, puts a muddy sneaker on the cover and shoves Todd's shoulder, sending him off balance so he lands on his butt.

'What's this, your diary?' he snickers, picking it up.

I'm about to snatch back the notebook myself and give the jackass a piece of my mind, when Todd shoots me a look to tell me not to interfere; I can see his point. A reaction is only going to encourage them.

Ian starts leafing through the book, and I can see the muscles in Todd's face twitching and his mouth contorts with a wince when Ian says, 'Oh, look at that, it *is* a diary!' He pulls out a Post-It note and I can see him wondering if he should read it out loud or not.

Todd's back on his feet now, and tries to snatch the book back – but Ian laughs, holding it up out of reach and then tossing it to Austin. I turn to him, and plant my hands on my hips, doing my best impression of Mom's stern glare.

'Give that back to him right now or I swear to God I'll—'

'What? Tattle on us?' the other guy, Kevin, jeers. 'Ooh, I'm so scared.'

Austin turns to laugh and add something, and I grab the book out of his hands before he notices I'm moving. I hand it back to Todd, who buries it in his backpack.

Josh pulls on my sleeve to get my attention, bringing me close enough that he can wrap an arm around my waist. I glare at him, pushing on his chest. 'Don't touch me.'

'Ah, come on, Ashley, let's just talk about this—'

I twist out of his arms, furious. 'If you really thought I was sleeping with Todd behind your back, you should have spoken to me about it, not beaten him up. You've just lost any chance of talking to me about anything ever again.'

Todd grabs my elbow gently. 'Let's just get out of here.'

'The kid's a total loser, Ashley,' Josh tries to tell me,

walking after us as I let Todd lead me out of the locker room.

'You're the losers here. Four against one? Hardly fair, is it? That's just cowardly.'

Josh stops in his tracks, taken aback, and the door swings shut on him.

Todd jerks up his hood to hide the extent of the damage in case we pass anybody. I want to say something, but feel so useless. This is all my fault. If I hadn't sat with him at lunch, Josh might not have decided to beat him up. All Todd did was be a good friend, and this is how he gets repaid for it. Almost like he knows I might say something, he pulls the headphones up over his ears beneath the hood.

With his head hung low, his hair flops over his face, hiding his expression from view. He takes his keys out of his pocket when we're in the parking lot, unlocks the car, and gets in, not saying anything.

I frown over at him, but get in the car.

'Todd?'

He either doesn't hear me, or simply pretends not to. He puts the key in the ignition, but doesn't turn it.

'Todd?'

Still no response.

If he's ignoring me, I'm not going to put up with it. I make to pull down his hood and headphones in one swift motion, but it's not as smooth as I'd anticipated, and the headphones stick on one side, so I have to reach over with my other hand to wrestle them down. He tries to swat me off, but it's useless: I'm determined.

'Ashley, get *off*.'

'Don't do this to me now, Todd. Please, I just want to talk.'

I grab his bony wrists, pulling them away from where he fights to pull his hood back up, and finally he gives up, sighing heavily, and turns his head toward me.

'Talk about what? Your ex-boyfriend cornering me after gym class to accuse me of sleeping with you? Or how you had to come and rescue me because I'm so pathetic I can't even take care of myself?'

'Sorry you think I interfered,' I reply calmly. 'I came looking for you, and it's not like I could just stand by and watch.'

He sighs again. 'I know. Sorry. It's not you I'm mad at.'

'Maybe you should be,' I mumble. 'This is my fault. If I hadn't—'

'It's not your fault, either. Josh is just a complete asshole,' he snaps, spitting out the words like they're poisonous. He twists the key violently, but the engine stutters, and he has to try again. When he tries to put the car in gear, it stalls. He smacks a hand against the steering wheel, and winces. I notice his knuckles are scraped raw, like he punched something.

I brush a fingertip lightly over the back of his hand. 'What happened?'

He takes a deep breath and starts the car again, this time properly.

He puts the car in gear and pulls out of the spot, taking us home and away from the school. 'I tried to punch him back, obviously, but some guy shoved me and I missed and punched the locker instead. It just really sucks. I mean, if he wants to act like a brat and say things like that to me, then fine, I can handle it. He's not the first guy like that to beat me up. But it's the fact that he thought you were cheating on him. Like that was the only reason why you'd break up with him. Not because he's a—'

I sigh and he cuts off, and I sink into my seat. 'I think I'm getting a headache.'

Todd flicks on the indicator as we pause at a stop sign and turn. I rub my temples. *Definitely* getting a headache.

'How are you feeling about the whole break-up thing, anyway?'

'I don't miss him,' I say. 'But it's weird, not having a

boyfriend, not being someone's girlfriend. We dated for more than a year and a half. I'm used to texting him goodnight and going over to his house after school to just hang out and snuggle with a movie. It's not him I miss, though, it's just those things.' I shake my head. 'It'll pass.'

'Yeah.' Todd looks at me quickly to smile, then winces as his lip starts bleeding again. 'Give it a week, and you'll wonder what you were feeling so nostalgic over.'

'Uh-huh. So, onto a slightly more pressing matter, my mom's starting to plan Thanksgiving dinner and wants to know: how do you feel about yams?'

# Chapter Twenty

I get a haircut on the weekend, and Mom takes me to the mall.

'You're single now,' she says with a smile. 'Time for a re-vamp and a new outfit. Out with the old, in with the new.'

'Is this new outfit for Thanksgiving dinner? And the haircut?'

'Yes, but that's entirely beside the point.'

'Can I have some new shoes as well?'

Mom gives me a sidelong look and lets out a melodramatic, 'Well, I suppose . . .'

It's a great day out, actually – I get a cute purple sweater dress and a brown belt, and some new Mary Janes to go with it. We go to the Chinese restaurant for lunch. At one point, I start to wallow in self-pity; I haven't had this much fun in ages, and I'm shopping with my mother, not friends – I don't even really have any friends at this point, I don't think.

But the self-pity party doesn't last long. I'm having too much of a good time.

It's been a while since my mom and I really spent some quality time together, and I think it puts us both in a great mood.

And I'm still in a great mood when I get out of bed on Monday morning, which is a surprising change. I mean, who wakes up in a good mood on a Monday morning, anyway?

I take extra time braiding my hair, and applying eye-liner with great care and a steady hand. I choose a plain black T-shirt and pair it with the silver scarf I bought Saturday at the mall, and pull on my ankle boots over skinny jeans.

When I go downstairs for breakfast, Dad is sat scrolling through the *Financial Times* on his iPad. Humming quietly, I pour myself some cereal and take a seat by him.

'You seem to be in a good mood,' he comments.

'Why shouldn't I be? The sun is shining, my hair looks good . . .'

'It's a Monday . . .'

'Ah, who cares?'

'Still not feeling bad about the whole Josh situation, then. I'm glad. It's nice to see you so happy for once.'

'What do you mean?'

'Well, the last few weeks before you two broke up, you looked so stressed out all the time, and you were always so distant. It's just nice to see you back to normal. And a little less sarcastic.'

'Pfft, when am I ever sarcastic?' I roll my eyes, and Dad laughs.

'Now, I won't be home till about seven, and your Mom has a meeting out of town, but she should be back just after six. If you get hungry, there's leftover lasagna in the refrigerator.'

I leave a couple of minutes early, waiting in my car with the engine running and the heater on, my stereo blasting the new mix CD I burned last night. Right now, it's playing 'Young Volcanoes'.

The passenger door opens and Todd tosses his backpack carelessly onto the backseat, and then his lanky legs slide into the car, and he ducks his head as he climbs in. 'Fall Out Boy?'

I grin. 'It's never a bad time to listen to Fall Out Boy.'

He laughs. His lip isn't as swollen today, and the split in it is healing. There's a faint bruise on the edge of his cheek, too, but that doesn't look so bad at least. Even so, it sends a pang of guilt through me. 'Your car, your music. It's just lucky we have the same taste. So, feeling okay about school today?'

'You know what? I really am.'

'And you're not going to eat lunch on your own?'

'Nope. But I'm not so sure I'm going to sit at your table. I don't know that I can face Allie.'

Todd sighs. 'Why don't you just talk to her? Apologize? I'm sure she'd understand . . .'

'She was the one who started the argument,' I say stubbornly, feeling a dent in my good mood. 'She—'

'Okay, okay, sorry I asked . . .'

'Sorry.'

'Never mind. So who are you going to eat lunch with?'

'Um, well, I . . . hadn't completely thought it through . . . But hey, there's always Jack, from biology. He's nice.'

'Uh-huh.'

'Todd, come on, I know you found it hard to try and make friends, especially being the new kid, but it's just as hard for me – only not in the same way. Sure, I talk to all these people in class and we get on, and I've known them for years, but that's kind of my point: I've known them for so long, isn't it going to be weird if I'm suddenly trying to hang out with them all the time? I don't want them to think that it's because they're second best, or anything. And I don't want them to pity me and pretend to enjoy hanging out with me.'

'Sometimes you just have to suck it up, and—'

'Yeah, yeah, spare me the pep talk, please.' I turn up the volume on the music, turn off the heater, roll down the windows, and sing along at the top of my voice.When we get out of the car at school, we're laughing. I'm not really sure why, but it's nice, and the stitch in my side doesn't even bother me.

We've calmed down a little by the time we're walking through the doors. Todd turns to me, his mouth open as if he's about to say something, but then he stops, and his expression softens.

'What?'

'You didn't put any cover-up on your freckles.'

I gasp, and cover my face with my hands, splaying my fingers just enough so I can see him. 'Oh my God. Oh, crap. How? How did I forget that?'

Todd, still smiling, chuckles and pries my hands away from my face. I'm blushing furiously, and looking around with wide eyes, waiting for someone to point and laugh.

'I have to go to the bathroom. I have some make-up in my bag . . .'

'Don't.'

'Todd, let go of my hands. I need to—'

'Why do you always cover them up?'

First bell rings, and lockers start slamming and the

volume of chatter increases, the noise of footfall joining it. I look at Todd, who seems genuinely confused.

'I hate them. They're so *ugly*.'

'I think they're cute.'

I roll my eyes, even though it makes me feel warm and fuzzy. 'You also think my hair is red, so shows how much you know.'

'It *is* red, and they *are* cute. I don't know why you always hide them.'

I put a hand over my cheek, which is still hot from blushing. 'I'm self-conscious. I'm a teenage girl, it's not exactly unusual.'

'Yeah, well, maybe you shouldn't be. There's a reason you forgot the make-up this morning, right? You didn't care. If you did, deep down, then you would've remembered to cover them up. Do I need to embrace my sassy inner self and tell you to embrace how you look?'

I laugh. 'Okay, okay.'

'If you make it to lunch without putting on make-up, I'll buy you a milkshake.' He holds out a hand, arching his eyebrows, daring me to take him up on the challenge.

I narrow my eyes. 'And a candy bar.'

The tardy bell rings as we clasp hands.

'Deal.'

* * *

As much as I keep wanting to run to the girls' bathroom between classes and cover my entire face in make-up to hide my freckles, I don't. I tell myself it's so I can prove something to Todd (even though I'm not totally sure what I'm trying to prove), but then I realize that I need to do this for me, too.

Plenty of people in my classes glance my way a few times – probably because they heard about me and Josh, but I'm terrified it's because they're laughing at my stupid freckles.

And as much as I want to duck my head and pull my hair over my face, I meet their eyes until they look away again.

It's kind of empowering, in a weird way. Acting like I don't care what they think.

Well, if I can't suck it up to sit with Todd and his friends at lunch, maybe I can suck it up and be myself for a change.

The bell finally sounds for lunch, and I head to my locker first to dump my textbooks. The hallway is mostly empty, and the sound of my locker door clanging against the one next to it as it bounces open echoes.

I get rid of my books, and put a hand on the locker door to shut it, and hesitate. There's a mirror taped to the inside, just a little one, and I pause to look at my freckles. My green eyes pop with my eyeliner (which I'm pleased to see is still perfectly intact from this morning), and I don't look as pale as usual, with all of my freckles on full display. Usually they're covered up enough that you can't really see them unless you're right up close to my face, but now . . . I look totally different.

And maybe it's not exactly a bad different.

I smile at my reflection.

There are some photos tacked to the inside of my locker door. Some family ones, from Christmases and Thanksgivings, and one from my sixteenth birthday; a couple more recently of me and Todd, and some of me and Josh.

I take a deep breath and lift my head higher.

*Out with the old . . .*

I rip one of the photos of Josh and me from last Christmas down, and it tears slightly. It's a satisfying sound. Grinning, I pluck away the rest of them, leaving the big one of us at the Sadie Hawkins dance last year until last.

I let the handful of photos flutter to the floor, my grip on them slipping when I realize what the big Sadie Hawkins photo was covering.

My smile falls away at the sight of the old, slightly

torn and crinkled photo strip tacked to the top of my locker. It's from the junior high prom. They had a photo booth in the gym, and Allie and I paid the three dollars between us to take five photos. One of them was serious, with us trying to look cool, but the other four are us falling around laughing and looking so happy.

I take it down, looking more closely at the photos. Her hair is brown in them, not black, and longer. Her big sister helped her straighten it for the prom. We have our arms around each other and I want to screw the photos up in my fist, but I can't bring myself to do it.

I bend down and pick up the photos of me and Josh, and walk toward the trash can near the water fountain at the end of the hallway.

'Ashley?' a familiar voice behind me says.

I stop, the photos hovering over the trash can. Footsteps come closer, and I sigh before turning around. 'Josh. Hi.'

'Um . . .' He clears his throat and rubs the back of his neck. 'How – how are you?'

'Great. And you?'

'I miss you.'

I should've been expecting that. But I really, really wasn't. I was expecting an 'I'm fine', not an *honest* answer. So my response of, 'Good,' dies on my lips and my mouth hangs open for too long before I remember to close it.

This time it's my turn to say, 'Um.'

'Ashley,' he says, stepping closer and giving me a pitiful look, 'what happened with us? I just – I don't understand.'

'I told you, when you called the other night. I don't feel the same way about you any more. I haven't for a long time. It just took me a while to realize it. Maybe it's my fault – maybe I should've told you sooner. And before you ask, it has nothing to do with *"that O'Connor kid"*,' I add, glaring and putting a hand on my hip as I say it. 'And by the way, I need to speak to you about that.'

Josh at least has the good grace to look a little ashamed about it. 'If this is about Friday—'

'Hell yes, this is about Friday. You beat him up, and accused him of sleeping with me – which, by the way, is not true, and I'm offended you think I'd cheat on you, or jump into some guy's bed just after we broke up when we haven't even done anything like that in almost two years of dating.'

'I just—'

'Stop, okay? Just *stop*! You can't talk your way out of this, Josh – or back into a relationship with me. I'm sorry that things didn't work out. I'm sorry that this upset you so much and that I hurt you. But I'm not sorry for ending things with us. I did what was right for me. And it wasn't a selfish decision, it wasn't intended to hurt you. It was what I needed to do.'

I'm breathless after my little speech, but feeling distinctly proud of myself.

I guess the haircut and shopping trip did give me some kind of confidence boost.

I turn away from Josh, and look at the photos of us. My fingers tighten around them a little; I could always keep them, maybe in a shoebox on the top of my closet, or something, as a memento of our relationship, but . . .

*Out with the old . . .*

I toss them in the garbage, and it's like a weight off my shoulders.

'Were those photos of us?'

'Yeah, they were. And now they're in the trash can.'

I breeze past him, my new Mary Janes clacking loudly on the floor. I hold the strip of photos of Allie and me tighter, glad I didn't toss them out, too. I put them back in their place in my locker, smiling as I shut the door.

Josh is walking away, hands buried deep in his jean pockets, and my smile falls away again. As comfortable as I am with my decision, it hurts to see him looking so dejected.

But he'll get over it, right?

'Tough love, huh?'

I spin around so fast I make myself dizzy.

'*Allie?*'

# Chapter Twenty-one

She gives me an awkward, half-hearted smile, and an equally awkward wave. 'Hi.'

'What . . . what are you doing here?'

'This might come as a surprise to you, given that we haven't acknowledged each other in a while, but I actually *do* go to school here.'

'No, I – I mean . . .'

'I know what you meant.' The awkward smile twitches again, and she walks closer, very slowly, and stops a short distance away. I'm glad the hallway is empty. This is the kind of thing anyone would feel second-hand discomfort over. My heart is pounding so hard and fast that my breath is a little shallow.

'I, uh, I didn't mean to eavesdrop, or anything, I just, sort of, heard you guys talking, on my way to my locker, and didn't want to interrupt.'

'Well, thanks. I . . . appreciate it.'

There's a long pause, and I gulp. God, I hate this. We

haven't spoken in almost two years, haven't so much as met eyes and smiled at each other, and all of a sudden she's talking to me again?

I thought she hated me.

'So, you, uh, you guys . . . broke up,' she says hesitantly, and clears her throat. At least this is just as awkward for her as it is for me. I stop biting my lips and gulp again, trying to come up with a coherent answer.

'Yeah.'

*Oh, God, come on, you can do better than that!*

'I mean, we – we just . . . I didn't feel the same way. Any more.'

'I heard. It was a nice little speech you gave.'

'Oh, well, thanks.'

'It must've been difficult for you to break up with him.' She steps a little bit closer again, and then scuffs the toe of her pink Converse against the floor, peeking up at me from under her hair. It's more of a dark brown now – she must've dyed it again. 'You guys were together for so long, and even if you didn't want to be with him, it can't have been easy to do.'

'It wasn't, but . . . you know, had to be done. Actually, it wasn't all that bad. Making myself tell him was the hard part, but once I was really doing it and talking to him, it was pretty easy.'

'So what changed things?'

'I changed, I guess.'

'In a good way.'

I smile. 'Yeah. In a good way.'

She gives me a tentative smile, and then moves to her locker, taking some books out of her backpack to leave in there. 'So how have you been?'

Allie sounds so normal saying that, like nothing's changed, like we're back in freshman year before I started dating Josh and we stopped being friends. Her tone is breezy, amicable, and she sends me an easy smile that reaches her eyes and makes them crinkle a little in the corners.

I stare at her for a second. She raises an eyebrow at me as if to say, 'What?'

'We don't talk for nearly two years and now it's "*How have you been?*". What's going on? Why are you talking to me all of a sudden?'

She shrugs. 'Why not?'

'Well we aren't friends. And you're acting like we are.'

'You're the one who stopped being my friend.'

I gasp in disbelief. 'You stopped talking to me after we had that fight about me dating Josh.'

'Yeah, because you acted like I didn't exist any more. Everything was all Josh, Josh, Josh. I put up with it for a while, but I couldn't take it any more. I wanted my best friend back, but you thought I wanted you to stop seeing Josh.'

'Of course I did, because that's how it sounded! And then you didn't speak to me again, and after that . . . You know. Suddenly we just weren't friends.'

She shuts her locker. 'It was never up to me who you dated. I *was* a little harsh on you. But listen – people change. They drift apart. It happens. That's just high school for you.' She bites her lip for a second before carrying on. 'I wanted to try and fix things, but I didn't know how. I was mad at you for ages, and then it seemed like it was too late to fix things. I bought you a birthday present a few months later, but I chickened out of bringing it over. I was scared you'd just laugh at me and slam the door in my face.'

My shoulders sag a little. 'That's why I never tried to talk to you. Assuming you hated me and wanted nothing more to do with me was easier than you shutting me out completely.'

'We always thought alike.' She smiles, and I manage a half-hearted laugh. 'So do we need to argue over who should apologize to whom, or can we just . . .'

'Go back to how it was?'

She nods, looking down at her feet and glancing up at me with a hopeful smile tugging at her lips.

'Can we do that?'

She shrugs. 'I don't see why not.'

'Really?' I shake my head, and almost pinch myself. She's crazy, right? This is all some humiliating prank and as soon as I say yes she's going to laugh in my face and leave. That, or I'm dreaming.

'This is a joke, right?'

'I know, I know, I'm really pathetic, but I can't help it. Todd told me that you and Josh were going through a rough patch, and I wanted to be there for you. I wanted to have girly nights in eating Ben and Jerry's and watching *Mean Girls* and talking about all the little things you were stressing about – like we did when you had a crush on Bobby Harper in seventh grade – and I just missed you a lot.'

She draws in a deep breath, and I can see her giving herself a mental pep talk – she's got that crazy look in her eyes and she's scowling, like she used to before a pop quiz, and like when I saw her ask a guy to the Sadie Hawkins dance last year and pretended I hadn't noticed her there.

When Allie starts talking again, she's babbling so fast it's hard to keep up, but I listen carefully to make sure I don't miss anything.

'Todd said that you'd broken up with Josh, and he told me earlier that you wanted to talk but you were too scared, so I thought I'd make the first move. I figure we're way past apologizing to each other now, but maybe we can just skip past all the weirdness and hang out again? We don't have to go back to being best friends or anything but—'

'I'd like that.'

A muscle in her cheek twitches. 'Which part? The hanging out and not being best friends, or—'

'No, I mean, I – I want to be friends again, and skip past all the weirdness.'

She left out a huge, audible sigh of relief, and her frown disappears, her face brightening. 'Really?'

'Yeah.'

A grin spreads across her entire face, and I notice that she's still got her gap-tooth. She always used to say she wanted braces to get rid of it, but I guess she never did get them.

'So we're friends again? Just like that?'

I smile as well, not able to help myself. 'Just like that.'

Maybe not out with *everything* old. Some things you just can't get rid of.

We walk to the lunch hall together, not talking much. It's kind of awkward, and I keep trying to think of something to say, but I have so much I want to say to her that I don't know what to say. I keep opening my mouth, but then thinking that I'll just say the wrong thing, so I don't bother.

It's not a totally uncomfortable silence, though. The walk to the cafeteria seems much longer than usual, but we keep sharing clumsy smiles and then laughing when we realize how silly we're being.

We walk side by side, and I get a waft of her perfume. It's the Marc Jacobs one her aunt bought her for Christmas a couple of years ago. She always used to wear it, every day, so whenever I passed someone else wearing it, I automatically assumed it was Allie.

Once we've picked up sandwiches, we make our way to her usual table, near the left-hand side of the room. It's crowded, and some people are playing Uno, and there's a guy doing homework, and another doing a Sudoku puzzle, but everyone is animated and smiling and laughing – except the guy doing homework, who is scribbling furiously and looking at his watch like he's counting down the minutes to his impending doom.

'Um, hi, guys,' I mumble.

'Hey,' Allie says, louder than me, and shoves gently at the homework boy's shoulder. He says hi, and scoots his chair over so that we can all fit, pulling up some empty chairs from the next table.

'Hey, Ashley,' someone says, and a few people look up and notice me for the first time, greeting me as well – either with a simple hi, or with a smile. I say hi back and smile, trying not grimace too much. I feel like a fish out of water, even though, really, this is just where I want to be.

I'm talking to one of the guys about the chemistry homework we have due in tomorrow, and I stop mid-sentence when hands clap over my eyes.

I pull them away, and then Todd leans over, his face upside-down in front of mine. 'Are those freckles I see?'

I laugh. 'They are indeed.'

'I'll buy you a milkshake and candy bar tomorrow. I forgot my wallet, and I only have five dollars for lunch today.'

'Sure.'

He pulls a hand out from where I'm holding them, and then he looks over at Allie, who's shouting across the table to one of the other girls. He straightens up and pulls a chair over, squashing it in between the two of us. 'So you two are talking, I take it?'

Allie's still talking and doesn't realize that Todd's speaking to her as well, so she doesn't respond, but I nod. 'Yeah. Thanks for talking to her for me.'

'You were both being so down about missing each other, but not talking to each other. I tried to give you a push but you weren't there yet, but Allie was.' He shrugs. 'It's no big deal. I just thought I'd help you guys out. I did the right thing, didn't I?'

I smile, and bump my shoulder into his. 'You did. Thanks, Todd.'

He puts an arm around my shoulder, and steals a tomato slice out of my sandwich, popping it into his mouth. He gives me a wide, innocent smile, and I can't help but feel that breaking up with Josh was the best decision I ever made.

# Chapter Twenty-two

'You're home late,' Mom says, as I drop onto the couch next to her, my satchel landing with a muffled thump on the carpet.

'*You're* home early,' I reply. 'Dad said you wouldn't be back till gone six.'

'My meeting got pushed back until Wednesday, so I didn't have to take the train out of town. Home usual time. You, however, are not. *Busted*, young lady. And I believe I grounded you? So unless you were cleaning up trash as part of a community project or you had detention, you'd better have a good excuse for being out.'

'Actually, I was at Denny's.'

Mom raises her eyebrows over her coffee mug. 'Does the word "grounded" mean nothing to you? I take it you went with Todd.'

'Actually . . .'

'Oh, you haven't got back together with Josh, have

you? I thought you were adamant that you were happy and better off without him. All this high school drama, it's like an episode of *90210* . . .'

'Mom!' I interrupt, laughing. 'I went with Allie.'

Mom stops, mid-rant. 'Allie as in Allison Lewitt, your former best friend?'

'That's the one.'

She puts her mug down on the coffee table and leans forward towards me. 'I want to hear everything.'

So, I tell her everything. Including talking to Josh, and throwing away photos of the two of us, and how Todd talked to Allie about how I missed her and said that she should talk to me.

Mom smiles when I tell her Todd's role in it. 'He's a good guy.'

'Yeah, he is.'

'He looks out for you a lot.'

'Well, like you said, he's a good guy.'

'I'm glad you two are such good friends. And it's so nice to hear that you and Allie are friends again. I've missed having her around. She was always so sweet.'

'Uh-huh. So anyway, we both had last period free, and . . .'

'Wanna go to Denny's?' Allie asks me, hugging her binder to her and smiling tentatively. 'It's just, you know, we both have study period now, and . . .'

'And we used to go to Denny's a lot,' I finish, closing my locker and jiggling my bag to get my books to sit better inside it. She gnaws on her lip. 'Sure, why not?'

She smiles brightly, tucking some hair behind her ear. The metal bar through it glints under the harsh lighting in the hallway. 'Okay, great! Um, do you have your car? I got a ride in with my mom this morning, because my car has a flat tire.'

'That sucks. Yeah, I have my car. We'll have to be back to pick up Todd, though, if he can't find a ride home.'

Allie nods. 'That's fine. I just thought it'd be nice if we could spend some quality time together a little like we used to. And not surrounded by people, like at lunch. Milkshakes are on me.'

It's not a particularly long drive to Denny's, but we spend the ride arguing amiably over the music on my mix CD. Allie and I had a lot in common, but our music tastes always differed. She was always into more acoustic, indie stuff, and big, bass-y house music; and it's kind of nice to see she hasn't changed much.

When we get into Denny's and find a booth, we both order pancake stacks and milkshakes. And not once do we stop talking – except to shovel pancakes in our mouths, or slurp at our milkshakes.

We talk about everything: about embarrassing things that happened recently; the books we're reading for English class; which colleges we're thinking about applying to. It doesn't even matter what we're talking about (like when Allie starts whining about how her nail polish is always chipping, no matter what she does) because it's just so great to be hanging out again.

I realize, as she's telling me with such wild and passionate arm gestures she almost takes out a passing busboy all about how misogynistic this guy in the debate team is, how big a part of my life I've been missing without my best friend.

Neither of us tries to even imply that the other is to blame for our friendship being wrecked in freshman year, and I'm glad. I don't know if I could take it if she turned around now and blamed me for everything.

I keep waiting for an awkward silence to settle, or for something to happen that breaks this fragile connection we've found again – but nothing ruins it.

Todd texts me to let me know he's found a ride home with a guy in his French class, so we don't have to leave after just the one milkshake.

We stay for three, in the end, and when I stop the car outside Allie's house, she grins at me.

'I missed you, you know.'

'I missed you, too. It's weird, how normal this was, right?'

I laugh. 'Definitely. But good weird.'

'Well, thanks for the ride.'

'Thanks for the milkshakes.'

'Anytime, Ashley.'

She climbs out of the car, and on impulse I roll down the window and call out to her before she has chance to unlock the front door.

'Hey, Allie?'

She turns. 'Yeah?'

'Thanks for being my friend again.'

She laughs. 'Like I said – anytime, Ashley.'

Mom smiles at me. 'Sounds like you had a good time.' She drinks some more coffee, and then picks up the TV remote, switching from the news channel to an episode of *Breaking Bad* that's playing. 'But you're still grounded. So no more Denny's.'

I sigh. 'Yes, Mom.'

She sets down the empty mug, and picks up a notebook off the coffee table, flicking it open. 'So, I was going through everything ready for Thanksgiving. Callum is taking care of dessert, and your father's doing the cranberry sauce and the turkey. Grandma will be over on the Tuesday – she's staying in the spare bedroom – and Gran and Grandpa are arriving early Thursday morning. Aunt Janice and Uncle George will be here around noon with your cousins, and—'

'Whoa, okay, Mom, slow down. What do you want me to do, take notes?'

'No, I want you to be available to peel and chop vegetables.'

I laugh. 'Now that, I can do. And Todd and Callum don't have any allergies, I checked.'

Mom pats my knee. 'Good girl.'

She always gets worked up over Thanksgiving. The one year we went to Aunt Janice's house, it was a complete disaster. She's not the greatest cook, and Uncle George was too busy watching the football to pay much attention to what was going on in the kitchen, and we ended up with an incinerated turkey and undercooked vegetables. After that, we went back to Thanksgiving at our house.

But I think, in a way, Mom thrives on the stress of Thanksgiving.

We asked Todd and Callum a little while ago what their Thanksgiving plans were – I guessed they'd be going back to Idaho, maybe spending the day with Todd's mom. But she's going to the Bahamas for a long weekend with her fiancé, and it turns out that Todd doesn't have that many cousins – an eight-year-old cousin on his dad's side, who lives near his grandparents in Nevada, who he sees maybe once a year during summer vacation, but that's it. I never realized what a small family he had.

When I asked on behalf of my parents (well, mostly my mom) if they wanted to join us for Thanksgiving, I was surprised when Todd jumped at the chance and agreed before his dad had chance to even open his mouth.

He told me why afterwards, when we were sitting in his room making flash cards.

'I don't think either of us want to spend Thanksgiving just the two of us. It'll seem a little lonely.'

I'd patted his knee. 'Don't you worry, Todd O'Connor, I've got your back.'

The rest of the week at school feels like something out of a dream, or a movie. After that first lunchtime I spent at Todd's table, I join them every day, and they all seem genuinely happy to see me. I know everyone's name, of course, but I never got to know many of them properly, aside from the few people I've sat by in classes.

Tuesday lunchtime, I sit on the end of the table next to Todd, only talking to him and Allie really because I don't know how the rest of them feel about me, if they even want me there.

But on Wednesday, I show up at their table before Todd and Allie, and they make space for me right in the middle, making me a part of their conversation and dealing me in the game of Uno they're about to play.

I'm reserved and quiet those first few days, shy and awkward when somebody who isn't Todd or Allie speaks to me – yes, *me*, the newbie at the table – not knowing what to say to them.

'We're going bowling this Saturday,' says Kelly, laying down a green three on the pile of Uno cards in the center of the table. 'Are you coming, Ashley?'

I jump at the sound of my name. 'Who, me?'

'Yeah,' she says, smiling at me brightly. 'Come on, it'll be fun.'

'Um, I don't know . . .'

'Aw, we don't bite,' pitches in Mike, smiling at me as well.

'No, it's just – I'm grounded, and I don't know if my mom will let me . . .'

'Can't hurt to ask her. It's no biggie if you can't come, but it'd be nice if you can.'

'I'll ask,' I promise, and I do, over dinner later that night. Dad tells me of course I can go, why am I even bothering to ask? – and I have to remind him that I'm grounded. So Mom declares my punishment officially over on Saturday, and I go bowling with my new friends.

It's the most fun I've had in a long time.

By the end of the week, I feel like one of them. And I realize I've been missing out on something for a long time – I just didn't know what it was.

It's so great to be part of a group of people I can talk to so easily without being afraid of them looking at me like I'm a complete loser, or that by trying to strike up conversation about something I find interesting I'll kill the conversation completely.

I still see Josh's friends around school, but they all give me the cold shoulder. Not Naomi so much – she did smile at me when she saw me in the hallway between classes on Tuesday – but the rest of them pretend I don't exist. But at least they aren't saying mean things whenever they brush past me in the corridors.

I don't miss Josh, or his friends, not once.

I'm *happy*.

# Chapter Twenty-three

The whole of Wednesday is spent making sure we have enough chairs to go around the dining-room table, ironing the giant tablecloth (and then ironing it again because Mom found a crease in the middle), and preparing some of the food that can just be re-heated the next day.

'It's not cheating,' Mom tells me adamantly, just like she does every Thanksgiving, 'it's just making tomorrow easier. It's still home-cooked.'

That evening I take Todd to pick up Allie and take them to Denny's to meet up with everyone else there. Todd stays in the car while I go knock on Allie's front door.

Her mom answers, and the stressed-out frown on her face disappears when she sees it's me. 'Oh, Ashley! Come in a sec, Allie's almost ready.' Leaning over the banister, Mrs Lewitt shouts up, 'Allie, Ashley's here!'

'Thanks.' I wipe my feet on the welcome mat and step inside. 'Smells good.'

'Ah, you mean the Chinese take-out we ordered?' She laughs. 'The refrigerator is looking pretty empty, aside from the four apple pies I had to make for tomorrow.'

'Take-out was a sensible decision,' I agree.

'I'll be down in a second!' Allie yells, a belated reply to her mom.

'When are you leaving?' I ask, even though Allie's already told me. They're going to her grandparents' place, opting for an early start on the road due to all her cousins from Maine staying in the spare bedrooms and couches.

'Hitting the road at seven,' her mom tells me, looking surprisingly upbeat about it. 'How's school going?'

'It's fine, yeah . . . Plenty of homework, but it's okay.'

'It's good that you two are friends again,' Allie's mom says after a pause, smiling fondly at me. 'She's really missed you.'

'I missed her, too.' I smile, even though I want to roll my eyes. It feels like I have this conversation every time I've been over Allie's house since we started to hang out again – and I know that when she's been over my house, my mom says the same thing to her, too. It's crazy.

I guess it's a mom thing.

Allie runs down the stairs, one arm in the sleeve of her jacket and her purse between her teeth. She manages to get the other half of the jacket on by the time she's reached us, and takes the purse out of her mouth to kiss her mom on the cheek.

'Don't be out too late.'

'We won't. I'll text you when I'm on my way home.'

'Have fun!' her mom calls out after us as we make our way to my car. Allie climbs into the backseat, and says hi to Todd. We're meeting a few people at Denny's – those who haven't already left to visit family, or who aren't being held hostage to spend quality time with the relatives they see maybe twice a year at most. Grandma, my grandmother on my mom's side, is already here, but exhausted from her trip. She's been asleep since six, so mom couldn't object to me going out with my friends.

Not that she would have anyway; she's ecstatic I have a group of friends I actually want to spend time with.

'So what time do I need to have you back home?' I ask Allie.

'Ten at the latest,' she says. 'But preferably earlier, because I need to wash my hair.'

'No problem.'

'Thanks. How's your mom doing with the Thanksgiving preparations?'

'Surprisingly well.'

The three of us talk mostly about the holidays and how much homework school has given us over our long weekend off, and once we get to Denny's and meet the others, the conversation isn't much different.

I squeeze into the corner of the booth, Todd sliding in next to me, and Allie sits on the other side, next to Kelly, Ben and Logan. Amanda arrives not long after us, and we all order drinks.

At one point, I have to go to the bathroom, and squeeze out of the booth. Amanda stops slurping her milkshake, grabs her purse, and says, 'Ooh, I'll come with you.'

'Why do they always have to go to the bathroom together?' I hear Logan mutter. 'Like, is there some incredible secret to the girls' room we're missing out on?'

'Like the teachers' lounge in junior high,' Ben agrees, and they both start laughing.

'Boys,' Amanda mutters to me, and I laugh. In the bathroom, we both avoid the middle stall, which has the door mostly shut but a vomit-inducing stench emanating from it. After I wash my hands, I lean over the counter to look in the mirror and get rid of the smudged eyeliner at the corner of my eye with a fingertip.

Amanda leans into the mirror as well, checking her teeth.

'It's nice, having you around,' she says, out of the blue.

'Oh, um. Thanks.'

'You're actually really fun. Don't take that the wrong way, it's just – you know, you always looked a little grumpy. I thought you were just one of *those* girls.'

'Right . . .' I blink, a little lost, but I listen anyway.

'Sorry, that came out wrong. I'm just trying to say that it's nice having you as part of the group.'

She doesn't add something about Allie, or Todd – she just grins at me. And I beam right back at her.

They really do think of me as part of the group by myself, not just an extension of somebody else, someone they'll hang out with for the sake of their other friends.

'So,' she says, lowering her voice a little, and taking some ChapStick out of her purse, 'you and Todd.'

*Oh*, there *it is*.

'What about me and Todd?'

'You two are pretty cozy.'

'You think?'

She giggles, and rolls her eyes at me. 'Don't look so

freaked out. I'm just *saying* – you broke up with your boyfriend, and you and Todd . . .'

'Oh, no, we're not – we aren't – not like that,' I stammer.

She shrugs. 'Okay.'

'Why? Are you interested in him?' I smile, a confidential sort of smile that encourages her to tell me a secret. The kind of smile I haven't been able to share with anyone in a long time. I didn't realize how much I missed girly chats like this. I'd always listen to Naomi and Eliza and Danielle talking and gossiping like this, but I never felt like I could really join in, even if I tried.

'No!' She shakes her head, like she finds the idea amusing. 'I was just really curious, and I figured that you'd be better at answering than Todd. Sometimes boys aren't so great at realizing when a girl likes them.'

'But I don't like him – not like that.' I push the door open, walking out of the bathroom and holding it for Amanda. 'Really.'

'*Really?*' She scoffs, and raises her eyebrows at me, but not in a mean way. 'Are you sure? Because your face is almost as red as your hair.'

I stop in my tracks for a second. She didn't say it nastily, more in a teasing, friendly way, but the words themselves hit me hard. She strides past me and I stumble after her, and wriggle back into the corner of the booth, half-sitting on Todd's lap before I get to my spot.

'You okay?' he mumbles in my ear.

'Sure I am, why?'

'You just look a little flustered. Did Amanda say something to you?'

'No, it's – never mind.' I smile. He doesn't look convinced, but he doesn't push me, and I'm glad. But I'm distracted the rest of the evening – suddenly acutely aware of his leg pressed against mine and my foot resting over his, and our arms overlapping on the table.

I remember when I first started dating Josh, and my palms would turn clammy whenever we held hands. He was my first proper boyfriend: I'd had a date for the junior prom, and that was awkward and exciting, but things with Josh were different. They were so much more serious.

I felt clumsy when it came to guys, and not in that adorable rom-com way. Being with Josh was a learning curve for the first few months – becoming comfortable with a kiss on the cheek before parting ways for class, or holding hands in the hallways, and not clashing teeth when I tried to surprise him with a kiss.

It makes me realize that it's the complete opposite with Todd – all of the casual, familiar touches; even if they are totally platonic, and just come so easily and feel totally natural. Even if I don't like him in that way.

When it's nine fifteen, I reach across the table and give the sleeve of Allie's cardigan a tug to get her attention. 'Hey, we should probably head off now.'

'What time is it?'

'Like, nine fifteen.'

She nods. 'Sure, I'll just finish this' – she stirs the straw around the last bit of her milkshake – 'and then we'll head off.'

So the three of us finish our drinks – and sundae, in Todd's case – and shuffle out of the booth, leaving the others to it.

'I plan on staying out for as long as I can get away with,' Ben says. 'The less I'm around to hear the entire family arguing over the best way to cook turkey, or whether we should watch the parade or the football, the better Thanksgiving will be.'

I shove my purse at Todd so I can put my jacket on more easily, and he swings it over his shoulder.

I grin. 'It suits you. Red is definitely your color.'

'Yeah, I guess so.' He tugs on one of my curls pointedly, and I bat him away.

'Jerk,' I mutter. I take my purse back, and catch Amanda's eye past Todd's shoulder. She gives me a *look*, with that secretive smile, and I know she's thinking about our conversation in the bathroom.

I give her a look in response – one with cynical eyes and a smile that says 'Oh, *please*' and then we leave, waving goodbye one last time as we head outside to my car, our breath fogging up in the chill air. I shiver, and zip my jacket all the way up to my chin. Allie's well prepared, her hat and gloves on already.

'Here.' Todd drapes his scarf around my shoulders, and gives me a wide smile.

'Thanks.' It smells like him. I resist the urge to bury my nose in it and inhale deeply.

My engine stutters when I turn on the car, and the heating doesn't kick in until we're halfway home. 'I should probably get that checked,' I say out loud, as we pull up at Allie's house and the engine makes a chugging sort of noise.

'It can't hurt,' Allie agrees. She leans between the seats to give us both awkward, one-armed hugs. 'Okay, so I probably won't see you guys until Sunday, but have a great Thanksgiving and eat way too much food and have fun!'

'You too! Say hi to all the family from me!' I yell as she gets out.

'See you around!' Todd calls.

On the drive back to our houses, Todd says, 'You know Jennifer? With the short blond hair, glasses.'

'Jennifer Carter? Yeah, she's in my art class. What about her?'

I can see him twirling the guitar pick around his fingertips in a gray blur. 'We went on a date last week. Two, actually.'

I almost slam on the brakes, I'm so shocked, but I manage to maintain my composure and keep driving. My mouth suddenly feels like I've swallowed sawdust. 'Huh. Why didn't you tell me?'

'I didn't want to make a big deal out of it in case it was a disaster. You were busy hanging out with Allie, so you didn't notice. We went to the movies one night, and out for dinner on Sunday.'

The milkshake suddenly isn't sitting so easily in my stomach. 'Do I take it from the fact you're telling me that these two dates went well?'

Jennifer is bubbly and outgoing and one of those people who gets on with everybody. Somehow I just can't see her and Todd together, not in that way. She's nice – but suddenly I feel a certain dislike for her that I can't explain.

*Not jealous, not jealous*, I tell myself. *Not jealous.*

'I think they did, actually.' He sounds so happy I feel guilty for not being able to be excited for him.

'Have you . . . kissed her, yet?'

He blushes. I've never known a guy who blushes so

easily. 'Yeah, I kissed her goodnight after our first date, so . . .'

'Cool.' Cool? *Oh, crap, I'm such a dork.* 'I mean, good for you, Todd.'

'You don't mind, do you?' he asks, after a too-long, undeniably awkward pause.

'What? No!' I say, a bit too loudly and forcefully, and force a laugh. 'Don't be silly. I'm – happy for you, really.'

A few minutes later, after complete and total silence, we get out of the car at my house. 'So we'll be over about two tomorrow, right?'

I nod, locking my car and walking up the driveway to my front door. 'If things are taking a turn toward disaster, I'll let you know.'

'Okay. See you tomorrow then.'

'Yep. Night, Todd.' I have to raise my voice a little for him to hear me, since by now we're both on our porches unlocking the doors.

I'm not jealous, because if I were then that would mean I'd have to like Todd as more than a friend, and . . .

I think back to when he almost kissed me at the Freemans' house, and how much I'd wished he had kissed me then.

It's only when I'm inside and taking off my jacket,

my arms a little numb and stiff from the cold, that I realize I'm still wearing Todd's scarf. I ball the soft fabric in my hands and hug it close, the smell of his Old Spice deodorant and his shampoo lingering in my nostrils even as I climb into bed.

Stupid Jennifer Carter.

Stupid me.

# Chapter Twenty-four

I don't have a crush on Todd. Definitely not. It's just *not* possible.

So maybe I wanted to kiss him when we were babysitting the Freeman twins and he almost kissed me. And maybe it made me feel weirdly, deliriously happy that he gave me his scarf yesterday and forgot to ask for it back. And maybe I am a little jealous of Jennifer Carter.

But none of that means I *like* him.

Ugh, I let Amanda get in my head about this too much. That's the only reasonable explanation, right?

I roll over again in bed, looking at the time. It's 07:13, four minutes since I last checked, and I've been awake for almost thirty minutes now. I had the weirdest dream, where I was playing baseball in the park with Todd, and he did that cheesy thing and stood behind me, arms around me, to show me how I should swing the bat – which is ridiculous in itself, because even if I can't pitch or throw a ball to save my life, I'm awesome at batting. And then there was one of those kiss-cams, and . . . I woke up just before dream-Todd kissed me.

Since I woke up, heart pounding, I haven't stopped thinking about it.

I'm driving myself crazy.

I just got out of a serious, long-term relationship. I don't need to think about jumping into another one just yet. And with Todd, especially . . . it could ruin everything. I value him too much as a friend.

And obviously, I'm just a friend to him. I mean, what's stopping him from asking me on a date now that I broke up with Josh? Nothing. But he chose to ask out Jennifer instead.

And so what if he gave me his scarf, and puts his arm around me sometimes when we're walking into school? He's just being nice, nothing more than that. So what if he wanted to kiss me? That was only the one time, and it doesn't mean he *really* likes me in that way. It could've just been a spur-of-the-moment thing.

I can't risk losing him as a friend. Even if I possibly maybe have a teensy crush on him, it's just a silly crush. I don't need to make a big deal out of it. And I should be supportive of his relationship with Jennifer.

I take a deep breath, and roll onto my back again, staring at the ceiling. It's raining outside, and the sound is soothing as I lie there and tell myself to stop stressing out, it's no big deal, I'm thinking too much into things.

Anyway, I'm better off not having a boyfriend for a while. After things went so wrong with Josh, maybe I should avoid relationships at the moment. I'm happy with my new group of friends, and with Allie back in my life. I don't need a boyfriend to make me happy.

I stay in bed a little while longer, scrolling through my Twitter feed (which at this time of the morning is dead) until I hear Mom getting up ready to start cooking dinner, and I get up too, take a shower and then go and help out.

My grandmother is asleep still – I can hear her snoring in the spare bedroom as I walk past. Jeez. Either the jet lag really got to her, or it's an old people thing. I don't remember the last time I slept more than ten hours – never mind the almost fourteen hours she's been asleep.

Downstairs, I find Mom with her hair knotted loosely at the base of her neck and an apron tied on already. She's running through a checklist of food, checking things off and putting stars by other things.

'Oh, good, you're up,' she says. 'Wait – why are you up so early?'

'Couldn't sleep.'

'Is everything okay?'

'Yeah, I'm fine,' I say, honestly. 'I guess I'm just so excited about chopping vegetables for dinner that I couldn't sleep.'

'In that case . . .' Mom turns to the refrigerator and tosses me a bag full of carrots. 'You can get started on those.'

'Great.'

'Is Grandma awake yet?'

'Nah. Do you think we should wake her up soon?'

'If your dad's not up in an hour, I'll go kick him out of the bed. He needs to clean the bathrooms, and vacuum the hallway and lounge. I'll wake her up then.'

'All right.'

Mom's phone rings, and she takes a look at the screen before sighing. 'It's Grandpa. Again. You know this is the third time he's called this morning?' She answers, and as she repeats probably for the third time this morning that yes, it's okay, he *is* on the right interstate . . . but no, don't take the first exit, it's the *second* exit . . .

I don't hear the rest because she takes the call out in the hallway, but I bite back a laugh. Part of me wonders if Grandpa only does it for a joke. I wouldn't put it past him.

Every time he visits, Mom tells me he's where I get

my sense of humor from; and she doesn't say it like it's flattering.

Gran and Grandpa arrive about an hour later, only five minutes before my aunt, uncle, and cousins. They weren't supposed to show for another few hours, so the stress is visible on Mom's face when we have guests and Dad is still cleaning the upstairs bathrooms.

She's trying to catch up with Aunt Janice and her parents-in-law, and make coffees and put out some snacks, and remember to baste the turkey. Her eye twitches a little, and her hair's falling out of its knot.

'Mom, calm down.'

'I should've pre-prepared more food yesterday,' she mutters, ripping open a bag of chips and pouring them into a bowl for people to snack on, and then doing the same with some walnuts. 'Can you take these out?'

'Uh-huh.' I take the bowls into the lounge, and on the way back, I linger in the hallway to make a phone call.

'Happy Thanksgiving,' Todd answers as soon as he picks up.

'Yeah, you too. I need you to come over now. Like, put on some pants over those ridiculous SpongeBob boxer shorts and put on some shoes and come over.'

'Huh. Am I going to be cutting vegetables?'

'Yep.'

'And what's in it for me?'

'Um, I'll really appreciate the help and I'll owe you one?'

'Good enough for me.' He hangs up, and rings the doorbell eight minutes later.

Mom's head shoots up from mashing potatoes. 'Oh, God, who's that? I thought your uncle Patrick was on holiday, he's not—'

'It's Todd, don't worry.'

'Oh. He's early.'

'Well, I thought we could do with a little help.'

Mom looks ready to scold me, but I bounce out of the kitchen to let Todd in before she gets the chance to. I introduce Todd to my family in the lounge, first, before whisking him away to the kitchen.

After the chips and nuts have been demolished, Uncle George brings the empty dishes out, and sticks around to help with the cooking. The four of us makes the kitchen pretty crowded – especially when Dad comes in every so often to get more drinks for everyone – but it's nice. Homely.

We don't see my cousins much, except over summer vacation. Having them around the house like this, even if it's only once a year, is great.

Todd and I are doing some dishes, alone for a short time while my parents sit in the lounge talking to the rest of the family. He nudges me gently to get my attention.

'Yeah?'

'Thanks, for having us over. I appreciate it.'

'No problem. You and your dad are practically family now anyway, right?'

He smirks, but looks away. 'Right. Your family are so great though. I haven't heard one argument all day – except for your cousins fighting over which was the best float in the parade, but I don't think that really counts. It's so different to what I'm used to. Even before the divorce, Thanksgiving dinner was hell. My parents would try to get on for my sake and they'd only end up arguing about the amount of butter in the mash potato or how the carrots had been cooked.'

I'm not totally sure what to say to that. 'Well, I'm glad you're having a good Thanksgiving for a change.'

He dries the last plate and I put it away, and then we go into the lounge with the rest of my family.

'So, you're the famous Todd we've heard so much about,' Grandpa says.

'Uh, I guess so, sir.'

Grandpa chuckles. '"Sir!" It's been a long time since somebody who wasn't serving me food called me sir.'

'Technically, I have helped cook some of the dinner,' said Todd with a grin.

'Ah, damn. And here I thought you kids respected your elders like we used to.' Grandpa laughs loudly, which turns into wheezing, and he has to take a drink of water. 'Ashley's told us a lot about you, you know.'

'All good things, I hope.'

'We haven't heard a bad word about you yet,' Gran says, smiling at him. Todd's sitting on the arm of the couch my cousins are occupying, and I'm on the floor at his feet. Laughing, Todd ruffles my hair – but not too much; he knows that today I put in a lot of effort (and a lot more product) in making my hair look curly and cute, not frizzy and wild.

I pat my hair back into place and when one of my cousins – Gemma, the nine-year-old – starts telling Grandpa, very loudly with a lot of outrage, about a girl in her class that cheated on her test, Todd leans down to talk in my ear.

'So you talk about me a lot, huh?'

'Maybe,' I mumble, deliberately not looking at him.

'What kind of things do you say about me?'

'Hmm, mostly about what a jerk you are . . .'

He shoves my shoulder, laughing again, and I lean back against his knees.

Having managed to not think about my dream all day, I'm beyond irritated when it flashes through my mind again. I tense up, and will myself not to blush.

God, I'm such a dork sometimes. I don't even have anything to be embarrassed about!

Todd notices my sudden reaction, and leans down again. 'Everything okay?'

'Uh-huh. I'm fine.'

I check my cellphone; a text from Allie, pleading with me to save her from another game of Scrabble, and a couple of 'Happy Thanksgiving!' texts from my new friends. I haven't had much chance to check my phone today, what with helping my mom to juggle the cooking and washing up dirty dishes as soon as they appeared, so I reply to all the texts now.

I consider texting Josh, only to say a brief Happy Thanksgiving, but think the better of it. He seemed hurt enough by the break-up as it was; a text, however innocent, will only rub salt in the wound.

The turkey is ready by five, and we all sit down to eat. I didn't realize just how starving I was until it was all laid out in front of us – a dozen or so dishes of vegetables and bread and gravy boats and potatoes, and the turkey in the center.

Before Dad carves it, we do the silly family tradition of going around the table and saying one thing for which we're thankful. Mostly, it's 'good health' or in the case of Aunt Janice, the new baby she's expecting.

My cousins come up with slightly more trivial things – like 'my new Nintendo 3DS', making us all laugh.

Then it's my turn. 'I'm grateful for . . . for good friends.' I can't help but glance at Todd out of the corner of my eye, and I see a pink flush sweep over his cheeks.

It's his turn next, and he clears his throat. 'And I'm grateful for good neighbors that take us in at Thanksgiving.'

I laugh. Callum sighs, 'You make it sound like we're homeless or something.'

Grandpa finishes with the last 'I'm grateful for . . .' and then Dad stands to carve the turkey, and we finally get to eat.

My cousins are staying in a hotel overnight, and Aunt Janice and Uncle George bundle them into the car around eight o'clock, ignoring their pleas to stay longer with the reasoning that they'll need to have a bath and get to bed at a decent hour.

Gran and Grandpa leave shortly after, and Grandma makes herself another cup of peppermint tea and goes to bed.

My parents and Callum open another bottle of wine, pouring themselves very full glasses, and then pour smaller glasses for Todd and me. We sit in the lounge for a while with them, but after about ten minutes it starts to get pretty dull, so we take our few mouthfuls of wine and go over to Todd's house, away from the tipsy, rowdy laughter of our parents.

I pick up my coat from the coat hook in the hallway, and see Todd's scarf underneath it. 'Oh, hey, your scarf,' I say, holding it out to him. 'I forgot to give it back.'

He takes it from me and smiles, and we head over to his house, hurrying a little because it's cold out. When we get in, the house isn't much warmer.

'Damn,' he mutters. 'He turned the heating off.'

I rub my arms, my sweater dress not keeping me warm enough now.

'I'll grab a blanket.' Todd sets his wine on a coaster on the coffee table. 'How about you find something to watch on TV?'

'Sure.'

Todd's a while, but I hear him pottering around in the kitchen as well. When he comes back, I've found some rom-com on that I've never heard of, but it looks pretty decent, and Todd's holding a large bowl of toffee popcorn that smells amazing.

I put a hand to my bloated stomach. 'Ugh, seriously? I don't think I can eat any more.'

'But it's toffee-flavored . . . your favorite . . .'

I scrunch my nose. 'Damn you, Todd O'Connor.'

And I dip my hand into the bowl, taking a small handful and shoving it into my mouth all at once, making him laugh. He falls into the spot on the corner of the couch, next to me, and leans forward to pick up his wine and takes a sip, then pulls a face.

'I'd say you look very sophisticated with your red wine, but when you make a face like that after drinking some, it kind of ruins the effect.'

He's still grimacing, and scraping his tongue along his top teeth like he can scrape the taste of it away. I laugh again. 'I'm sorry, and no offence to your grandma for her choice in wine, but this is disgusting.'

I nod. 'That's why I haven't drunk the rest of mine.'

'You want some chocolate milk?'

'God, yes.'

He takes away the wine glasses to pour the vile stuff away, and returns with two large glasses of chocolate milk instead. He takes his seat again, and I lean into his side without even thinking about it. Like it's the most normal thing in the world. He stiffens at first, and I wonder if maybe I shouldn't have done that. And then he puts his arm around me, and I pull the blanket over us.

Toward the end of the film, I feel my eyes drooping, and struggle to keep my head up, letting it loll back against Todd's chest instead. I feel him move the empty bowl of popcorn to the floor, slowly like he doesn't want to disturb me.

As I get more drowsy, I curl in tighter to his side, and the last thing I'm aware of before I fall asleep is Todd kissing the top of my head.

# Chapter Twenty-five

I wake up in the most awkward position possible. *God, my neck is killing me!* I groan, and try to stretch the soreness out of it, raising a hand to rub at it. Then I lean back down, sighing and wishing I could go back to sleep.

There's a heartbeat by my head, strong and steady and even. I nuzzle closer before realizing where I am, and who I'm sleeping on, and my eyes flash open.

Todd's slumped down against the couch, leaning sideways and his head dropped back, mouth hanging wide open. He's drooling, and snoring intermittently. I bite back a laugh, but can't hold in my smile. One of my legs is over his, and the other is curled underneath me – and it's completely numb where I've been sitting on it for hours.

The blanket's still covering us, but the empty bowl of popcorn and our empty glasses of chocolate milk have disappeared. I can only assume that Callum cleared them away.

Slowly, I peel myself away from Todd. Cozy as it is, I can't stay there for ever. I should probably go back home.

I remember his dates with Jennifer at that point as well, and curse myself for falling asleep on Todd when he's got a girlfriend (of sorts) and how she'd probably hate it if she knew.

Despite my best efforts not to disturb him, Todd's snore turns into a startled grunt and he jolts awake, blinking drowsily and mumbling unintelligibly.

I give him a sheepish smile. 'My bad. Sorry, I didn't mean to wake you.'

'S'okay,' he murmurs. He wipes the back of his hand across his mouth and chin, grimacing. 'Oh, man, was I drooling?'

'Yep.'

'Did I drool on you?'

'I hope not.'

His eyes close again but he smirks. 'Good.'

I sit up straighter and stretch, rolling my head around to try and work the crick out of my neck. 'I can't feel my butt.'

'Tell me about it.'

'Sorry I fell asleep on you.' I stand up to try and get a little feeling back.

'That's okay, it wasn't – I mean, I didn't mind. Sleeping with you wasn't – no, I mean . . .'

'Todd?'

'Yeah?'

'You can stop talking now.'

His ears are bright red, and he clamps his mouth shut, taking a deep breath through his nose before saying, 'It was kinda cozy. I didn't mind.'

I smile, and start folding up the blanket. 'Well, I should probably head home. Take a shower, wash the drool out of my hair . . .' He looks away, embarrassed. 'Have some breakfast.'

'Why don't you have breakfast here? I bet I can convince my dad to make waffles and bacon.'

'If your dad's awake, then sure.'

Todd goes upstairs to see, and I go to the bathroom. I take a look in the mirror and wonder how Todd didn't say anything; my eyeliner and mascara is smudged, and my hair is on the unruly side of curly. I take a couple of minutes to fix myself up, having to wiggle my bra around because it's out of place from sleeping.

I can hear the sounds of cooking in the kitchen, and figuring that I look as good as I can in yesterday's clothes and make-up, I go to the kitchen.

'Morning!' I greet Callum.

'Hey, Ashley. Coffee or OJ?'

'Some coffee would be great, please.'

'On it,' Todd says, getting out another mug as he waits for the coffee machine to finish. I take a seat at the table.

'Thanks for letting me stay over last night,' I say, because I feel like I should say something.

'It's no trouble. I didn't want to wake you up. You two looked very *cozy*, asleep on the sofa.'

I don't know why, but I blush. Lucky for me, Callum's got his back to me as he pokes the bacon around the frying pan. Todd catches my eye as he puts the coffee down in front of me, and I have to look away.

We fell asleep on the couch watching a movie. No big deal. It's not like we *actually* slept together, in the not-so-innocent sense of the phrase.

'Do you want some eggs as well, Ashley?'

'Um . . .'

'I'm doing some for myself anyway,' he adds.

'Yes, please, then, if it's not too much trouble.'

'None at all.' After a pause he says, 'Did Jennifer have a good Thanksgiving, Todd?'

I glance at Todd as discreetly as I can, in time to see him squirm uncomfortably. 'Uh, yeah. I texted her a couple of times.'

'Any more dates planned?' his dad asks.

'Not yet.'

We eat breakfast, and it's almost, but not quite, as tense and uncomfortable as I was expecting. I try my best to offer to help with the dishes before I leave, but Callum won't hear of it – insisting that it's no trouble, that it's fine, really, so eventually I give in and go put on my shoes to go back home.

Todd follows me into the hallway. 'So do you, um, have any plans for later?'

'I might catch up on a little homework, but not really. Why? Do you wanna hang out? We could always hit the Black Friday sales? Or we could go see a movie?'

He looks a little uncomfortable, and rubs the end of his nose with his knuckles. I give him a confused frown, but before I get to ask him what's up, he gestures for me to step outside, and we both go out onto the porch, Todd shutting the door behind us. He crosses his arms over his chest, but I think it's because it's cold rather than a gesture of hostility.

'What are we doing, Ashley?'

Okay, now I'm definitely confused.

'What do you mean?'

He looks down at his feet, and wiggles his toes. I notice he's not wearing shoes, only socks. His feet must be cold.

I shake myself. Not the thing to be thinking right now, when he looks so serious.

'Does this have anything to do with Jennifer?' I ask, and then I find I can't stop. 'Why did you ask her out on a date, anyway? I mean, I thought . . . Like when you tried to kiss me, it . . . And you . . .' I can't form a coherent sentence, and bite my lip, hard. 'Do you really like her?'

'It wasn't some ploy to make you jealous, if that's what you're asking.'

'I think I got a little jealous anyway,' I mutter, half-hoping he doesn't hear.

'I don't know if I'm getting mixed signals from you or what, but I thought you weren't interested in me like that. You *told* me you weren't.' He gulps, Adam's apple bobbing anxiously. 'Look, I know I was out of line trying to kiss you a while ago. But when you broke up with Josh, you didn't treat me any different, and I thought you only liked me as a friend. And I thought, that's okay, because I'd rather you be my best friend and nothing more than not have you in my life at all.'

'Todd . . .'

My stomach is suddenly all butterflies, making me feel a little woozy after such a hearty breakfast, and I feel a little breathless, my heart somersaulting. I dread that he's going to say that now he's decided he's over his crush on me and wants to date Jennifer more.

'No, let me finish.' He sighs. 'I like you, Ashley, a lot.

But I'd rather know how you feel before I mess anything up.'

He looks mildly terrified, but even so, he manages to look me in the eye.

'What about Jennifer?'

His mouth twists into a worried line. 'It's not serious, not yet. But that's my point – if I keep dating Jennifer – and don't get me wrong, she's an amazing girl and I had a great time on our two dates – and things do get serious, but the whole time you've wanted to be more than friends, then it's going to mess everything up.'

'So you'd break up with her?' I clarify.

'We never said we were officially together,' he concedes.

And I can only say, very lamely and feeling totally pathetic, 'I don't know.'

God, I'm such a loser. I can't just leave him with an answer like *that*!

'I'm sorry, and I don't know if I've been leading you on, but I just – I don't really know what I want. I like you a lot, but I'm scared that we might make a total mess of things if we try something more than friendship.'

Because what if this crush is nothing more than that: a passing crush that I'll be over in two weeks? And what if we start taking things more seriously and acting like a couple and everything becomes weird?

He nods. 'Yeah, I know.'

I look away then, feeling awful. I want to be able to give him a clearer answer, but I really don't know what to say. Sure, I wanted to kiss him when he tried to kiss me; and it feels totally natural when he puts an arm around me, or like last night when we fell asleep cuddled up on the couch, that felt so not-weird.

I run a hand through my hair, and curse under my breath when my fingers stick against a tangle of knots. I wriggle my hand out of and sigh, looking back at Todd.

'I'm sorry,' he says. 'I just made everything really weird, didn't I?'

'No, you didn't. I've kind of been thinking the same things lately.'

He looks relieved at that, but doesn't say so.

I bite my lip before continuing. 'Can I have a little more time to think about this?'

'Sure. I mean, it's . . . it's no big deal. I only wanted to try to clear the air, because I didn't know how you felt, and . . . and you know, there's Jennifer . . .'

I nod. 'It's okay, Todd, I get it.'

'Okay.'

'So how about the movie later? Casual, of course. Or the mall. You pick.'

He grimaces. 'I'm not really up for fighting the hordes in the sales, so how about the movie?'

I nod. 'Sure. You pick the movie – just let me know what time, yes?'

'Yep. See you later Ashley.'

'Bye, Todd.'

Back home, once I've showered and changed into fresh clothes, I go into the lounge where my parents and grandma are watching the news. 'I'm going to the movies later, with Todd.'

'Are any of your other friends going?' Mom asks.

'No, just us.'

She turns her gaze toward me with a barely concealed smile of excitement. 'Like a date?'

God, did she overhear our conversation on the porch or something? I roll my eyes, scoffing. 'No, Mom. Why would you even say that?'

'Callum called last night to let us know you were staying over. He said you and Todd were passed out on the couch under a blanket, looking very sweet.'

'I'm sure Callum didn't say it was sweet.'

'Well it sounded very sweet,' Mom argues. 'You two were acting very . . . couple-y, yesterday, that's all. Your Aunt Janice didn't believe me when I told her you two weren't dating.'

'We're *not*.' I huff. 'God.'

'I'm just curious, since you're not dating Josh any more, that's all,' Mom barrels on, 'and you and Todd are so close, if you're—'

'I don't know, Mom,' I say, a little snappier than I'd intended. 'It's complicated.'

'Why? Does he like somebody else?' my grandmother pitches in, turning up her hearing aid. Dad looks between us all before reaching for the TV remote – presumably to change to a sports channel, or maybe to find a documentary.

'Don't you dare,' Mom tells him, not even looking his way. Dad shakes his head, smiling, but puts the remote back regardless. 'Well Ashley? Does he like someone else?'

'That's kind of the problem; he likes me. But, he just started dating this other girl at school because he thought I wasn't interested. I haven't figured out if I like him back yet, in that way. Like, I think I do, but I really don't know. What if it's just, like, a rebound crush and in a couple of weeks I'll be over it? I don't want to ruin things with him.'

'You've liked Todd since before you and Josh broke up,' Dad pitches in, to my surprise. 'Even I could see that.'

'But—'

'I know you don't want to wreck your friendship,

but you two act like a couple already, aside from the kissing,' Mom says. 'I think he was an idiot to ask this other girl on a date – but that's boys for you.'

'Unless you have kissed him,' Grandma adds.

I grit my teeth, but blush a little.

'Oh my God, you have, haven't you?' Mom laughs, grinning. 'Oh, I knew it.'

'We haven't!' I insist, but I get the feeling she doesn't believe me. 'Okay, so we *almost* did, once, but we didn't. I was still dating Josh at the time, and I pushed him away before he could kiss me.'

Mom raises her eyebrows, skeptical, but she doesn't voice her doubt out loud.

'Look, I just . . . I don't know.'

'There's an easy solution to see if you do like him, you know,' says my grandmother with an easy smile. 'Next time he tries to kiss you, don't push him away.'

Todd and I leave around five for the movie – it's a DreamWorks animation. I can kind of see why he picked it: because it's not exactly a date movie; we've steered clear of the holiday romances they're showing, and the action movies that are bound to have some kind of passionate, romantic embrace in the midst of explosions or near-death experiences. Plus, we're both suckers for cartoons.

We share some nachos, and our hands keep brushing when we go to take some, but I don't pull away like I'm fourteen-years-old and on my first date with a boy. But neither do I make an effort to avoid brushing his hand. I want to keep things normal.

Afterwards, Todd drives up onto one of the hills that overlooks the town. I packed some leftover-turkey sandwiches, and we sit on the hood of his car eating them and slurping the milkshakes we picked up on the way.

We talk, like we always do, drifting from one topic to another effortlessly, and not mentioning our discussion this morning – but I do make a joke about finding some drool in my hair, over which Todd groans and buries his face in his hands, laughing.

From here, you can see the Christmas decorations lighting up the mall like a giant, gaudy beacon for Santa Claus and holiday shoppers. It's a cloudless night, and you can see the stars, too.

Our breath fogs up and, after a while, my teeth start to chatter.

Todd notices, and unwinds the scarf from around his neck, draping it around mine instead with a fond smile. 'You look colder than me.'

I smile back. 'Thanks.' I tie it, tucking the ends inside my coat for a little extra warmth. We talk a while longer, and Todd starts telling me about constellations. He sounds so passionate about it, his voice hushed and almost breathless with awe, and even though I know a bit about the major constellations from when I researched them last year for a project, I let him talk, and I listen attentively.

'You really love the stars, huh?'

'My granddad taught me about them. He used to have a telescope, but my mom got that when he died. Apparently he used to talk to her about them too – not that she really cared about the stars much, but she wanted the telescope because it reminded her of him.'

I nod. 'That's understandable.'

Todd leans back onto his elbows, tilting his head up to look at the stars again. 'You can't see so much here, with the light pollution—'

'Damn Christmas lights,' I pitch in.

'Right. But they're still beautiful, don't you think? Look, you can see Orion's belt there – see that one? And the star underneath—'

I scoot closer, trying to look where he's looking and pointing. I point as well. 'By there?'

'Yeah.' He takes my extended arm and moves it a little. 'And over there, that one? It's . . .'

He goes on, pointing out the constellations we can find, and then we start making up our own, saying that the cluster of stars over there looks like a water bottle – and those ones over there like a cupcake.

'I tried counting the stars once,' I admit. 'We went camping on vacation for a few days one summer, and my dad had this map of constellations he was trying to use, and my mom kept laughing because they couldn't agree on where the constellations actually were in the sky. So I decided to count the stars.'

'How'd that go?'

'Not so great.'

'You'd have better luck counting all those freckles,' he teases, dragging a fingertip lightly across the bridge of my nose and cheek. I laugh, and push his hand away. After a while, it gets too cold to stay out on the hood of the car any longer, and we get back inside, letting the heater warm us before we go anywhere.

He gets the guitar pick out again and starts tapping it in a steady rhythm on the dashboard. The object is like his security blanket, but it's also his nervous tick. I wait to see what he has to say.

'I've driven up here a couple of times, since we moved. If I missed home, and my granddad, and if playing my guitar wasn't helping, I'd come up here. It made me feel a little closer to him. I like to write when I'm here, too. This is where I wrote that song for you, too.'

He smiles at me, but I can see the sheen of tears in his eyes. Quickly, he sucks in a breath and blinks, shaking it away.

'Sorry.'

'It's okay. You know,' I add, 'you never did get to finish that song you wrote for me.'

'It had another verse to it,' he says. 'It was harder to write it once we started talking again. I can sing you the other verse though, if you want? I don't have my guitar, but I can sing it to you.'

I smile, and say, 'I'd like that.'

He nods, and closes his eyes, tapping his fingers on his thigh, and then he starts singing. It sounds a little weird without the guitar to accompany it, but I don't mind: this way I can focus more on the lyrics. He starts from the beginning of the song, and then the new verse.

*'It cuts me to the core*
*That we're not talking any more*
*And it cuts me to the quick*
*That you might leave me by myself*
*Because on days that I don't*
*Have the strength to move.*
*All I can do is wait for one more*
*Sleepless night*
*To miss you.'*

* * *

I smile, feeling a little tearful because I'm touched by the song he wrote with me in mind, and it's good to know I mean so much to him that he not only writes about me, but sings the songs he writes to me.

He doesn't sing to me often, but sometimes he'll show me a new song he's working on, and ask me what I think of the lyrics – or if we're both sitting in our window seats, he'll play something, and then shout across to my open window to ask what I thought.

Todd puts the car in gear, but doesn't go anywhere. 'I don't know what I'd do without you, Ashley.'

The ride home is pretty quiet, but not the bad kind of quiet. It's more the soft kind of quiet, like cotton wool wrapped around us and hugging us tight, with no tension crackling in the air and no semblance of discomfort.

After a while, he says, 'I spoke to Jennifer earlier.'

My whole body tenses up. How had I managed to forget about her? 'Oh, yeah? How is she?'

'She's good, yeah. She's still over at her grandparents' house from Thanksgiving, and seemed like she had a pretty nice day with her family.'

'That's nice.'

'She asked if I wanted to go over for dinner sometime next week.'

This was exactly what I'd been worried he'd say.

My mouth is dry and I don't know how I manage to actually speak. 'What did you say?'

'That maybe it was best we didn't carry on dating. She's brilliant, but I told her I didn't want to lead her on, and I wasn't sure that I could see things going very far with us. She understood. Actually, she thanked me for – quote – *being man enough to admit that*. And she said if I changed my mind about it later on, I had her number.'

'Oh.'

'She wasn't upset,' he adds. 'I don't think she thought things were serious yet, either.'

I can't help but feel relieved when he tells me this. I mean, I hadn't expected him to talk to her today, so soon after our conversation, but I'm glad he did. It makes me feel a little more sure about what I want.

I glance over at Todd, and when he sees me looking he shoots me a smile. I remember when we first met, and it was a fight to get even one smile out of him, and how I thought he was so stand-offish and pretentious, and how different he is now I've gotten to know him. How much more open he is and how he smiles so often, and they're big smiles, not small, reluctant ones he wipes away as soon as he can.

I think about how when I first found out about his

book of songs, he was always ready to snatch it away and hide it somewhere I couldn't even see it; and now he'll leave it lying around and sometimes play me snippets of songs he's written. He opens up to me now.

We pull up on his drive, and Todd puts the car in park and turns off the engine. 'I guess I'll maybe see you tomorrow?'

I nod. 'Why not? You're welcome to come over for more leftover-turkey sandwiches.'

He laughs. 'Can't wait.' Then he bites his lip, nervous.

'What?'

'I'm just – glad that things weren't weird tonight. You know, after what we talked about this morning. Crap. See, now saying that made things weird, didn't it? God, I keep messing this up so bad—'

'Todd—'

He's getting really flustered now, and the muscles in his jaw jump as he clenches it in exasperation at himself. I can't help but smile, just a little.

'I should just keep my mouth shut and I know as I'm about to say it that it's going to make things weird, but I say it anyway and make an idiot out of myself, and – and I probably should have mentioned that I spoke to Jennifer a little sooner, but—'

'Todd!'

'Yeah?'

I'm leaning across the car to put a hand over his, where his right hand rests on his knee, and smiling at him. 'It's okay, you didn't mess anything up.'

I expect him to nod, but he doesn't. Instead, he just stares at me really intensely. His eyes look gray tonight, almost silver, and those incredible cheekbones are thrown into sharp relief by the glare of the streetlight outside. Todd's fingers move a little underneath mine, and his gaze flickers to my lips.

*There's an easy solution to see if you do like him . . . Next time he tries to kiss you, don't push him away.*

He leans a little closer, moving his face nearer to mine. I suck in a sharp breath, almost a gasp but not quite. He turns his hand around so our palms are touching, and he links our fingers together.

Both of us edge our faces a little nearer to each other, and I can feel my hands sweating, but I don't pull my hand away from his; I don't want to spoil the moment. My heart is racing so hard I think that most of the street must be able to hear it. It feels like my first kiss all over again.

Todd keeps his eyes locked on mine, and his breath tickles my cheek. His voice is barely louder than a whisper when he asks, 'Are you going to push me away this time?'

I shake my head, not able to get the word out, and very softly and tentatively, he kisses me. It's a feather-light touch of his lips against mine, and it sends a spark through me that I never felt when I used to kiss Josh. I kiss him back, and our teeth bump and the handbrake sticks into my ribs when I lean his way more, and he runs a hand through my hair only to get caught against a knot and has to apologize for pulling my hair, and we're both laughing.

The windows are steamed up and if my mom is peeking out of the window to see why I'm not in the house when Todd's car is outside, she'll be under no illusions.

Todd's forehead is still pressed against mine. 'Was that weird for you?'

I shake my head, bumping my nose against his. 'No. Was it weird for you?'

'No.'

'Good,' I murmur, and kiss him again.

# Epilogue

'Come on,' Todd says, urging me over with a wild hand gesture. 'Look.'

I bend in front of the telescope, putting my hands under my armpits for extra warmth. The mittens my mom bought me for Christmas are cute and all, but right now they're not doing a brilliant job at keeping my fingers from going numb. Todd's hand rests on my shoulder as he stands behind me.

'That's Cassiopeia?'

'Yep.'

'That's amazing.' I stand up, and he puts his arms around me, holding me in close. 'So I did a good job on the Christmas-present front?' I ask, referring to the telescope. After we went to look at the stars that night when we first kissed, it was easy to know what to buy him for Christmas. He got me some gorgeous hardback books, and a necklace with a star hanging from the chain.

'You did an amazing job,' he reassures me, and kisses my freezing cold nose.

We're both bundled up against the cold, in thick coats and gloves and scarves (this time, I'm wearing my own scarf, not Todd's) and hats. There were a couple of New Year parties going on, but our friends were just hanging out at Kelly's house for the night. We were there for a couple of hours earlier this evening, but decided to bail and do our own thing instead for when it turned midnight. Then maybe go back to Kelly's afterward to hang out for a few more hours, if everyone was still there by the time we left the hill.

When I told Allie and Kelly yesterday that we were going to spend a night under the stars – like we did on what was technically our first unofficial date – they cooed and grinned and Kelly told me not to worry about ditching them for an hour or so, that what we were doing was totally romantic and way better anyway.

After that night we kissed, it wasn't like things changed much. There was no pressure for us to suddenly spend all our time together being a couple. We just were. Everything was just like it always had been – joking around and teasing each other, talking about anything and everything. Except now there was more kissing involved.

I kept expecting for things to feel weird between us, for us to kiss and things suddenly feel wrong. But it didn't.

Kissing Todd was the kind of thing I felt I could never get used to.

It all just felt so right with him, and so wonderful, and I felt suddenly alive again – back in tune with the world.

We didn't exactly announce that we were suddenly dating, either. I mean, I'd told Allie the night we'd kissed that we'd *kissed* and it was a huge deal and I was on cloud nine, but she was the only one who really knew; after my mom, of course, who wanted to know exactly why I'd been sat inside Todd's car for a full twenty minutes once we'd got back.

I'd just blushed furiously and let her tease me about it before begging off to call Allie and tell her everything.

Aside from Allie, none of our friends knew that we'd transitioned from 'just friends' to 'couple'. We acted totally normal on the Monday morning we were back in school, and then when the bell rang to signal us all off to homeroom, Todd gave me a brief kiss on the lips and said, 'See you later.'

I didn't miss the looks we got, but nobody said anything immediately. At lunch, when we exchanged a few more light and casual kisses, they still didn't say anything. Aside from the 'I told you so' look I got from Amanda, none of them seemed even remotely surprised.

I'd found a thick ground mat and picnic blanket in the garage to lay out on the ground next to the telescope for us to sit on now, and we have chocolates and coffee in thermoses to keep us going. I sit back on the mat, and Todd looks through the telescope a while longer, until I get his attention.

'Todd, it's almost midnight.'

'Oh, right.' He sits down next to me, and puts an arm around me at the same time as I lean into him. I turn to give him a kiss before drinking a little of the coffee. It's still warm, at least. I pass him the thermos and we both take turns sipping from it while we wait for the fireworks.

He holds his left arm out in front of us, so we can see his watch.

'Four . . . three . . . two . . .'

'One,' I finish, and kiss him, smiling, heart racing, as the fireworks explode around us.

# Acknowledgements

This book was probably my most challenging, simply down to the fact that I was balancing working on it with settling into my first year as a university student, so there's a long list of people to thank with this book . . .

As always, a massive thanks to my brilliant editor at Random House, Lauren Buckland, and my publicist Clare Hall-Craggs, for your help in publishing my books, and to the rest of the team, too, for all your hard work.

Thanks to all my fans, new and old; particular thanks to Wattpad and my fans from there, who have been with me since the beginning of my journey into becoming a published author. I owe my success to you!

Thanks to Mum and Dad, who have done a late-night dash down to university to give me a laptop to write on when mine broke, and for everything else you've done to support me; to my sister for putting up with me stealing the spotlight every so often; to Auntie Sally and Uncle Jason for your crazy (and occasionally useful!) input; to my granddad, to whom this book is dedicated, for being probably my biggest fan and telling everybody you meet about me and my books.

To my flatmates, who introduce me to their friends and families as 'the one who wrote the books', you've been great at distracting me and lifting my mood when I've been working too hard, so a big thank you for that!

Tara and Ffion, you both need a mention here, for keeping me sane in my moments of madness trying to juggle problems sheets for classes and editing this book. Colebrook and Caroline, you've always been there for me, too – and Aimee J, I don't know what I'd do without you!

And finally, a big thank you to James: you're always encouraging me, inspiring me, and motivating me when I hit a wall with my work, and I definitely owe you a big hug and batch of brownies for that!

**The first published book by Beth Reekles –**
**the internet sensation everyone is talking about!**

**Meet Rochelle Evans.**
**Pretty, popular – and never been kissed.**

**Meet Noah Flynn.**
**Badass, volatile – and a total player.**
**And also Elle's best friend's older brother...**

When Elle decides to run a kissing booth for the school's Spring Carnival, she locks lips with Noah and her life is turned upside down. But this romance seems far from fairy-tale and headed for heartbreak . . . Will Elle get her happily ever after in the end?